Praise for Woman of the Ashes

'From the myths that swirled around Ngungunyane (and still do), Couto conjures what he has described as the "many and small stories" out of which history is made, offering a profound meditation on war, the fragility of empire, and the ways in which language shapes us'
The New York Times

'*Woman of the Ashes* is a beautiful and grotesque force interweaving history with myth. Couto's prose carries the weight of a creation story in nearly every passage'
World Literature Today

'In their exploration of myth, dreams, power, and fear, Couto's books draw from the tradition of storytelling across Africa. In the use he makes of stories—about dreams and superstitions, spiders and stones that talk—Couto has created a work of rare originality and imagination. Read it and remember'
The Economist

'Mia Couto has combined brilliant folkloric prose with extensive historical research to write a novel on the colonial history of Mozambique at the end of the nineteenth century. *Woman of the Ashes* exposes the nature and impact of colonial power in Mozambique. It is one of the best historical novels published in 2018. You will learn more from *Woman of the Ashes* than from several scholarly books on Portuguese colonialism in Mozambique'
The Washington Book Review

'A beautifully written and spirite
Run Spot Run

D1440631

'In this excellent book, Couto feathers history with folklore; while readers with some knowledge of Mozambican history will get the most out of the novel, this is still a fascinating, intricate story'
Publishers Weekly

'A rich historical tale thick with allegory and imagery that recalls Marquez and Achebe'
Kirkus Reviews

'Couto's mastery lies in his ability to turn his exploration of this slice of history into a commentary on all of human civilization. Richly translated by Brookshaw in words that suggest more than they say, Couto's tale evokes a sense of timelessness, especially in the world seen through Imani's eyes. An intriguing combination of folklore, history, and magic realism, and the first in a trilogy, this is a novel to be read and reread, savored and analyzed'
Booklist Online

'*Woman of the Ashes* is the sort of novel in which fish fly through the air, the soil bears the footprints of angels, and a bundle of animal pelts hides a deep abyss. The book's richness stems from its recognition that many forms of conflict rend nations and their people. This is a wise and powerful novel about war and its consequences'
BookPage

'While Couto treats his characters to a world of blazing specificity, Imani—in *Woman of the Ashes*—is also a vessel for our more contemporary battles'
Vanity Fair

MIA COUTO, born in Beira, Mozambique, in 1955, is among the most prominent writers in Portuguese-speaking Africa. Besides writing, he is a biologist and teaches at the Eduardo Mondlane University in Maputo. Mia Couto has been awarded several important literary prizes, among them the Camões Prize 2013 and the Neustadt International Prize for Literature 2014. He was a recent finalist for the Man Booker International Prize and for the International Dublin Literary Award 2017. His work has been translated into 20 languages.

DAVID BROOKSHAW is a professor emeritus at the University of Bristol, England. He has published widely in the field of Brazilian and Lusophone postcolonial studies, and has also translated the work of various authors from Portuguese, including Mia Couto's *Confession of the Lioness*, which was shortlisted for the 2017 International DUBLIN Literary Award.

Woman
of the
Ashes

Mia
Couto
Woman
of the
Ashes

Translated from the Portuguese
by David Brookshaw

WORLD EDITIONS
New York, London, Amsterdam

Published in the UK in 2019 by World Editions Ltd., London

World Editions
New York/London/Amsterdam

Printed by Mullervisual/Mart.Spruijt, Amsterdam, Netherlands

This book is a work of fiction. Any resemblance to actual persons, living or dead, or actual events is purely coincidental.

British Library Cataloguing-in-Publication Data
A catalogue record for this book is available on request from the British Library.

ISBN 978-1-64286-039-9

First published as *Mulheres de cinza* in Portugal in 2015 by Editorial Caminho.
US edition published as *Woman of the Ashes* in 2018 by Farrar, Straus and Giroux, 175 Varick Street, 9th Floor, New York NY 10014, USA.

Grateful acknowledgment is made for permission to reprint an excerpt from "The Negro Speaks of Rivers" from The Collected Poems of Langston Hughes by Langston Hughes, edited by Arnold Rampersad with David Roessel, Associate Editor, copyright © 1994 by the Estate of Langston Hughes. Used by permission of Alfred A. Knopf, an imprint of the Knopf Doubleday Publishing Group, a division of Penguin Random House LLC.

Twitter: @WorldEdBooks
Facebook: WorldEditionsInternationalPublishing
www.worldeditions.org

Book Club Discussion Guides are available on our website.

But it seems that for our sins, or for some arcane judgment of God, at all entrances into this vast Ethiopia round which we sail, He has placed an angel with a sword aflame with all mortal fevers, which hinders us from penetrating its youthful gardens, whence spring the rivers of gold that flow out to the sea.

—JOÃO DE BARROS

Contents

Introductory Note

This is the first book of a trilogy about the last days of the so-called State of Gaza, the second-greatest African empire ruled by an African. Ngungunyane (or Gungunhane, as the Portuguese knew him, or Mudungazi, as he was sometimes known locally) was the last emperor to govern the whole of the southern half of the territory of Mozambique. After his defeat in 1895 by Portuguese forces under the command of Mouzinho de Albuquerque, the emperor Ngungunyane was deported to the Azores, where he died in 1906. His mortal remains were supposedly taken back to Mozambique in 1985.

There are, however, stories suggesting that it was not the emperor's bones that were returned, but lumps of sand. All that remained of Portugal's great adversary were grains of sand in Portuguese soil.

This narrative is a fictional recreation inspired by real facts and people. My sources of information consisted of extensive documentation produced in both Mozambique and Portugal and, even more important, various interviews I conducted in Maputo and Inhambane. Of all those interviewed, worthy of particular note is Afonso Silva Dambila, to whom I owe my deepest gratitude.

The road is a sword. Its blade slashes the earth's body. Before long our nation will be a jumble of scars, a map forged by so many blows that we shall be more proud of the wounds than of the unblemished body we may yet save.

1

Unearthed Stars

Mother says: Life is made like string. We need to braid
it until we can no longer distinguish its threads from our
fingers.

Each morning, seven suns would rise over the plains of
Inharrime. In those times, the firmament was much
larger, and all the stars were contained within it, the living and the dead. Naked just as she had slept, our mother
would leave the house, a sieve in her hand. She was going
to choose the best of the suns. With her sieve, she would
gather up the remaining six stars and bring them back
to the village. She would bury them next to the anthill
behind our house. That was our graveyard for heavenly
creatures. One day, if we ever needed to, we would go
and unearth stars. With such a bequest, we were not
poor. That's what our mother, Chikazi Makwakwa, said.
Or just *mame*, in our native language.

Whoever visited us would be aware of the other reason for this belief. It was in the anthill that we buried
the placentas of newborn babies. A mafura tree had
taken root on top of it. We would tie white cloths around
its trunk. It was there that we talked to our dead. But the
anthill was the opposite of a cemetery. It was a guardian
of the rains, and within it dwelt our eternity.

One day, when the morning had been well sieved, a
boot trampled on the sun, the sun that Mother had
chosen. It was a military boot, like those worn by the
Portuguese. This time, however, it was worn by an Nguni

soldier. The soldier had been sent by the emperor Ngungunyane.

Emperors hunger for land, and their soldiers are mouths that devour nations. That boot shattered the sun into a thousand pieces. And the day turned to darkness. All the other days as well. The seven suns were dying under the soldiers' boots. Our land was being gobbled up. Devoid of stars to nourish our dreams, we learned to be poor. And we lost our eternity too. Knowing that eternity is merely another name for life.

◆

My name is Imani. The name I was given isn't a name. In my mother tongue, *Imani* means "Who's there?" You knock on a door, and from inside someone asks:

"Imani?"

So my identity was merely a question. As if I were a shadow without a body, the endless wait for an answer.

In our village of Nkokolani, it is said that a newborn's name comes from a whisper heard before birth. In a mother's womb, it is not just another body being woven together. A soul, the *moya*, is being produced. While still in the darkness of the womb, this moya is gradually made from the voices of those who have already died. One of these ancestors asks the new being to adopt his or her name. In my case, the wind whispered *Layeluane*, the name of my paternal grandmother.

As tradition required, our father went to consult a medicine man. He wanted to know whether we had captured that spirit's genuine wish. And the unexpected happened: the soothsayer refused to confirm the legitimacy of my baptism. It was necessary to consult a second medicine man, who, generously and in return for a payment of one pound sterling, assured him that everything was in order. However, because I cried ceaselessly during the first months of my life, the family came to the conclusion that I had been given the wrong name. Auntie Rosi, the family's own soothsayer, was consulted. After she had cast her magic bones, our aunt declared, "In this girl's case, it's not her name that's wrong, it's her life that needs to be put right."

My father withdrew from his duties: my mother needed to deal with me. And that is what she did, naming me "Ash." No one knew the reason for such a name, which in fact didn't last long. After the death of my sisters, swept away in the floods, I was given the name "Live Girl." That's how they referred to me, as if the fact that I had survived were the only feature that distinguished me. My parents would tell my brothers to go and see where the "Live Girl" was. It wasn't a name. It was a way of not admitting their other daughters were dead.

The rest of the story is even more nebulous. At some stage, my dear old father reconsidered, and eventually reached a decision. I would be given a name that was not a name: *Imani*. At last, the order of the world had been reestablished. The attribution of a name is an act of power, the first and most decisive occupation of some foreign territory. My father, who complained so bitterly of other people's empires, reaffirmed his status as a little emperor.

I don't know why I am spending so much time explaining all this, for I wasn't born to be a person. I'm a race, I'm a tribe, I'm a sex, I'm everything that stops me from being myself. I'm a black woman, I belong to the VaChopi, a small tribe on the coast of Mozambique. My people dared to oppose the invading VaNguni, warriors who came from the south and installed themselves here as if they were the owners of the universe. In Nkokolani, people say that the world is much too big for one owner alone.

Our land, however, was disputed by two rival overlords: the VaNguni and the Portuguese. That was why they hated one another so much and were at war: they were so alike in their motivations. The VaNguni army was much larger and more powerful. As were their spirits, which ruled on both sides of the frontier that tore our lands in half. On one side, the Empire of Gaza, controlled by the Nguni chief, the emperor Ngungunyane. On the other side, the Lands of the Crown, ruled by a monarch that no African would ever see: Dom Carlos, King of Portugal.

Our other neighbors had adapted themselves to the language and customs of the black invaders arriving from the south. We VaChopi are among the few who inhabit the Lands of the Crown and who allied themselves with the Portuguese against the Empire of Gaza. We are few in number, protected by our pride and surrounded by the *khokholos*, wooden palisades that we build around our villages. We were so hemmed in by these protective measures that we knew every stone by name. In Nkokolani we all drank from the same well, and one drop of poison would be enough to kill the whole village.

◆

Countless times we were awoken by our mother's cries. She would sleep and shout, wandering through the house with a sleepwalker's gait. During these nocturnal fits of delirium, she would lead her family on a journey across marshlands and streams and through the landscapes of her imagination. She would return to our old village on the shores of the ocean, where we had been born.

In Nkokolani, we have this proverb: If you want to know a place, speak to those who aren't there; if you want to know a person, listen to that person's dreams. Well, this was our mother's only dream: to return to the place where we had been happy and where we had lived in peace. Her longing was infinite. In fact, is any longing not infinite?

The digressions that occupy my mind are of a very different order. I don't shout or wander through the house. But not a night goes by when I don't dream of being a mother. And today I dreamed yet again that I was pregnant. The curve of my belly rivaled the arc of the moon. But this time, what happened was the opposite of a delivery: it was my child who expelled me. Maybe that is what the newly born do. They free themselves from their mothers, tear themselves away from their mothers' lone, borderless bodies. Well, my dreamed-of baby, a creature without face or name, was ridding itself of me in violent, painful spasms. I awoke in a sweat, with terrible pains in my back and in my legs.

Then I realized: it wasn't a dream, it was my ancestors paying me a visit. They were bringing me a message. I was fifteen years of age, and they were warning me that I was late to motherhood. All the girls of my age in Nkokolani had become pregnant. Only I seemed condemned to a barren fate. In fact, I wasn't just a woman without a name. I was a name without a person. Without substance. As empty as my belly.

◆

In our family, every time a child is born, we leave our windows open. It's the opposite of what the rest of the village does. Even when the heat is at its greatest, other mothers wrap their babies in thick blankets, imprisoning them in the darkness of their rooms. In our house, we don't do this; the doors and windows stay wide open until the newborn's first bath. This unbridled exposure is, in fact, a form of protection: the new creature is filled with light, sounds, and shadows. And that is how it has been since time itself was born: only life can defend us from the business of living.

On that January morning in 1895, the windows we had left open made people think a child had been born. Once again, I had dreamed I was a mother, and the smell of a newborn child permeated the whole house. My attention was gradually drawn to the rhythmic sweeping of a broom. I wasn't the only one waking up: that gentle sound was rousing the whole house. It was our mother, cleaning the yard. I went to the door and watched her, slim and elegant, in a swaying curve, as if she were dancing, and in the process turning to dust.

The Portuguese don't understand why we take such care to sweep around the outside of our houses. As far as they are concerned, it makes sense to sweep only inside buildings. It never occurs to them to take a broom to the loose sand in the backyard. Europeans don't understand: For us, what's outside is still inside. The house isn't the building. It's the place that is blessed by the dead, inhabitants who ignore doors and walls. That is why we sweep the yard. My father, however, never accepted this explanation, which he found too complicated: "We sweep the sand for a much more practical reason: we want to know who's come and gone during the night."

On that morning, the only footprint was that of a

simba, a feline creature that snoops around our chicken coops in the dead of night. Mother went to check on the hens. There were none missing. The wildcat's lack of success reflected our own failure: if the creature had been seen, we would have promptly hunted it down. The spotted skin of the females was sought-after as a sign of prestige. No present could give more pleasure to a great chief, above all to the commanders of the enemy army, who adorned themselves in such a way that they lost their human form. That is why a uniform is worn: to rob a soldier of his humanity.

The broom firmly wiped away evidence of the nighttime intrusion; the memory of the simba was erased in a matter of seconds. After that, Mother walked off down the path to fetch water from the river. I stood watching her disappear into the forest, elegant and upright in her brightly colored cotton. My mother and I were the only women not to wear the *sivanyula*, a material made from the bark of trees. The clothes that covered our bodies were bought at the Portuguese store, but they made us the target of women's envy and men's desires.

When my mother got to the river, she clapped her hands, asking for permission to draw near—rivers are the dwelling places of spirits. Leaning forward over the riverbank, she peered along the edge to make sure there wasn't a crocodile waiting to ambush her. Everyone in the village believes that the great reptiles have "owners" whom they alone obey. Chikazi Makwakwa collected water, facing the mouth of her pot downstream so as not to go against the current. When she was getting ready to return home, a fisherman offered her a beautiful fish, which she wrapped in a piece of cloth that was tied at her waist.

When she was already near home, something unexpected happened: a group of VaNguni soldiers burst out of the thick bush. Chikazi took a few steps back, at the same time thinking, I escaped the crocodiles only to be devoured by even more violent monsters. Ever since the war of 1889, Ngungunyane's forces had ceased ranging over our lands. For half a dozen years, we had enjoyed peace, thinking that it would last forever. But peace is a shadow on impoverished ground: all that's needed to make it disappear is the passage of time.

The soldiers surrounded our mother and soon realized she understood them when they spoke in Xizulu. Chikazi Makwakwa had been born in the south, so the language of her childhood was very close to that of the invaders. Mother was a *mabuingela*, one who walks ahead to brush the dew from the grass. That was the name the invaders gave to the people whom they used to clear their path across the savanna. My brothers and I were the products of this mixture of histories and cultures.

But now, some years after the peace had begun, the intruders returned, as menacing and arrogant as ever. Confirming all our old fears, those men surrounded my mother with the strange intoxication felt by adolescent boys simply because they are in a pack. Though her spine tingled with fear, Chikazi bore her load of water with vigor and elegance. She maintained her dignity in the face of the strangers and their threat. The soldiers felt insulted and were propelled ever more strongly by a desire to humiliate her. Suddenly, they knocked the pot from her head and whooped with glee when it hit the ground and shattered. And they laughed when they saw the woman's slender body drenched with water. After that, the soldiers required no effort to tear at her clothes, which were now transparent and clung to her skin.

"Don't hurt me," she begged. "I'm pregnant."

"Pregnant? At your age?"

They saw the little bump under her clothes, where she was hiding the fish she had been given. And, once again, they spat their doubt into her face: "Pregnant? You? How many months?"

"I'm twenty years pregnant."

That's what she felt like saying: That her children had never left her body. That she was harboring all five of her children. But she contained herself. What she did instead was feel around for the fish under her clothes. The soldiers stood watching her explore the secret parts of her body under her *capulana*. Unnoticed by any of them, she grabbed the spiny dorsal fin of the fish and used it to tear her wrist. She waited for the blood to flow and then opened her legs, as if she were giving birth. Gradually, she pulled the fish from under her clothes, as if it were emerging from her insides. Then she lifted the fish up in her blood-soaked arms and announced:

"Here is my child! My little boy is born!"

The VaNguni soldiers stepped back in horror. This was no ordinary woman. She was a *noyi*, a witch. And there was no more sinister offspring she could have produced. A fish, for these occupying soldiers, was a taboo creature. And as if the animal weren't enough, its appearance was compounded at the same moment by the worst of all impurities: the blood of a woman, the filth that soiled the universe. The thick, dark stickiness ran down her legs and stained the soil around her.

When they were told about this episode, the invading hordes were disturbed. It was said that many soldiers deserted, fearing the power of the witch who gave birth to fishes.

◆

And so it was with ripped clothes and shredded soul that my mother, Chikazi Makwakwa, arrived back home around noon. At the door, she recounted what had happened, neither weeping nor displaying any emotion. Blood dripped from her wrist as if her tale were being spelled out with every drop. My father and I listened to her, unsure how to react. As she finished her story and washed her hands, Mother muttered in a voice that was unrecognizable:

"Something must be done."

My father, Katini Nsambe, frowned and argued: The best way to respond would be to remain calm and quiet. We were a nation under occupation, and it would be better if we remained unnoticed. We VaChopi had lost the land that was ours, the land of our forefathers. Before long, the invaders would be strutting through our cemetery, where we buried our placentas and our stars.

Mother reacted forcefully: "It's a mole that lives in darkness."

My father shook his head and retorted in an undertone: "I like the dark. You don't notice the world's defects in the dark. A mole is what I always wanted to be. When it comes to how the world is, all we can do is give thanks to God that we are blind."

Stunned, Mother gave a loud sigh while she bent over the fire in order to stir the *ushua*. She moistened the tip of her finger, pretending she was testing the heat of the saucepan.

"One day, I'll be like a mole. I'll be all covered in earth," my father muttered, anticipating with sorrow the news he was about to announce.

"That'll happen to us all," Mother said.

"It won't be long before I leave for the mines. I'm going to do what my father did—I'm going to leave this place and try life in South Africa. That's what I'm going to do."

It wasn't a prediction. It was a threat. He took a pinch of tobacco from his pocket and an old cigarette paper. With surgical care, he slowly began to roll his cigarette. There wasn't a black man in the entire village who could boast of the ability to roll his own smokes in this way. Only my father could. With kingly demeanor, he approached the fire and drew out an ember to light his cigarette. Then, standing stiffly and jutting his chin out, he blew a puff of smoke into his wife's indifferent face. "You, my dear Chikazi, insult moles, knowing that it will offend my late father."

My mother hummed an old song, a time-honored *ngodo*. It was a woman's lament, a complaint that she had been born a widow. Disdained, my father withdrew noisily.

"I'm leaving," he declared.

He wanted to show that he was hurt, that his wife wasn't the only one bleeding. He slipped out of his own shadow and removed himself to the great anthill, where, though absent, he believed his family would notice him more.

Then we watched him walk around the house, and eventually set off toward the valley. The tiny glint of his cigarette gradually disappeared into the darkness, as if it were the last firefly in the world.

◆

We sat there, my mother and I, weaving our silences together in a way that only women can. Her thin fingers scratched around in the sand as if confirming their intimacy with the ground. She spoke with the accent of the soil when she asked:

"Did you bring wine from the Portuguese store?"

"There were still some bottles left over. Are you scared Father will hit you?"

"You know what he's like: he drinks, he hits."

An unexplained mystery, how Father could reconcile within himself two such opposed souls. When he was sober, he was as gentle as an angel. When he was under the influence of alcohol, he turned into the most vicious of creatures.

"It's incredible how Father has never suspected you of lying."

"Me? Lie?"

"Of course you lie. When he hits you and you cry out in pain, Mother. Aren't you lying?"

"This illness of mine is a secret, and your father mustn't suspect. When he hits me, he thinks my tears are real."

The malady was congenital: Chikazi Makwakwa didn't feel pain. Her husband was puzzled by all the burn marks on her hands and arms. But he believed that her obliviousness to pain was the work of amulets she got from her sister-in-law, Rosi. Only I knew it was a birth defect.

"And what about your other pain, Mother?"

"What other pain?"

"The pain in your soul."

She laughed and shrugged her shoulders. What soul? What soul did she have left after two of her daughters had died and her two sons had left home?

"Was your mother beaten?"

"Your grandmother, great-grandmother, great-great-grandmother. It's been like that ever since women were women. You'd better get ready to be beaten as well."

A daughter doesn't contest her elders' certainties. I

imitated her movements and held up some sand in my cupped hand, then tipped it out so that it fell to the ground in a cascade. In the tradition of our folk, this red sand was the sustenance of pregnant women. What was slipping away between my fingers was my wasted existence.

Chikazi Makwakwa interrupted my thoughts: "Do you know how your grandmother died?" She didn't wait for me to answer. "She was struck down by a flash of lightning. That's how she died."

"So why have you just remembered this now?"

"Because that's how I want to die as well."

This was how she wanted her end to be: free of body, weightless, without a trace of her to bury. As if a painless death might erase all the pain in her life.

◆

Every time a storm broke, our mother would rush out into the fields and stand there, her arms spread, in imitation of a withered tree. She was waiting for the fatal thunderbolt. Ash, dust, soot: that is what she yearned to become. Her desired fate was to be reduced to an invisible powder, light, so light that she would travel the world, carried on the wind. It was my grandmother's wish that justified my original name. This is what my mother wanted me to remember.

"I like 'Ash,'" I said. "I don't know why, but it reminds me of angels."

"I gave you that name to protect you. When we are dust, nothing can hurt us."

Men might well beat me, but no one would ever hurt me. This was the intention behind that baptism of mine.

She scratched at the ground with her hands; four

rivers of sand cascaded from between her fingers. I stood dumbstruck, overwhelmed by the dust emanating from her hands.

"Now go and get your father. He's jealous of us."

"Jealous?"

"Of me for not giving him all my attention; of you because you were educated by the priests. You belong to a world he can never enter."

That's what men are like, she explained. They are scared when women talk, and even more scared when women are silent. I must understand this: My father was a good man. He was just scared of not being equal to other men.

"Your father was angry when he left here. Learn one thing, my girl. The worst thing a woman can say to a man is that he ought to do something."

"I'll go and get Father."

"Don't forget the wine."

"Don't worry, Mother. I've already hidden the bottles."

"Quite the contrary, daughter. Take him a bottle!"

"Aren't you scared he'll beat you afterward?"

"What that stubborn old mule mustn't do is sleep in the bush. Bring him back here, sober or drunk. After that, we'll see what happens."

Then Mother returned to her sadness, like a domestic animal returning to its pen. She was already on her way when she spoke once more:

"Ask him to take us back to live in Makomani, ask him to take us back to live by the sea. He listens to you. Ask him, Imani, for the love of God!"

2

The Sergeant's First Letter

Lourenço Marques, November 21, 1894

Your Excellency Counselor José d'Almeida

I write to you, Your Excellency, in my capacity as your humble servant, Sergeant Germano de Melo, appointed captain of the garrison at Nkokolani to represent Portuguese interests on this frontier with the enemy State of Gaza. This is my first report to Your Excellency. I shall do my best not to tire you, and shall restrict myself to the facts of which I believe Your Excellency should be aware.

I arrived in Lourenço Marques the day before the city was attacked by the Landins, local rebels, from the immediate area. It happened early in the morning. We heard shots, and soon Negroes, Indians, and whites had filled the streets in panic. I was staying at a boarding house run by an Italian woman, right in the heart of the town. The guests battered on my door, shouting and screaming, demanding that I defend them at the entrance to the inn. They had seen me arrive the previous night, armed and in uniform. I was an angel fallen from the heavens in order to protect them.

The proprietress of the inn, who goes by the name of Dona Bianca, took control of the situation, assembled the guests, and locked them in a cellar. Then she invited me to follow her onto a terrace from which one could look out over most of the city. Here and there were columns of smoke, while farther over toward the estuary one could hear gunfire and explosions. It was clear that our opposition to the assault by the natives was almost nonexistent.

Before long, the only focus of resistance was the Fort. The assailants—who were Landins and not Vátuas, as people seem to insist—were operating in the streets at will. After they had overcome all the defensive lines around the city, they attacked shops, looted stores, and could have killed more people but simply chose not to. Here at the inn, we avoided the maelstrom produced by the kaffirs because they thought all the Portuguese had taken refuge in the Fort.

From the terrace where we watched our approaching fate, I saw a scene that left a great impression on me: Among the thick curtains of smoke, two galloping horses appeared. They were ridden by two Portuguese, one in uniform and the other in civilian attire. It was this latter individual who sparked my curiosity, because he had only one arm, and remained mounted thanks to the strength of his legs. With his one hand, he both clutched the reins and held a gun, which he fired more or less at random. The owner of the boarding house identified him as One-Arm Silva, a deserter who had fled to the Transvaal, where he had suffered an accident while handling a consignment of dynamite. He had returned to Mozambique, and was pardoned for his desertion because of his acts of bravery.

Behind this man Silva was the soldier, mounted on a white horse, trotting along in a much more restrained fashion. As the distance between the two horsemen increased, the dashing soldier was surrounded by a horde of Negroes brandishing spears and shields. In a panic, the man fired his gun a number of times, until he had all but run out of bullets. Seeing himself ever more tightly encircled, and guessing what his end would be, the horseman shot himself in the head. Alarmed by the shot, the horse accelerated, dashing forward in leaps and bounds. Later, it slowed down, allowing its almost headless rider to remain seated in his saddle, blood spurting from him like some abundant fountain. And so the horse advanced slowly until it disappeared in the mist. It occurred to me that this funeral march would continue out of the city and lose itself in the African veld until the body of the suicide victim was no more than a skeleton swaying in the saddle of that solitary animal.

I was awoken from these gloomy flights of the imagination by the sound of cannon fire. Our ships out in Espírito Santo Bay were shelling the town. That was our last line of defense. And it worked, thanks be to God. The kaffirs eventually retreated, leaving behind them a trail of destruction and chaos.

Allow me, nevertheless, to record the absurdity of it all: in order to get rid of the enemy, we were obliged to bombard our own city, one of the largest settlements on the coast of Portuguese East Africa. The boarding house where I was staying was hit by a cannonball. As she looked at the ruined wall, the owner of the establishment wept in despair, knowing that she would be unable to claim damages from anyone. Bianca was crying so intensely that she did not notice the body of a Portuguese soldier lying next to the razed wall. As I knelt down to cover him with a sheet, I noticed that on his forearm he bore a tattoo of a heart with the words "A Mother's Love" written across it. I was more moved by that tattoo than I was by the sight of the dead man.

Your Excellency will benefit from more detailed accounts of this unfortunate incident that befell the city of Lourenço Marques. I suggest you seek to establish the true causes that provoked the revolt of the local chiefdoms around the city. However, do not rely on the usual sources. I discovered, by both direct and indirect means, that the royal commissioner himself requested a report from a Swiss missionary by the name of Henri Junod. This report was drawn up on the basis of statements provided by black Christians, who the origin of the revolt to causes that do not cast us in a favorable light. I suggest Your Excellency study this report.

Whatever the true explanation may be, the fact is that my presence in Africa has got off to the worst possible start. On the terrace of that inn, the Italian lady showed me in a matter of minutes what I had already suspected was the case: our domains, which we so pompously call "Lands of the Crown," have been consigned to a state of lawlessness and immorality. For centuries, we have failed to maintain a true presence in these territories. And in those areas where we have left our imprint, the situation is even more serious, because we have allowed ourselves to be represented by deportees and criminals. Among our officials, no one believes we are capable of defeating Gungunhane and his State of Gaza.

The new royal commissioner, António Enes, has an exceedingly difficult mission, surrounded as he is by adversaries as well as adversities. The commissioner is viewed badly by most of the military, who consider him to possess the paltry skills of a civilian, and a writer and journalist at that. On the other hand, it is obvious that our commissioner will receive no replies or support from the Lisbon government. The monarchists are too busy trying to survive. And the military advisers who have been assigned to him by the Admiralty and the Ministry for the Colonies know nothing of Africa. We are thankful to have people such as Your Excellency, with years of experience in Mozambique, Angola, and Guinea. I ask you, in all humility, not to deprive me of your timeless and precious counsel.

It is because of these concerns that I leave with an anxious heart for Nkokolani, which is more than five hundred miles from here, in the vast hinterland of Inhambane. I hope the military authorities will remain true to their promises to convert that unfinished outpost into a proper garrison. And I have faith that they will send me a contingent of Angolan soldiers, so that I may exercise my functions in a prompt and appropriate fashion.

The Italian woman, who knows many of our officials intimately, told me I should forget any promises made to me. For, according to her, I am a military man only in my appearance. She told me that the serenity of my gaze was enough for her to be sure of this. Her rash opinion aside, the truth is that Dona Bianca began to list other reasons for her hasty conclusion. She asked me to whom I was answerable, and I took the liberty of telling her that the superior to whom I sent my reports was the counselor José d'Almeida. She laughed. And then she commented with a degree of cynicism: "You'll never fire a shot. And you'll be lucky if you don't get shot yourself."

Then she added that she knew of other cases involving an endless wait for a garrison. When she took her leave, the Italian woman promised that she would visit me at Nkokolani. She would undertake the journey because she knew that Mouzinho had been appointed to the regiment at Inhambane. She wanted to meet the gentleman again, as if that were her sole aim in life.

I began to think about Bianca's prediction, and I feared that there might be some truth in it. Everyone here is aware of my republican past, and they all know the reason for my presence in Africa. Nor, surely, is my participation in the revolt of January 31 in Porto unknown to Dona Bianca. I cannot complain about the sentence I received, given that most of the rebels were jailed indefinitely. In my case, they decided I should be deported to the remote interior of Inhambane. They did so in the hope that there I would encounter a prison without bars, a prison which, for that very reason, I would find more suffocating than any other. They were, however, prudent enough to make me responsible for a bogus military mission. The Italian woman is absolutely right: It is not a soldier inside this uniform. It is a political exile who, in spite of everything, has agreed to bear the responsibility of his duties. On the other hand, I have no desire whatsoever to sacrifice my life for this timeworn, mean-spirited Portugal, for this Portugal that made me leave Portugal. Mine is another country, which is waiting to be born. I know that these outbursts exceed the tone that should be guiding me in this report. But I hope Your Excellency will understand the utter solitude that is my current lot and appreciate how my isolation is starting to deprive me of my powers of discrimination.

Just this by way of conclusion: This morning, I was received by the royal commissioner in a brief courtesy meeting. Although sparing in his words, Commissioner António Enes confessed that he was relying heavily on two trusted individuals he had chosen to work in Mozambique: Captain Freire de Andrade and Lieutenant Paiva Couceiro. He even announced that, immediately after our meeting, he and his two faithful advisers were going to draw up the so-called Plan of Action for the Southern Districts of the Colony. Neither Ayres de Ornelas nor Eduardo Costa had been invited. I thought this detail should be brought to Your Excellency's attention.

Although he was apprehensive, there was for a moment joy on the face of António Enes, visible in the fleeting glint behind his spectacles, which failed to conceal his slight squint. This joy became clear when he showed me a telegram from Paiva Couceiro revealing that the settlement of Marracuene had been renamed Vila Luiza, in honor of the commissioner's beloved daughter. His expression glowed soulfully when he recalled that, farther north, we had founded a town and named it after Queen Amélia. From what one can gather, among all the individuals in Lisbon, only the queen bothers to give the abandoned commissioner moral support. From the king and other prominent Lisbon personalities, he receives not a word of comfort. Poor kingdom of ours that rules neither here nor in Portugal. Poor Portugal.

I apologize, Excellency, for this long, sad catalog of confessions that are personal in character. I believe you will appreciate that I see in Your Excellency the tutelary father figure whom, I must confess, I always lacked.

3

The Soil's Page

This is how glory ensnares: The greater the victory, the more the hero will be hunted down and besieged by his past. This past will devour the present. It does not matter how many honors he has received. The only medal he will have left in the end is his tragic, fatal solitude.

Darkness was already widespread when I left in search of my father, carrying a basket in which there swayed a bottle of wine sporting, in bold letters, this label: "Black Man's Wine." The full moon lit up the slumbering landscape. My feet followed the recent footprints of old Katini. Who else in the village wore boots? I became more and more surprised at how far away he'd gone. My quivering calls faded, echoless and unanswered:

"Father! Father?"

Eventually, I arrived at a limitless field. It looked like land for growing crops. As if to confirm the landscape's purpose, there was my father, busy scratching away at the soil. Only VaChopi men till the land alongside their women. But, in truth, my father was less a tiller and more of a distiller.

As I drew near, I noticed that what looked like a hoe was in fact a stick with a sharpened point. He wasn't loosening the soil, but, rather, scratching it as if he were drawing on a huge canvas.

"I'm writing," he said as he sensed me approaching.

"Writing?"

"You're not the only one who writes ..."

"And what is it you're so busy writing, Father?"

"It's the names of all those who've died in the war."

I looked at the ground and saw that the earth he had gouged extended beyond the horizon. But even in the bright moonlight, his sandy scratchings were illegible.

"So who is going to read all this?"

"God!"

He pointed his stick in no particular direction, a gesture more vague and indistinct than his own voice. He repeated with a stutter: "God! God is going to read me!" He spun around and sat down on the ground, as if knocked over by some invisible force.

"That mother of yours ..."

He didn't complete his sentence; he had become blind to words. This blindness assailed him every time he tried to talk of his wife. He chewed his silence as if it were some bitter fruit. And there he remained, vanquished and motionless.

The moon was hidden by passing clouds. The names of the dead, scrawled in the earth, had been swallowed up by the gloom when Father spoke again: "Have you come to get me? Well, tell your mother I'm not coming back. She's got to learn to have some respect. I'm her husband. And, besides, I'm the most senior member of the Nsambe family."

"I've brought you this, Father; it was Mother who told me to give it to you." And I offered him the bottle of wine.

His eyes lit up. He uncorked the bottle with his teeth and, with deliberate ceremony, poured the first drops on the ground. Then he took a loud and joyous swig, and he continued to drink as if that were his only task in this world. His bony hands turned the bottle round and round as if he were trying to make the wine dizzy while it was still inside its glass cradle. The letters on the homemade label were gradually erased, until the only words left were "Black Man." My father had no color, but as he went on drinking, he grew ever darker. I was scared that he too would be swallowed up by the night. I held out my hand to save him. When he felt my fingers, he asked: "Are you afraid, Imani?"

I nodded. Touched, he tried to allay my fears. Could it be that I was like my mother, fearful that he might drink too much?

"Everyone says I'm a drunkard. What do you think it is that I drink, you who know me well?"

"I don't know, Father. You drink wine, you drink *nsope*. You drink so many things."

"So many things" told only part of the story. Old Katini drank everything. Once, he even swallowed a whole bottle of eau de cologne that he stole from the sergeant's house. We had to bring him back to life, and his breath was so perfumed that it pervaded the night air. But he seemed to have a completely different explanation: "I'm a solitary, fearful man. Your mother doesn't understand. I only drink people. I drink the dreams of others."

In our family, alcohol had the most ancient roots: we would drink to escape from a place, and we would get drunk because we didn't know how to escape ourselves.

◆

At long last, my poor old father gave in to sleep. I snuggled up to him, paying no attention to the smell of liquor that emanated from his body. I was seeking protection, but the opposite happened: he was the most fragile, the most vulnerable of us all.

A pack of hyenas worked up the courage to lay siege to

our hiding place. The more like humans wild animals are, the more they scare us. And the hyenas seemed to be in a far greater state of drunkenness than my father.

Their brawling chorus must have rung an alarm bell deep in Katini's subconscious domains. The truth is, he awoke with a start. He went into the bush and, with his back turned to me, took a long pee. He wasn't just answering a physical need; he was marking the borders of his tiny empire with urine. Then he waved his arms vigorously and let out a few shouts. The hyenas moved away, cackling like witches.

◆

Those who are familiar with nights in my country know that when the crickets fall silent another, deeper night begins. This other darkness is so thick that dreams lose their way. My father listened to this silence and said:

"Now even God has fallen asleep."

"Let's go, Father. Let's go home. I'm scared."

"First, let me see to the last one."

"What last one?"

"The last of the dead."

With painstaking care he scratched his father's name, Grandfather Tsangatelo. A shiver ran through my soul, and in my despair, I rushed to hold his long arms: "Don't do that, Father."

"Keep quiet, Imani. This is a ceremony, and you're not old enough to be here ..."

"Grandfather hasn't died!"

"He has died. Of that, there's no doubt."

"Has anyone seen the corpse?"

"There aren't any corpses in the mines. It's all stone, earth, and people, the living and the dead: all earth within the earth."

He mumbled some kind of prayer before we set off along the path that could now be made out in the meager early-morning light. We had just reached the first clearing when we were startled by voices coming from the bush. In a matter of seconds, we were surrounded by half a dozen men shouting in Xizulu. It was clear to us—their pierced ears and the wax crowns fastened on their hair left no doubt as to their identity—they were VaNguni soldiers, and their intention was to terrify us. My father whispered to me:

"Were you scared of the wild animals? Well, the real hyenas have just arrived."

Our biggest fear was that they were timbissi, the ill-famed brigades used by the emperor to carry out massacres. *Timbissi* is the Zulu word for "hyenas." However, our assailants were not wearing the typical adornments of that godforsaken group: two goat horns hanging on each of their chests. Luckily for us, these brigands were no more than common soldiers. They were collecting the taxes they said they were owed. The biggest, doubtful whether we had understood, stuck his hand out next to Katini's face and declared, "Listen, you dog, we're here to collect the animal skins."

"Who are these skins for?"

"Who do you think they're for? For the owner of these lands, the emperor Ngungunyane."

"But we've already given our skins."

"Who did you give them to?"

"To the whites."

"Which whites?"

"The Portuguese."

"The Portuguese no longer rule here."

"We didn't know. The Portuguese intendant came to collect the skins. Now we don't have any left. Unless you want our own skin."

"Get busy looking. Ngungunyane isn't going to like it when he knows you disobeyed him. And the girl," the soldier asked, pointing at me, "who does she belong to?"

The soldiers surrounded me and began to nudge me and feel my thighs. To my surprise, my father intervened, his chest puffed out and his arms stretched so wide that he seemed like one of the walls that protected our village.

"This young girl is my daughter!"

"She may be your daughter, but her body has already begun to take shape. What were you two up to in the dark?"

"No one touches my daughter!"

Katini Nsambe's ever more furious stance was an unacceptable insult as far as they were concerned. One of the VaNguni came at us, a look of loathing stamped on his face. The man roared as he straightened himself, preparing to give my poor old father a kick. As he was doing this, the soldier suddenly tripped and fell to the ground in a heap. He struggled on the sand for a moment, but was unable to get up. The others had to help him regain his composure. That was when I saw what had happened: the aggressor had fallen over as he had trodden on the names written in the ground. The other VaNguni also noticed there was something strange about the sand. All together, they trampled the ground as hard as they could. Then, once again, they pointed at me, declaring: "Next time, we'll take her as a gift for Ngungunyane. You know only too well that the emperor takes a virgin from each place he conquers. Or do you need reminding?"

They spat on the ground and disappeared, all the while hurling their invective. Their saliva bubbled in the sand like some toxic curse. When they were far away, we could still hear the soldiers' guffaws. There was no doubt about it: they were hyenas. Or, worse still, they were creatures who only felt alive in the excitement of the kill.

◆

When we were finally alone, my old father, seized by fury, drew himself up, spun around on the tips of his toes, and screamed in Portuguese: "You may have weapons, but I've got all this ground here, where I've written the names of the dead. You'd better watch out ..."

He mumbled to himself, as if chewing poison, "Miserable wretches, you don't even have a word for 'paper' in your language." And, leaning on his staff, he quickly set off in the direction of home. I hurried after him along paths moistened by the dew.

"Don't speak about what happened when we get home; it will only worry your mother. And it will feed Uncle Musisi's appetite for war."

For a moment, I thought it might not be so bad if they had abducted me, and taken me to where a king might choose me as his wife. I would, at long last, be a woman. I would finally be a mother. And, as a queen and a mother, I would have power over the VaNguni. And I would bring peace to our nations. My brothers would return home; my sisters would live again; my mother would stop wandering through the darkness in her sleep.

Maybe this king whom everyone feared, having created such a vast empire, was no more than a friendless victim. Who knows, maybe love was the only empire Ngungunyane sought? Or maybe he had other motives throughout all these years of war: to find a woman like me, capable of infinite passion. That might explain his endless marriages. People said the emperor had so many wives that he believed all the children in the world were his. I asked myself this: When I was presented at his court, would he take me as a wife or as a daughter? Or would he have me killed, to give substance to the fear that kept him on his throne?

◆

In our part of the world, we know we are near a human settlement because of the sound of children's voices, their singing and wailing. This is what we could hear when we were still some distance away from the village: the cries of children reached our ears before we reached the dwellings.

Chikazi Makwakwa was awaiting our return at the door of our house. Even from some way off, I realized that this time she too had been drinking. Anticipating her husband's rebuke, she came toward us, jabbing her finger: "You don't love me, Katini!"

"Who said so?"

"So why is it you've only got me? There are so many men around who've got more than one wife ..."

"I'm not like those VaTsongas who collect wives as if they were heads of cattle ... Besides, didn't we decide we were going to be civilized?"

"You're the one who did the deciding. And because of that, our children have given up on us ..."

"We've still got Imani."

"Imani will go away. In fact, she hasn't been here for a long time."

She was talking as if she couldn't see me. I ran up to her and touched her on the arm.

"I'm here, Mother."

"You've already gone, girl. You speak to us in Portuguese; you sleep with your head toward the west. And only yesterday you were talking about the date of your birthday."

Where had I learned to measure time? The years and months, she said, have names and not numbers. We give them names as if they were living beings, like those that are born and die. We call the months "fruit-picking time," "the time when the paths are closed," "the time of birds and ripening corn." And many other such names.

More serious still was my growing estrangement: my dreams of love would never be expressed in our language or directed toward our folk. That's what my mother told me. She paused for some time before addressing Katini: "You know my greatest wish, husband. I want us to return to the sea. We lived in peace there, far from this war. Why don't we go back there?"

"You're asking the wrong question, wife. Your question should have been: why did we leave there? You know that answer only too well, for it fills you with fear. And this fear is greater than your wish."

Then he got up, staggered about for a few seconds, and held his wife's arm. He looked as if he were leaning on her for support, but he was forcing her into the bedroom. I also retired to my room. I lay down and covered my face with my capulana, afraid that the thatched roof might collapse. Houses are living, ravenous creatures. At night, they devour the residents and in their place leave stumbling dreams wandering here and there, stumbling like my drunken father. More than any other house, ours had an insatiable appetite. All night long, we would see the dead entering and leaving. In the darkness, our house would swallow us up. When morning came, it would spit us out again.

◆

My brothers were the other half of my world. But they now lived far away from our home. This was why the house had been split down the middle. Mother dreamed of the sea. I dreamed that my brothers were coming back. At night, I would wake up calling their names: Dubula and Mwanatu. As I sat there in the darkness, I would remember when they were children and shared our space.

From an early age, Dubula showed himself to be intelligent and active. He was given a Zulu name, and the choice explained his strange fascination for the invading VaNguni. *Dubula* means "gunfire." My father gave him this name because, when the baby was being delivered, he got tired of waiting and grabbed his old rifle and fired into the ceiling. His nerves got the better of him, he explained later. In fact, it was the crack of the gunfire that hastened the child's birth. Dubula was the product of a fright, a spark. He was like the rain, the son of a thunderclap.

Mwanatu, the youngest, was the opposite, sluggish and inept. Since childhood, he had been fascinated by the Portuguese. This attraction had been encouraged by our father, who sent him for catechism. And so he stayed with me as a boarder at the Mission. When he returned home, he was even more of a simpleton. Under instructions from Father, Mwanatu went to work as Sergeant Germano's adjutant, while still continuing his previous job, helping at the Portuguese store. He lived night and day in the military quarters, and no longer visited us. He occasionally took on guard duties, pretending to keep watch on the Portuguese man's front door. He had been given an old military tunic and a sepoy's cap. He adored his uniform, unaware that his performance was a source of amusement for passing Portuguese. Mwanatu was a mere outline of a person, a soldier in caricature. His efforts merited pity: no one had ever taken such tasks so seriously. On the other hand, no one had ever been made such a source of amusement.

More than the uniform itself, he clung to a promise made to him: one day, he would set sail for Lisbon and, once there, he would enroll at a military school. This journey was imagined for its eventual return. He would come back to live among his "people." Mwanatu's loyalty to the Portuguese Crown filled everyone in our family with shame except our father, who had another view: as long as we were under the protection of the Portuguese, that devotion, whether sincere or feigned, was very useful to us.

◆

The differences between my two brothers reflected the two sides of the border that separated all our family. Times were hard and required us to choose allegiances. Dubula, the elder of the two, didn't need to choose. Life chose for him. When he was still a boy, he obeyed the rituals of initiation, in accordance with age-old traditions. When he was six, he was taken into the forest, where he was circumcised and instructed in matters of sex and women. For weeks, he slept in the forest, covered up with sheaves of grass so as not to be recognized by the living or the dead. Every morning, our mother would take him food, but she would never enter the forest where the initiates were gathered. Everlasting misfortune would befall the woman who trespassed in this forbidden territory.

The same prohibition was being repeated now, ever since Dubula had fled home to live a wandering existence. It was said he slept each night in a different part of the forest. In the half-light of dawn, our brother would prowl around our backyard, knowing that our mother had secretly left him a plate of food on top of the anthill. The footprints that our father looked for in the sand weren't those of wild animals. They were his own son's.

As for Mwanatu, he was educated to read and use numbers. He went through the same rituals as a white Catholic Portuguese. Our mother would warn us: the soul he'd been given was now no longer suited to our patch of ground. The language he had learned wasn't just a way of talking. It was a way of thinking, living, and dreaming. In this, he and I were alike. Our mother's fears were obvious: We had consumed so much of the Portuguese language that our mouths would have no room left for any other way of speaking. And, in time, those mouths of ours would devour us.

Nowadays, I think our mother was right to have such fears. Where her son saw words, she saw ants. And she dreamed that these ants crept out of the pages and gnawed away at the eyes of the reader.

◆

So often have I relived Dubula's last visit home that it is as if he had never vanished into the world. I still remember that distant evening when I got home and saw my elder brother sitting there, his back to the door. The abundant sweat running over his shoulders gleamed in the rarefied light. As I drew closer, I realized that it wasn't sweat. It was blood.

"Was it Father?" I asked, already in tears.

"It was me," he replied.

I walked up to him and circled his statuesque body. The blood was seeping, thick and slow, from his ears.

"Why did you do this, Dubula?"

His torn lobes left no room for doubt: Dubula had inscribed his body with the marks of a new birth. He was no longer one of us. He was an Nguni, the same as the others who negated our existence. I hugged him as if for the last time. And I asked him to leave before our father arrived.

I watched his slender figure disappear down the path, and I slid my hands down over my breasts as if I myself were lost. Then I felt my brother's blood on my skin.

4

The Sergeant's Second Letter

Chicomo, December 15, 1894

Your Excellency Counselor José d'Almeida

I shall begin by requesting Your Excellency's lenience regarding the account of my meeting with the royal commissioner. Please accept my sincerest apologies. My account was absolutely impartial and bears no relation to any particular sympathy I may have for the person of António Enes. I was completely unaware of any mutual hostility between Your Excellency and the royal commissioner. I now know that the animosity is long-standing, and dates from the first mission to Mozambique undertaken by the commissioner, in 1891. I shall never interfere in this conflict, and shall maintain my complete devotion to Your Excellency, to whom I respond with a sense of rectitude that far exceeds the duties required by rank.

However, I could not fail to convey to Your Excellency the hostility displayed by António Enes when I spoke to him about the duties I shall carry out at Nkokolani, providing a presence alongside the peoples who, at such risk to themselves and in such a spirit of sacrifice, give us their support. Clearly, the commissioner was not criticizing me by making his views felt. It was against Your

Excellency and against the negotiations undertaken by you with the State of Gaza, which, in the commissioner's opinion, appear to be overly protracted. It was clear, though never explicitly declared, that the commissioner suspects that we are making too many concessions to Gungunhane. Also to be lamented was that taking so much time will severely compromise the efficacy of our military campaigns. Finally, António Enes complained about the military command at Inhambane, currently the responsibility of Colonel Eduardo Costa, who, in his view, finds every excuse not to make any territorial advances.

"This delay could prove fatal for us," were Enes's words. And he said more, this time with malicious insinuations concerning Your Excellency's good intentions. His exact words were as follows: "José d'Almeida has never cared a fig for the nation's interests!" Whereupon he suggested that Your Excellency was benefiting Gungunhane's policy, which is to make us lose the war long before there has been any battle. According to him, this war will be lost if we concentrate our military resources in the cities, with neither the desire nor the aptitude to place our troops in the heartlands of the enemy's territory. We shall perish in our encampments, besieged by inertia and fear, and assailed by fevers and the despair of waiting. And our European enemies, with England at their head, will rejoice triumphantly, because we will have provided them with proof of our inability to possess colonies in Africa. "War requires warriors, and all I have been given are functionaries," António Enes complained. This is what the commissioner said. And this is what I feel the need to communicate to you in this already lengthy report.

Permit me to say, Your Excellency, that as a military

man I cannot remain indifferent to the arguments of António Enes. In truth, the worst way to lose a war is to wait endlessly for it to occur. It has to be said that our victories in Marracuene, Coolela, and Magul improved morale and promoted our image among the natives. Throughout this journey to Nkokolani—a journey that I shall relate in due course—I have encountered numerous local chiefs in many places who, in the wake of these glorious battles, switched their allegiance. They are now with us. But it must be said that we won our victory against the Vátuas, who are the slaves of the Ngunis. It did not involve a victory over the forces of Gungunhane. As for this latter potentate, we still have much work to do.

I will now relate the details of my journey to Nkokolani. Yesterday we reached Chicomo, after a two-week trek through an interior that both fascinates and terrifies me. Every time we go through a forest, I imagine us being ambushed. In the darkness of each night, I sense a trap. Whether he is attacked by monstrous beasts or savage Negroes, what is the difference for the one who is going to die?

I must admit that, in spite of my fears, the journey has progressed without any great mishaps. Along the way I have passed kaffir villages, and everywhere I turn, I am struck by the way terrified children run away screaming when they see us. Alarmed mothers grab their children by the arm and drag them into their huts. It is true that one word from the local chief is enough to make their fear vanish. There have even been instances when initial terror has turned to effusive cries of welcome, when they learn that we have come to fight Gungunhane. But one question haunts me: why do they fear white folk so much? I can accept that they might be frightened, because, in most cases, they have never seen a European before. But the horror that we seem to inspire in them can only be explained by our being, in their eyes, tormented souls.

And this has led me to more extensive thoughts: What do these blacks think of us? What stories do they dream up to explain our presence? I know very well that as a soldier I should not be bedeviled by such questions. Perhaps I ask too many questions for a military man. Maybe I shall never become a proper soldier—at least, to serve this regime. Not because I am a die-hard Republican, but because, as I have already told you elsewhere, I did not enter the Military Academy from a sense of vocation. My family gave me no alternative. They left me with my packed suitcase at the front gate of the college. And they never paid me any visits while I was there. Nor do they know or want to know where I am now. It was the army that took care of my education. And, for sure, it is the army that will take care of my funeral.

At the encampment in Chicomo, where I have spent the night and from where I am sending you this letter, I had the opportunity to meet Captain Sanches de Miranda. As I listened to his stories about Africa, I could not help asking myself these questions: Who, among our officers, has this type of knowledge of Africans? How can we rule them if we know so little about them? What army can we defeat if we are so ignorant of our enemy?

I told Sanches about the terror I cause upon arriving in a village. He smiled and said that the fear they have is no different from ours in our belief that blacks eat human flesh. It is just that these people believe we are the ones who are the cannibals. And that we take them away on our ships in order to eat them on the high seas.

We Europeans and Africans are very different, to be sure. No one doubts— not even the poor Negroes—the superiority of our race. On the other hand, how similar we are in our fears, whatever side of the ocean we come from.

Moreover, Captain Sanches de Miranda added this: He had read the reports on the attack on Lourenço Marques, which he considered more than a little confused. It was not Gungunhane's troops who attacked us. Our enemies, at this precise moment, are certain Tsonga chiefs, not the Vátuas of Gaza. They invented Gungunhane's soldiers where there were none. And Sanches de Miranda wondered why we obstinately failed to understand. Why we persist in placing them all in the same basket when it would be to our advantage to divide them up.

One final word on this great Portuguese, this valiant Sanches de Miranda. The natives believe that he is the son of Diocleciano das Neves, the famous "mafambatcheca." As Your Excellency knows very well, he was a traveler and an ivory trader, well respected among the kaffirs and a close friend of Muzila, Gungunhane's father. This mistake is so convenient that Sanches de Miranda has wisely never denied it. Quite the contrary, our captain insists that Diocleciano made certain confessions to him on his deathbed. And that he, as a favorite son, promised his poor father he would do justice to his African legacy and would respect the affectionate nickname given him by the locals, *mafambatcheca*, which in the language of the blacks means "he who travels joyfully." I do not consider the physical similarity that the kaffirs find between the two Portuguese unreasonable. I realize that we all have the same mustache and haircut—a black man asked me if the Portuguese were born like this, already with a mustache.

Sanches de Miranda makes much of being the son of the late Diocleciano das Neves. He is certainly unaware of how much this piece of opportunism would disgust Diocleciano himself. And Miranda is also ignorant of how much his adopted progenitor had distanced himself politically from our authorities, protesting against the arrogance of our administrators and the continuing practice of selling slaves. Moreover, he is completely unaware of how much Diocleciano detested the city of Lourenço Marques. Among my papers, I came across a statement written by Diocleciano in which he refers to the city in the most unflattering terms. I include an excerpt here:

... Lourenço Marques consists of very little sand and a great deal of mud; once a fortnight, it is totally covered by the high tides. The pestilential emanations inhaled by the wretched inhabitants soon poison their lungs. Within three years of their arrival, two-thirds of the Europeans succumb; and the health of those who survive has deteriorated to such an extent that they can be of little use to themselves or to their country.

I too am happy to escape this disease-ridden city. Tomorrow I shall be joined by Mariano Fragata, Your Excellency's adjunct, and together we shall descend the River Inharrime in a dugout. It will take us some hours before we finally disembark at our destination, where I hope to carry out the mission assigned to me with energy and courage.

In closing, I have been told that in Nkokolani there is a Chopi family closely allied to us and completely devoted to our struggle against the devil Gungunhane. I have also been told that the head of this Christian family has placed a son and a daughter at my disposal, both of whom speak Portuguese and have been educated in accordance with our Portuguese values. I thank God for this providential support.

5

The Sergeant Who Listened to Rivers

Lucky are those who, having forsaken their humanity, become creatures of the wild. Unlucky are those who kill on the orders of others, and even more unlucky those who kill on the orders of no one at all. Finally, wretched are those who, having killed, look at themselves in the mirror and still believe they are people.

I remember the day Sergeant Germano de Melo arrived at Nkokolani. In truth, it was immediately obvious that this Portuguese was different from all the other Europeans who had visited us. As he climbed out of his pirogue, he quickly rolled up his trousers and walked ashore. The other whites, whether Portuguese or English, would avail themselves of a black man's back to carry them to dry land. He was the only one who didn't bother with these services.

As he did this, I approached him, curious. The sergeant gave the appearance of being taller than he was, his mud-coated boots adding to his height. What I noticed most was the shadow that covered his face. His eyes were clear, almost devoid of color. But his expression was darkened by a cloud of sadness.

"I am Imani, boss," I introduced myself, giving a clumsy bow. "My father sent me to help you with whatever you need."

"Ah! Are you the girl I heard about? How well you speak Portuguese, and with such good pronunciation! Heavens above! Where did you learn it?"

"It was the holy father who taught me. I lived for years at the Mission at Makomani Beach."

The Portuguese man stepped back to take a better look at me, and said, "You've got a really pretty face!"

I looked down, adding shame to guilt. We were walking along the riverbank when the visitor stopped and closed his eyes, asking me not to say anything. We stood there in silence until he suddenly spoke again:

"Where I come from, we don't have this."

"You don't have rivers?"

"Of course there are rivers. It's just that we have stopped listening to them."

The Portuguese was unaware of what was a well-known fact in Nkokolani: Rivers are born in the skies and flow across our souls in the same way that the rain crosses the sky. When we listen to them, we feel less alone. But I said nothing, and waited for my turn to speak.

"It's good to be greeted by a river," he remarked in an undertone. Then he added: "By a river and by a pretty girl like you."

Then he told me to wait there with him. It was at that point that I noticed another Portuguese, farther back, a dark-skinned, distinguished-looking civilian. I was told that his name was Mariano Fragata, and that he was the adjunct of the Portuguese intendant responsible for relations with the State of Gaza. Fragata was being carried on the back of one of our villagers, but his position was unstable and ridiculous, as he slid down his porter's back. The black man didn't seem to want to let the Portuguese go, while the latter pleaded ever more vehemently: "Put me down! Put me down this minute!"

They didn't get as far as both falling over, because I told my kinsman to stop, while he, amused, confided to me in Chopi: "That's to teach them that the one on top doesn't always boss the one down below."

The intendant's envoy regained his haughty posture, rolled down his trousers, and looked at me inquisitively. The soldier proceeded to introduce us: "This is the girl Minami ..."

"Imani," I corrected him.

"This is the local girl who has come to welcome us. You won't believe how well she speaks Portuguese ... Say something, girl. Go on, say something for my colleague!"

All of a sudden, I was dumbstruck, all my Portuguese swept away. And when I tried to speak my native language, I faced the same emptiness. Suddenly, I was left without any language at all. All I had were voices, indistinct echoes. The soldier saved me from embarrassment: "She's shy, poor little soul. You don't have to speak; just take us to our quarters."

Judging by his baggage, I realized that the sergeant would be lodged with us for a while. The other, the civilian, wouldn't be staying long. I escorted the visitors to the store belonging to Sardinha, the only Portuguese resident in our area, whom we had renamed Musaradina.

The two Europeans took their time examining every corner of the village.

"Just look at this village, my dear Fragata. It's all clean and well swept. I'm amazed—the streets are wide and lined with fruit trees ... Who are these blacks, so different from the ones we've seen so far?"

◆

Francelino Sardinha was standing at the door and greeted his compatriots effusively, as if, after centuries of isolation, he had discovered the only two human beings on the planet. The storekeeper was a short, fat man, always clutching a greasy kerchief, with which he would wipe away his abundant sweat. In fact, it would be true to say that this sticky handkerchief had become an integral part of his physique. At the entrance, he spoke to me harshly:

"You, little miss, stay outside. You already know your people can't come inside just like that."

"And why can't she come in?" the soldier asked.

"It's just that here, my dear sergeant, they know very well, there are rules here. These people can't come in."

"From now on, I'm the one drawing up the rules, the sergeant declared. This girl speaks Portuguese better than many Portuguese. And since she has come with me, she's going to come in with me."

"Very well, very well, then, if that's what Your Excellency wants." With his back turned to the soldier, he addressed me again: "Sit down over there, in the kitchen, on that little chair."

After that, they paid me no more attention. I contemplated the roof and noticed where the tiles had been repaired. And I was afraid about what was said in the village: The building had remained forever unfinished because at night an invisible hand undid what the Portuguese had built by day. Ghosts still lived there, hanging from the ceiling like huge bats.

The two newcomers wandered around the store with some difficulty, taking care not to stumble over the merchandise that was scattered carelessly across the floor. The days were long past when I would peep through the window of the store, attracted by piles of cloth and shoes. The disorder, however, was worse than ever: heaps of boxes and bundles; boxes torn open, allowing cans and bottles to tumble onto the floor.

My eyes paused on a roll of material with a blue-and-white check pattern. The soldier, guessing my thoughts, directed his question to me in a loud voice:

"Do you know what this is?"

"They're clothes, boss."

"Call me 'sergeant.' Did I hear you say these were clothes? The label states that this is striped denim, but to call them clothes requires a considerable degree of imagination. The thing is, no one in Europe, not even the poorest of the poor, would wear something made out of this."

He ripped a piece of the material and dangled it in front of the horrified storekeeper's face. "Look at this: steeped in starch! When this is washed, the white powder will be released, and all that will be left is a cobweb. It's like that horrible concoction they call 'Black Man's Wine.'"

The trader swallowed the insult. After all, the visitor was a member of the occupying power. Military opinion held more sway than his private business interests. When he gave his reply, his tone was contained, confirming his demotion from Sardinha to Musaradina: "These cloths, Excellency, are what we can sell here. Blacks aren't interested in the comfort of their clothes. As far as they are concerned, clothes are ornaments."

The people of Nkokolani, he went on to complain, didn't buy as much as other blacks. We VaChopi were happy enough with the resources of the land and the forest. "These guys even eat snakes. The others, the Vátuas, are right to look down on them," the storekeeper lamented.

"They aren't Vátuas, there is no such thing as Vátuas," I dared to correct him from my corner, in a faint thread of voice that no one heard. The soldier stopped in front of the wooden counter and, with one sweep of his hand, sent the rolls of material to the floor. The serenity with which he spoke contrasted with the decisiveness of his gesture: "I don't know how to say this. But there's no other, pleasanter way to tell you. My dear Sardinha, I've come to inspect this store. But there's another reason why we are here: we came here to arrest you."

"Arrest me?"

"Tomorrow, some sepoys will take you to Inhambane."

"Sepoys?"

Not for a second did the storekeeper's brainless smile fade. It was as if he had paid no attention to the warrant. "I'd like to offer you a drink," he said while he rolled up the cloths scattered across the floor. "This wine is the best there is, this is a fine tipple," he commented as he poured his visitors' wine into metal mugs.

"You've come to arrest me? May I ask what I am charged with?"

"You know very well what you've been selling here. And it hasn't been to the Vátuas, or the Chopi ..."

"I know where these rumors have come from, from that Indian ... from that Indian darky Assane, who's got a store in Chicomo. I swear to God ..."

"Let's not beat about the bush. You know why you're being arrested."

"To tell you the truth," the storekeeper replied, "all that interests me is that Your Excellencies are here with me. Whether you're here to arrest me is of little consequence. It's so long since I've seen a white man that I was beginning to forget my own race. Living alone among these kaffirs, I already saw myself as a black. That's why I say to you: Your Excellencies haven't come to arrest me.

You've come to liberate me."

He took a bottle from the cupboard. He wanted to celebrate that moment, even though it was based on an inconvenient bit of misfortune. The strangers were initially cautious in their reaction. But, little by little, all three Portuguese emptied bottle after bottle, and as they drank they became a family, even though they occasionally drifted into heated arguments.

At a certain point, the sergeant made a move to sit down on a wooden crate. He was reeling from drink, and already indisposed because of the heat. The storekeeper Sardinha hastened to stop the soldier: "Don't sit there, Sergeant. That crate contains a valuable consignment: bottles of port wine. And do you know who they're for? They're for Gungunhane—the best wine for our worst enemy."

"Our worst enemy is someone else. And you know who that is ..."

Sardinha was overcome with embarrassment. Owls could be heard scudding through the night, the oil in the lamps was threatening to run out, and the storekeeper was assailed by a sudden fit of melancholy: "Am I going to be taken away by sepoys? Couldn't I go alone? I promise not to run away. It's just that to pass these people while escorted by two blacks ..."

"Who said there would be two of them?"

And Fragata and Germano laughed. "In any case," the intendant's adjunct added, "you'll be escorted by sepoys and not Gungunhane." And they laughed even louder.

"It's not 'Gungunhane.' We say 'Ngungunyane.'"

The Portuguese gaped at me in surprise. They couldn't believe I had spoken, much less to correct their pronunciation.

"What was that you said?" Fragata asked, astonished.

"It's supposed to be pronounced 'Ngungunyane,'" I insisted gently.

They looked at each other blankly. Fragata imitated my diction, mocking my purist intentions. Then they went back to their drinking and complaining in hushed voices. After a while, I realized the soldier was mumbling: "What disturbs me more than anything about this Gungunhane is not that he hates us, but that he doesn't fear us."

"Do you know what we should do?" Sardinha suggested. "We should put some poison in these bottles, the ones you people insist on giving him! We don't even need to fire a single shot—one drop is enough. One drop and the entire Gaza Empire collapses."

"We've got orders not to kill him."

"Now I'm the one who feels like laughing," Fragata remarked. "We've got orders not to kill him? We're lucky he hasn't killed us all."

The storekeeper left for a moment and returned holding a musket. He hurried to calm those who had come to arrest him: "Don't worry yourselves, gentlemen, it's not loaded."

It was the gun he fell asleep clutching every night. He showed it off as if he were the proprietor of an arsenal rather than a store. And he declared: "This is the only language they understand. Or are you hoping to win the war with gifts and good manners?"

And he mumbled and muttered improprieties until he announced that he was going to bed. He spread some cloths over a sleeping mat and collapsed on the floor, hugging his old shotgun.

Germano dragged a chair over to sit beside me. Then he stared closely at me, as if he were studying a map. He had a fiery look in his eye. I was reminded of moths fluttering around the light of a lamp. The storekeeper noticed the visitor's interest, and, with his eyes half closed, warned: "Take care with that little girl. She's young, but she's got a woman's body. Black women are skilled in the devil's arts. I know what I'm talking about."

It only took a few minutes, however, for the sergeant to stop paying attention to me and begin to contemplate the wall against which he was resting his feet. He sat there for some time until he murmured: "There, on that wall there, lies my country." He pointed to a stain on the paint. It was a faded rectangle, caused by dampness that had discolored the lime wash. "That's Portugal there, on that wall."

Balancing himself precariously, he climbed up on the chair and scraped the stain with his fingernail, then looked down at the lime scattered on the floor as if he were standing before a dying animal. The attentive storekeeper immediately pointed to a broom: "Come on, girl. You're supposed to clean the floor, and you sit there in a daze?"

But the sergeant took the initiative and lifted the broom in the air as if it were a sword, proclaiming: "I'm the one who'll do the cleaning. That's what I came here to do—to clean up the filth that others have caused."

In the silence that followed, I began to think about the best way to make my exit. My shyness had taught me that the timid and the invisible become terribly exposed when they take their leave. It was night, and I was merely a woman among strangers. The storekeeper got up from his improvised bed and came over to me, carrying a box.

"Take this port wine to your father. It's my gratitude for all he has done for me. Take care, because it's heavy."

Stooping under the weight, I started to stagger across the darkened yard, but Sardinha's voice stopped me:

"Wait, I'll go with you and give you a hand as far as the road." Turning to the soldier inside the store, he asked: "May I, Sergeant? It's just five minutes; I won't run away."

The moment the storekeeper had closed the door, he directed his fetid breath at me and made the strangest request: he asked me to speak to him in Chopi while he gathered some herbs.

"Go on, speak, girl. Speak to me, address me as Musaradina."

"What do you want me to say, boss?"

"Anything, just talk, don't stop talking ..."

And he bent down, examining the ground, like a dog sniffing. He gathered up leaves and seeds and held everything up to his face, breathing in deeply, with his eyes closed. Then he straightened himself up and declared, "I saw him here, out here, in this open ground."

"Forgive me, boss, Musaradina: who did you see?"

"Gungunhane. He was here. He wanted to kill his beloved. And he wanted to die as well."

"Gungunhane was here?"

"He came here secretly, looking for the poison from the mri'mbava tree, which grows around here, near the lagoon at Nhanzié."

I looked at the storekeeper and saw that he was dark, with Sardinha's skin and Musaradina's soul. This Portuguese was a Chopi, one of us. Not just because he spoke our language, but because he spoke with his whole body. And Sardinha pressed on, mixing his languages: "Ngungunyane thought I could help him. He wanted to die and to kill. And all because of love—he had a forbidden love. Beautiful, isn't it?"

"What's beautiful? I don't understand."

"A man like him, who has all the women he wants, ends up not having the only one he really wants."

"Tell me, Sardinha—is there something you want to tell me?"

He didn't answer, just returned home, and when he reached the door, he waved to me. Whether it was in farewell or an order to hasten my departure, I don't know.

I hadn't taken more than half a dozen steps when I heard the shot. From behind the curtains, I was aware of a sudden movement of shadows and low voices. I turned back and found Francelino Sardinha dying in a pool of blood. The storekeeper was in his death throes, still clutching his old musket. He died hugging his shotgun, lying in the same position as when he was asleep.

Aroused by the gunshot, my brother Mwanatu appeared from the part of the building where he was quartered. Without uttering a word, he helped the sergeant to drag the body around to the back of the building, and then ran to the store to get shovels so they could dig a grave. When he got back, he found the sergeant on his knees, his head bowed. Germano de Melo's eyes were so blue that we feared he would go permanently blind if he were to cry. There were no tears. The white man was merely praying for the dead storekeeper. Fragata reminded him that he should pull himself together and cease his prayers. "People who commit suicide have no soul. One doesn't pray for them." These were Fragata's words.

The soldier got to his feet and grabbed one of the shovels Mwanatu had brought from the store. He began to dig frantically among the hard clods of earth. As I watched the men toiling, I couldn't help noticing the two Portuguese men's lack of skill. And this set me thinking: We blacks know how to handle a shovel far better than any other race. We are born with this skill, the same that makes us dance when we need to laugh, pray, or weep. Maybe because, for centuries, we have had to bury our dead ourselves—our dead, who are more important than the stars. And perhaps there was another reason: Europeans were bound to have black slaves in their own countries who would do this kind of work. Who knows, maybe there was a man of my own race waiting for me in Portugal? Who knows whether love didn't await me there, where only ships and gulls can reach?

6

The Sergeant's Third Letter

Nkokolani, January 12, 1895

Your Excellency Counselor José d'Almeida

I write to Your Excellency in order to apprise you of my arrival at Nkokolani, which occurred midmorning yesterday, in the company of the adjunct, Mariano Fragata. The news I send you is not the best, and I beg forgiveness in advance for the following report, which surely does not correspond with what Your Excellency was hoping to hear. Contrary to what we hoped, the grocer, Francelino Sardinha, was not awaiting us on our arrival. The young girl I mentioned in my last letter proved very useful. She is well educated and speaks our language beautifully. It was she who welcomed us. Her name is Imani, and she will prove extremely helpful to me in my mission.

I should mention that I have been considerably impressed by the cleanliness and dimensions of the settlement, which bear no comparison with those of other, similar villages in the neighboring territories of the Bitongas and VaTsongas. I asked the girl whether she was proud of the size and orderliness of her village. And she gave me a strange reply: Everyone there felt this pride except for her. For her, there was only one reason for its growth—fear. Nkokolani had grown in proportion to the extent that its inhabitants had shrunk. This was what Imani said, using these same sophisticated words. Then she added that its folk had gathered together there under the illusion that they were safer in numbers. But it is our terror that rules over us, she said, pointing to the leafy orange trees bordering the streets. These trees are sacred for the Chopi. The kaffirs believe that orange trees defend them from spells and curses, their worst enemies. Who knows, maybe I shall plant a tree in my backyard? If it does not give me protection, it will always afford me shade and fruit.

In contrast to the rest of the village, the military post where I shall be stationed is an example of total and absolute decline. To describe the decrepit building as a "barracks" can only stem from some huge distortion that fails to distinguish between fact and desire. It would be best if that hovel were demolished, for it is an unacceptable cross between an armory and a store for selling junk.

Your Excellency knows the history of that dilapidated building. The Portuguese dug the foundations and erected the walls more than two decades ago. The intention really was to build a garrison, but they did not get as far as making a roof, windows, or doors. The garrison remained an aspiration, but it began to crumble, abandoned and forgotten. Years later, an audacious trader by the name of Francelino Sardinha completed the building and set up his shop there. At the moment, the construction gives the impression of some hybrid creature: half fort, half store.

Now, even as I write, sitting at a table in the ill-fated store, hairy spiders crawl across my hands and over my papers. The loathsome creatures, along with a variety of nameless insects, are attracted by the light of the lamps. The alternative would be darkness, an unhappy anticipation of death. And Your Excellency knows how night falls early in this part of the world.

Last night, I crushed one of these disgusting spiders with a paperweight. A thick, foul-smelling squirt of liquid flooded the tabletop, rendering the correspondence lying there useless. My face, hands, and arms were splashed with the greenish venom. I was scared the poison might be absorbed by my skin and spread throughout my body. Imani tells me I should not kill animals. And she has a curious theory about the uses of spiders. She says their webs close the scars of the world, and they heal wounds that I don't know exist within me. In short, superstitions unique to these ignorant folk.

It is not just the dilapidated state of the military quarters that is a matter of concern to me. I must confess, counselor, my surprise upon seeing such extensive areas of land devoid of buildings and of Europeans. In my naïveté, I had a very different picture of the colony of Mozambique. I was under the impression we actually ruled over our territories. In fact, our presence has been limited for centuries to the estuaries of certain rivers, and to the provisioning of fresh water to ships. The sad reality: the only inhabitants of this vast hinterland are kaffirs and Indian traders. The rare signs of our presence are adulterated, thanks to people like the storekeeper and his ilk.

The courier charged with conveying this missive is called Mwanatu and is Imani's brother. The boy seems somewhat stupid, but, to be perfectly honest, I prefer this to someone shifty who might not be trusted. Taking advantage of Mwanatu's role as Sardinha's errand boy, I have given the simpleton tasks befitting an auxiliary soldier. For example, I have given him an obsolete rifle that no longer fires shots, and he has proudly assumed the duty of guarding the building.

I have not yet checked the arsenal that was left to the grocer to guard, and which I do not think was very large in terms of quantity. The task will require time and effort, because, at the moment, everything is mixed up: merchandise along with munitions. As soon as I have carried out a survey of the store, I shall send you a detailed report on the ordnance held here.

I should, in truth, say that huge and exaggerated expectations have begun to develop in Nkokolani regarding the arrival of Mouzinho de Albuquerque. Not that anyone knows him, and, to be perfectly honest, the Negroes can barely pronounce our cavalry captain's name. But their boundless fear is the reason they persist in fabricating some messiah who will save them. It is, of course, true that, after our recent military victories, many local southern rulers have turned their backs on Gungunhane and have sworn allegiance to us. Though our recent increase in influence may well have brought hope to the natives, the change in their loyalty may prove fatal to them. If we do not confirm the effectiveness of our power, these rulers will vacillate and, fearing terrible punishment, will become subjects of the great king of Gaza once again.

This is one of the reasons why these people place so much hope in the arrival of Mouzinho and his cavalry. There are, in fact, other reasons feeding into their attachment to the figure of Mouzinho.

The first is that many people in Nkokolani are tired of conversations. And they are perplexed at our insistence in negotiating with someone who is untrustworthy, rather than in waging war against the common enemy.

There is, however, another reason why they have invested in the construction of an imaginary savior. This has nothing to do with Mouzinho. It has, Your Excellency will be surprised to hear, to do with horses. According to the kaffirs, horses are not earthbound creatures. The kaffirs know this from the way their hooves tread the ground: with a nervous, restless step like that of long-legged birds. They don't walk or run like zebras or wildebeests, the nearest animals to horses that they know, creatures that tread the untamed ground with familiarity. Horses have a different gait, and they scarcely make contact with the ground. They advance across the veld as if they were clouds crossing the sky. Hence the belief: horses, they insist, were brought from that distant place where the earth's frontier touches the firmament. The kaffirs must certainly have seen images of Saint George and other saints descending from the skies on horseback, on the postcards distributed around here by the former priest.

Whatever we may think, this is how the kaffirs see it; this is their perception of an animal they have never seen before. If for us horses are a weapon of war, for these people they provoke other battles, equally serious and mortal. Inhambane is gripped by a war of witchcraft, potions, and curses. There isn't a witch doctor around here who is not busy blessing the arrival of our cavalry. When I mentioned here in Nkokolani that some of the horses—such as the one belonging to Ayres de Ornelas—had died of tremors and fevers, there were those who immediately attributed the illness to the VaNguni spirits. Similar blame was invented when they discovered that where there were assumed to be extensive green pastures all the grassland had suddenly become dry and barren. Such a sudden, inexplicable change could only be the work of villainous sorcerers.

Do not therefore believe, dear counselor, that they have any particular fellow feeling for those for whom Your Excellency harbors no affection. For all these reasons, I must encourage you not to ponder too much what the military may be planning. Continue your enterprising efforts in carrying out negotiations with the blacks.

Some say that our policy of dialogue betrays our fear and lack of preparation. These malicious tongues are ignorant of the State of Gaza's capacity for waging war. There are tens of thousands of fearless warriors, fully prepared and ideally equipped for a war out in the bush. I see open confrontation with Mudungazi's forces as no more than a reckless adventure destined to failure.

What we think is arrogance among the Negroes is merely an awareness of their numerical and military superiority. In fact, their insolence did not begin with Gungunhane. Over fifty years ago, the king of the Zulus, Dingane, treated us as his subordinates. He believed he had the power to dismiss and appoint European chiefs to govern territories that were ours by right but which he seemed to think belonged exclusively to him. The whole of the south of Mozambique, in his twisted understanding, was a Zulu colony temporarily ceded to the whites to administer.

This was how, in 1833, Dingane decided to replace the governor, Dionísio António Ribeiro, based in Lourenço Marques. He appointed in his place Anselmo Nascimento, a well-known trader who provided goods and services to the neighboring territories. The Zulu king was exchanging one white for another. Dingane argued that the Portuguese controlled each other better. The execution of this measure was, however, suspended. By the end of 1833, the Zulu ruler had decided to keep

Governor Ribeiro in power, even though the latter paid him no tribute.

Then, during the course of one of their raids to capture slaves, the Portuguese killed some Zulus by mistake. That was when the rupture occurred. Since Dionísio Ribeiro refused to be dismissed by someone who had not appointed him, King Dingane invaded the city, obliging the governor to seek refuge on the island of Xefina.

As Ribeiro was trying to escape in a small boat, he was caught and killed. They executed him publicly by breaking his neck. What did the Portuguese authorities do in response to this outrage? They ignored it. His successor as governor presented apologies in advance to Dingane, arguing that the colony was poor and that Lisbon's empty coffers rendered him unable to pay taxes to the Zulu emperor.

Cowardly postures such as these merely lend legitimacy to the imperialist pretensions of the English, proving to them that Portugal does not possess the capabilities to govern her African colonies. I do not know whether I feel greater hatred of English ambitions or our own authorities' shameful submission.

7

On Bats' Wings

Our highways were once as timid as rivers and as gentle as women. They asked for permission to be born. Now these highways are taking over the landscape and extending their great legs over time, just as the owners of the world do.

The VaChopi owe their name to their skill at handling bows and arrows. My father, Katini Nsambe, was the exception, growing up as he did outside this tradition, far from hunting and waging war. His passion, apart from alcohol, was music—the marimba. Maybe it was this gift for creating harmonies that made him so averse to violence. My father was a tuner of the infinite marimba that is the world.

Everyone acknowledged that he was the finest maker of xylophones. He would make them as if he were making himself. It wasn't an act of creation but a process of gestation. Each stage in this long genesis was accompanied by a ritual of prayers and silences, so that other hands, so ancient that they were indiscernible, might guide his gestures.

From the time when I was a little girl, I would go with my dear old father to look for *mimuenge* trees, the only ones that provided high-quality material. I would help him cut the wood, tie the strips of leather linking the wooden boards, and look for the gourds to make the resonators, which are placed under the keys. Each gourd was tested a thousand times, until the right note was found. It was my job to look after the beeswax, which was then used to seal the gourds.

It was because of these marimbas that I got up early one particular day to accompany my father to the forest of the great fig trees we call *mphama*. Ever since I was a girl, I had been given a responsibility normally assigned to a boy: to climb the fig trees in order to catch bats and tear their wings off, without getting bitten by their venomous teeth. After drying, the membranes from their wings were used to line the resonators. This was the most precious secret in my father's technique for making marimbas.

I began to develop skills in catching the large bats, the ones that are such voracious eaters of fruit. In the upper branches, they hang upside down, swaying like living pendulums, alert but without any apparent fear. I would watch them hanging aloft in a row for some time before casting my net over them. It was impossible to tell which were alive and which were dead. Their claws clung so tenaciously to the branches that even after they died they remained hanging there, drying out until they were no more than shriveled shadows. Some of us humans share the same fate: we die inside, and are only held together by our similarity to the living we once were.

On the highest branches, clusters of females were suckling their young. They were so like tiny people that I avoided looking them in the eye, so as not to cause my hunter's instinct to falter. That feeling of compassion became more pronounced as my dreams of becoming a mother grew. Until that time when, facing the trunk I was supposed to climb, I plucked up courage and announced, "I'm sorry, Father, but I'm not going up there ever again."

My old father was astonished by my attitude. A father

in Nkokolani never takes no for an answer. But he smiled with unexpected sweetness. "Don't you want to go up?" he asked, with a bewildered look on his face. I refused silently but firmly. To my surprise, he accepted my refusal. "Have you taken pity on the bats? I understand, girl. And I'm going to tell you why I acknowledge your decision."

Then he told me an age-old story he had heard from his grandparents. In those days, bats crossed the skies with the pride of those who believe they are unique creatures in this world. On one occasion, a bat fell to the ground injured at a crossroads. Some birds passed by and said: "Look, there's one of ours! Let's help him!" So they took him to the kingdom of the birds. But when the king of the birds saw the dying bat, he remarked: "He's got hairs and teeth; he's not one of ours. Take him away from here." So the poor bat was taken back to where he had fallen. Then some mice passed by and said: "Look, there's one of ours! Let's help him!" And they brought him before the king of the mice, who declared: "He's got wings; he's not one of ours. Take him back!" So they returned the bat, by now in its death throes, to the fateful crossroads. And there he died, abandoned and alone, the creature who aspired to belong to more than one world.

The moral of the fable was obvious, which was why I was surprised when he asked me at the end, "Did you understand, girl?"

"I think so."

"I doubt it. For this isn't a story about bats. It's about you, Imani. You and the worlds that mingle within you."

◆

Katini's artistry wasn't limited to the creation of marimbas. He was a composer and the leader of an orchestra consisting of ten members. He put on shows in our village and toured others. I would attend his concerts and watch, fascinated, as dancers dressed as warriors pretended to fight, wielding shields and rattles. Lying on their backs, they would leap up as if possessed by spirits emerging from the depths of the earth.

"Why do we play at wars?" I would ask, frightened.

My father never answered. Maybe we were incapable of living without fear. By dancing with ghosts, we ended up taming them. The problem with ghosts is that they are forever hungry. One day, they devour us, and we turn into our own phantoms.

Whatever the case, the truth is that this display of virile rhythm tore me away from the world, and although the dance was performed exclusively by men, I swayed to its rhythm with my whole body, in spite of my modest status. It was as if another person were dancing inside me. Perhaps that person was "Live Girl," or perhaps she was "Ash." Maybe she was all those girls who had dwelt within me. At that moment, I was released from my body, freed from the obligations of memory. I was happy.

◆

When the dance was over, the dancers plunged helplessly to the ground, as if they had been struck through by death itself. Only then were women allowed to participate. One or two mothers stepped forward from the audience and pretended they were looking for their sons among the warriors sprawled on the ground. In contrast to the exuberance and joy of the dance, that moment dragged me down into a feeling of hopeless anguish.

And I invariably ended up crying.

"Didn't you like it, daughter?"my mother asked when it was all over.

I nodded and replied that, yes, I had enjoyed it. And she would put her arm around my shoulder and comfort me: "It's all a game, my girl." But in the tone of her voice and the weight of her arm, there was a much greater sadness than mine. And she explained the reason for her melancholy: Whether it was on the dancing stage or on the real battlefields, we never found a son who was ours alone. All those who have fallen are our sons. The mothers of my homeland mourn all sons lost to war.

◆

It was almost noon, and my father was sitting with an open book on his knees. On the cover were the words *Manual for Learning to Read*. I had found the book ages ago, among the old odds and ends left in the church, and made a point of giving it to him at the time. Never before had he been so touched by a gift. Not a day went by without his passing his fingertips over the pages as if he had just created them. "Instead of words," he said, "I hear music." And he would drum his fingers on the pages as if they were the keys of a marimba.

"Father, aren't you scared of the VaNguni?"

"We need to put fear into those who want to scare us. That's the reason why I'm learning, with the help of this book."

He closed the book with extreme care, and with the same solicitude he put it away in a leather bag. Then he gave a deep sigh.

"They say I surrendered to the Portuguese; they say I sold my soul to the whites. But let me ask you this: do you know the little bird that lives on the hippo's back?"

I knew the bird and, what was more, I knew the saying. My father repeated the old fable once more: Everyone says that little bird lives off the hippo's leathery skin. But when the bird leaves, the hippo dies within a few days. To which he concluded with the enthusiasm of one who had made a new discovery: "I'm that little bird on the hippo's back. I'm the one who sustains the VaLungu, the whites in the Lands of the Crown. As far as your mother is concerned, all I do is drink and make marimbas ..."

"Father, I'm not going to do those tasks anymore."

"Your tasks haven't yet begun. Let the Portuguese sergeant settle in, and then present yourself at the barracks, all clean, pretty, and nicely dressed. Ready for your tasks ..."

"It wasn't those tasks I was talking about. I'm telling you that I'm not going to climb trees anymore, I'm not going to kill any more bats ..."

"Ah, that work's over and done with. You've got other duties now. And I'll tell you this in advance: When the sergeant gives you a reward, it won't be out of generosity. It will be payment for the favors I've done him. I've handed them a daughter, and, what's more, I've given them a son. Hasn't what I've given them got a price?"

"I made a promise that I wasn't going back to that man Sardinha's store ..."

"Don't call it a store. It's a garrison. And it's there that you can help your brother. He's a good boy, my little Mwanatu, and he never fails to deliver the mail. You can't imagine what he goes through to bring those papers."

"You know perfectly well how dangerous the task is. Just imagine what would happen if my little brother lost a letter, slipped and fell into the river ..."

"That's nothing to do with you—it's men's business. What I want to know is this: you've read the letters, haven't you, my girl?"

"Some of them, yes."

"So satisfy my curiosity, then. When does this big Portuguese chief get here?"

As far as my father was concerned, all the Portuguese were big chiefs. But he understood my hesitation and explained himself better: "I'm talking about the one who left Lisbon to come and kill Ngungunyane ..."

"Mouzinho de Albuquerque? I don't know, Father. The ship he was traveling on was hit by a storm."

"A storm?"

"Just as he was leaving Lisbon, the ship was almost sunk by a storm."

His son Mwanatu had already told him of the early setback that had befallen Mouzinho de Albuquerque's voyage. No one should have any illusions, my old father confided: that wasn't a storm, it was the result of an invocation.

"Father, be careful. No one must know that I read the telegrams of the Portuguese."

"Do you think I'm crazy? Do you think I don't know what the Portuguese do to spies? I've exposed a good few myself."

"The news I've brought you is contained in secret messages sent from Lisbon and Lourenço Marques. No one else must know ..."

"I suspect someone is passing along information. And that someone has given a witch doctor, a maker of storms, some news."

"Don't ever say the name of your suspect. I beg you, Father, for the love of God! Even here, out here in this wilderness, I'm scared someone will hear us."

"He may be your brother, he may be my son, but one of these days I'll forget I'm his father and I'll turn him in."

"For God's sake, don't say that. It's not fair. Father, you always treated Dubula as if he weren't your son."

"Tell me this, then: who's his hero?"

"I've never asked him."

"The great hero of that brother of yours is the emperor Ngungunyane. So answer me this: can such a person be my son?"

"What are you thinking of doing? Turning him over to the Portuguese?"

"That's exactly what I'll do. One of these days, when I meet your brother, I'll do something that will make him regret he once stood up to me."

"But, Father, please think carefully. There have always been storms. Why should this one be any different?"

"Well, I'm going to tell you something, and it's this: I went to the *nyatisholo*, I consulted the soothsayer. I went there, to Aunt Rosi, to find out whether the storm had been invoked or not."

He had sat down before the prophetess, unfolding his legs out of respect, so sad and subdued that his legs went numb on the seating mat. He asked Rosi to listen more carefully than ever before, for he was about to read out loud the text that his daughter had brought from the sergeant's quarters.

"You took the report to Aunt Rosi's house, Father?"

"That's right."

"But that's madness! And what if the sergeant discovers his papers are missing?"

"There's only one paper, and that's the one I've got here."

He took a crumpled piece of paper from his pocket

and began to read it as slowly as someone deciphering one letter at a time. Turning the paper over and over, pretending that his difficulties in reading it were merely the result of fleeting shadows cast by the clouds, he uttered each sentence, stumbling over words so much that saliva dripped from his chin onto his shaking hands:

... The *Peninsular*, on which our Captain Mouzinho de Albuquerque was traveling, upon leaving the port of Lisbon, was struck by a storm such as had never been seen before along that coast. The sea plunged into chasms and rose as high as mountains, rendering the ship so tiny that not even God could see where it was. The waves were so high that the ship's propeller came loose and was lost at the bottom of the ocean. The Peninsular thus drifted, detached from human control. French and English ships came to her assistance. They threw her cables, but the cables snapped. They launched lifeboats, but these were unable to make headway, so rough was the sea. Eventually, without anyone being able to understand fully, the storm abated and Mouzinho's ship returned to Lisbon for repairs and thereafter to continue her journey with the Lord's blessing ...

"Are you surprised I've read all these words?" Katini asked with a mocking look. It was you who taught me, he concluded as he folded the paper and put it back in his pocket.

"But, Father, have you only got that one sheet of paper? What happened to the others?"

"The nyatisholo needed them."

Aunt Rosi, his most respected sister-in-law, didn't need to raise her voice in order to be obeyed promptly during his consultation with her: "Put those bits of paper in the water!"

The sheet floated in the basin that the woman had placed on her ample thighs. The paper swayed like a boat in a storm. Then the ink began to dissolve, and a storm cloud darkened the water. That stain would forever flood Katini's soul.

"That ink isn't coming from the paper," the soothsayer announced. "That ink is coming from your veins."

Katini Nsambe watched, aghast, as the now blank sheet sank into the water. Rosi asked him to give her the rest of the report.

"I need that writing," she said. "Written words are mighty spells, capable of potent magic. I want to use these papers for my task."

"I'll give you everything, but first I want to know the outcome of my visit."

"Of one thing you can be sure: The storm didn't come from the sea. The storm had an owner. Whoever arranged for this spell to be cast will repeat it. And the victim will always be this Portuguese, this man Mousey ..."

"Mouzinho," my father corrected.

"More witchery will follow, in Africa and in Portugal."

"Who arranged for the storm, Aunt Rosi?"

"You know that, Katini. The one who opens the door is the one who's inside the house."

◆

Katini handed me the only page left from the report on Mouzinho's voyage. He thought that this would mitigate my sadness. And it was to distract me that he began to talk again: "I'm going to tell you one thing. When the Portuguese army comes to our rescue, you'd better be careful, daughter."

"Why, Father?"

"Those whites will be riding horses. Have you ever seen a horse? I saw one in Inhambane. You've got to be careful with an animal like that, girl. Never look one in the eye."

The eyes of a horse are incandescent. They are made of dark water, like deep lakes, but water that's ablaze. Whoever looks into their eyes will be left with a soul that's no more than a cinder.

"That's where wizardry likes to dwell: in the eyes. On the day I first met your mother, our eyes met with such passion that you, Imani, were born at that exact moment."

He swatted the flies circling around his face. His gesture followed an arc, as if he had really captured something in the air.

"So have you gone to start classes with Sergeant Germano?"

"Yes, but he seems to have no wish to learn."

In the very first class, the Portuguese didn't even look up from the correspondence scattered across his desk. Without looking at me, he made it clear that he only wanted to learn the minimum—whatever he needed to know to give orders. In fact, he would never learn a single word. He was, after all, going to live in complete solitude. Who would he give orders to?

"The sergeant's right. I've never understood why they want to learn a black man's language," my father said with a sigh.

"They don't. They have their orders."

"Whether he has classes or not, always show up at his house. That man is going to be our guarantee. As long as the sergeant is here among us, we'll be protected."

"I'll make sure I do, Father."

"And let me say something else. If, one day, that white man wants something more from you, you know what to do."

"I don't understand, Father."

"What I'm saying is quite simple: you've got to be for him what all women are in this world. Do you understand?"

I silently dug my feet into the sand as if I were damming a river. And it was my tears I was damming. It would have been better if I had allowed myself to weep out loud. Our mother used to say that when we weep our soul follows the example of the earth under rain: it becomes clay. Clay gives us the house we live in; it is clay that shapes our hand.

8

The Sergeant's Fourth Letter

Nkokolani, March 13, 1895

Your Excellency Counselor José d'Almeida

I am deeply sorry that the letter sent in Fragata's care went astray. More than by its mere loss, I am beset by the thought that it might have fallen into unknown hands. Nonetheless, I have every confidence in the messenger responsible for delivering this missive. I have already mentioned him before. This auxiliary it has been my misfortune to be assigned goes by the name of Mwanatu. He is somewhat retarded but of absolutely proven loyalty. His sister, Imani, on the other hand, is lively and intelligent, and we all but forget that we are dealing with a young black girl.

I am grateful for your warning not to send any information directly to Lourenço Marques without referring it first for Your Excellency's appraisal. I would never have believed such discord possible in our administration. Your Excellency may rest assured; I shall be worthy of the trust you place in me.

I should add, sir, that there is no basis to Your Excellency's suspicion that our correspondence is subject to unexplained deviations and intrusions. The only person who could intrude upon the secrecy of this missive would be the aforementioned Mwanatu, the fellow who cleans and looks after my quarters. He is the only person who carries the mail. The lad learned to read, but only in very rudimentary fashion. However, I am sure that he would no more risk opening letters than give them to someone else to read.

I am therefore at liberty, without any fear of intrusion in this report, to furnish you with the details Your Excellency requested concerning the tragic event that followed the arrest of the grocer, Francelino Sardinha.

Here is how it happened. In carrying out the orders received in Lourenço Marques, we placed the grocer under arrest. We did not consider it necessary to hand-cuff him, and, in all honesty, he did not seem downcast by the news. On the contrary, he appeared so relieved to have our company that he did not even ask why he had become the target of suspicion. This absence of surprise was, for me, clear evidence of his admission of guilt.

His only request was that we spare him being exhibited in the streets, in chains and escorted by Negro sepoys. During the remainder of our conversation, he seemed friendly, though in complete disagreement with our co-lonial policy. Suddenly, however, his mood changed radically. He became aggressive, and even slighted our brave army. I remember his exact words: "To hell with your heroism. Defeating a horde of blacks who charge bare-chested against your rifles and machine guns!" I did not need to answer these outrageous provocations, for Fragata retorted in no uncertain terms, reminding him that many kaffirs already possess rifles and ma-chine guns.

But Francelino Sardinha, irate as he was, would not be budged from his arguments. With his firsthand knowl-edge of a reality we can only gauge through written reports, the storekeeper insisted that the vast majority of Vátuas refuse European weapons. These were his words: "They don't use the rifles they are given. They say that fighting from a distance is for cowards. What these people trust is their potions and amulets, which they are convinced protect them against bullets. God forgive me, but even I confess that I now believe in their superstitions."

I relate what happened on that fateful night with all the details of a recollection that is still at its most vivid, and I shall proceed with scrupulous care, because the conversation we exchanged may prove useful in assessing the tensions that divide us Portuguese. For example, the storekeeper spent much time confronting the impassive Fragata, asking him whether he spoke any of the languages of the blacks. He wanted to know whether our negotiators had ever bothered to learn any of these languages. He said that he, Sardinha, spoke the dialect of the kaffirs because life had required him to learn it. That he wasn't like the "others" who had been in Africa for years and didn't know a word of the local language. That is what the storekeeper said.

At this point, it was the envoy who lost his temper. And as he was addressing Sardinha, he lost control and blurted out our true intentions: "And you, my dear Sardinha, do you speak English when you go to South Africa to sell our military secrets to the English?"

The storekeeper remained silent for a time. He emptied his glass in one go to gain courage, and then asked: "Do you know what language we speak, me and the English? We speak Zulu." According to him, the English, unlike the Portuguese, learned to speak the kaffirs' languages. This was why they were on good terms with the court of Gungunhane and sat at his side as advisers. I have to confess that this praise for the English, in contrast to his attribution of some innate deficiency to the Portuguese, made my blood boil.

Perhaps it was because of this that I decided to salvage our honor and argue for the use of interpreters in our African territories. To speak Portuguese and to teach others to speak it was part of our civilizing mission. Ever hostile, the storekeeper warned us we would be naïve to trust interpreters. The same fatal gullibility had us distributing weapons among kaffirs we assumed were our allies. The crazed grocer's conclusion could not have been more harrowing: "We shall be killed by the very rifles we put in their hands. And the order to kill will be given in Portuguese, in the language we put in their mouths."

I have to say that, by this time, Sardinha was talking to himself. Both Fragata and I were busy unpacking the belongings we most needed from our bags. I was surprised at the storekeeper's enthusiasm when he saw me hang my rifle from a nail in the wall. In a loud voice, he uttered the following words: "Well, there it is, the only language these folk understand, hanging on that wall."

I asked him to watch his words, for the next day he would have to walk through the kaffir village escorted by two armed sepoys. The grocer kept up his arrogant demeanor and commented with irony upon the Portuguese and their inconsistencies: while he was being arrested, the Portuguese authorities were promoting Gungunhane to a rank above mine in the military hierarchy. And Sardinha even went on to pour scorn on Lisbon's appointment of the Vátua chief to the rank of colonel in our army, with a right to honors and privileges. Moreover, what he then revealed, I have to admit, filled me with anger: "Do you know how that black refers to us Portuguese? He calls us 'my white Shangaan subjects.' We're his slaves, the slaves of that man Gungunhane. That's all we are, his slaves ..."

The conversation continued late into the night. Imani, who had witnessed the whole discussion, took her leave, and the storekeeper asked permission to go outside with her for a few minutes. After a brief absence, the man returned home in an unseemly manner, to commit suicide right there in front of us.

Your Excellency cannot imagine the discomposure that followed this act of madness. I had to bury the unfortunate storekeeper immediately, and with my very hands cleaned away the blood that had spread across the floor of the shop that we call a barracks. Even today, as I write, I see blood covering my fingers.

I remember my friend Fragata, seeing me in such a state, coming to my assistance:

"Don't concern yourself so much, my dear Germano. Our wretched storekeeper didn't just kill himself because he was under arrest. The crime he was charged with was far more serious than the sale of arms and elephant tusks to the English."

"And what was that?"

"Spying for the English. As soon as he got to Inhambane, the man would have been put in front of a firing squad. And Sardinha knew that."

"Would we shoot a Portuguese? Would we kill one of our own?"

"That's precisely the point: The storekeeper had long ceased being one of ours. He was, indeed—how shall I put it?—he was a black man, just a bit lighter, that's all. That's why he spoke the language of the kaffirs."

"Apart from this," Fragata continued, "Sardinha wasn't detained over kaffir matters. The blacks," said Fragata, "are the phantom that haunts us, but they don't exist in their own right. It's the English who are behind them. They are our true enemies."

My colleague believed that he had removed the burden of guilt from me by inciting my animosity toward the English. But I remained riven by remorse. Then, as if as a last attempt, Mariano Fragata led me out to the back of the house and pointed to a stone wall. "Do you see those holes, all in a line? Do you know what that is?"

"I've got no idea."

"All those holes were made by bullets. That wall," he concluded, "was where the firing squad carried out its executions. In Inhambane, they told me it wasn't worth bringing the storekeeper to the city. We should execute him right here, against that wall."

"We were supposed to shoot him here?"

"You're the soldier; you're the one who would have shot him. So you see? It was much better that he shot himself."

9

Message from the Dead, Silence from the Living

The difference between war and peace is as follows: in war, the poor are the first to be killed; in peace, the poor are the first to die. For us women, there's another difference too: in war, we get raped by those we do not know.

We were in Nkokolani because we had fled, because of lies and cowardice. We had been happy by the sea, in Makomani. It was there that I was born, there that I grew up as a boarder at the Mission School, there that I learned to be the woman I am today. My mother, above all my mother, had been happy in that little village on the shores of the Indian Ocean. It was our grandfather Tsangatelo, the most senior member of our family, who one day, and for no apparent reason, ordered us to leave that place, and never to return. It was an unexpected decision, and it was as if we were being pushed away by ghosts.

This was how we came to settle in Nkokolani, an inland village, where only the presence of the River Inharrime allayed our longing for the vast ocean. Without ever talking about it openly, we hoped that our grandfather would one day explain things. Or, better still, that we might return from our exile. And that is what went through our minds when, a year ago, he ordered a meeting of the whole family.

We were all together, sitting in the yard of his house, when Tsangatelo emerged from his bedroom, carrying baggage, as if he were going on a journey: a sleeping mat, a blanket, a roll of tobacco, a goatskin bag full of manioc flour. And a gourd brimming with water.

"Are you leaving, Grandfather?"

"I'm going to emigrate; I'm going to the mines."

The family's initial response was to laugh. The mines require men of a certain age; the earth's belly feeds on youth. Tsangatelo was over sixty. He wouldn't even last the journey, which would be done on foot. At that time, there were still no recruitment companies of the type that later would be responsible for mobilizing the miners and organizing their transport.

Yet Tsangatelo had never been more serious. He was determined to go to work in the English domains. He was going to the Daimond, which was what we called the diamond mines of South Africa. Alarmed by the gravity of his announcement, the whole family huddled together in the yard of his house. They tried to dissuade him. They began by arguing the matter of his age. Then they resorted to other lines of reasoning. Grandfather should pay attention to the wretched state in which migrant workers returned home.

My uncle Musisi was the most vociferous of all our relatives: "Our people's departure for the Rand is worse than all the wars that have been waged against us."

Our young men, he argued, were no longer the same when they returned from South Africa. They never went back to being VaChopi. Grandfather Tsangatelo remained impassive, ignoring everyone. Uncle Musisi persisted: The mines of the Transvaal were killing our nation. In the old days, we would pay the bride price with our own cattle. Now the only things people wanted were those famous English pounds.

Another family member countered this, remarking that, although the Portuguese paid us in their own money, they made us pay them in English money. In that situation, how was it possible not to emigrate?

A heavy, resigned silence had fallen on everyone when Grandmother, her voice shaking, confronted her husband: "Is that the example you want to set for our family?"

"What family?" Grandfather asked.

And the woman said no more.

◆

Before he left Nkokolani, my grandfather summoned me. He was violating the rules of our village: no one talks of serious matters with a child, especially if that child is female. At the time, I couldn't have been more than ten years old. Today I understand the reason for the summons: our elder just needed to listen to himself. Standing there in front of me, he recalled the moment he had been called to visit his dying father. He didn't have the courage. He was unable to contemplate a destiny that would, in the end, be his own as well. Now, so many years later, he looked at me and opened his heart:

"Now, with these new Nguni invasions, it's the same thing. I don't want to be summoned to witness an even greater death: the death of my homeland."

I looked at his callused feet. At that moment, I felt ashamed of my sandals, and my legs were heavy with guilt. With the exception of my household, no one in the village wore shoes. That was enough for us to be called VaLungu, or whites.

Then Tsangatelo asked me to go and get one of the notebooks I kept at home. He wanted to dictate to me a dream that was haunting him. He wanted me to write down his exact words. Then I was to tear up the paper so

that he would be free of his nightmare. I did what he
asked.

◆

"Write, granddaughter, write down my dreamed beings.
You, granddaughter, may ask, 'Dreamed beings?' And I
shall reply: 'Yes, dreamed beings.'

"Because I dreamed them. I say I dream them and not
I dream of them. The dead soldiers come to me every
night, more awake than I am, come to me from all the
battles ever fought anywhere. And then they shake me
with their gangling arms in order to tell me that they
have come because of this new war.

'What war?' I ask them in alarm.

'The one that's about to begin,' my dreamed beings
reply.

"I take a quick look outside the house. But it's just to
distract them, for they know I can't see beyond my own
self. I am a ransacked field, a cemetery larger than the
world itself.

"All these dreamed beings weigh so heavily upon me
that they sink my dream, for they travel carrying the
weapons that cut them down.

'Give me some respite,' I beg them.

'It wasn't us who opened the door,' they reply. 'It was
you. You are the dreamer.'

"I point to the walls of my room and show them how
limited the space is: 'In no time at all, I won't be able to
accommodate any more of you.' And they answer: 'When
that happens, you are the one who will have to leave the
dream.'

"I then realized I needed to appeal to their good sense.
I waved to the one who was nearest and was getting

ready to whisper something in his ear when he declared brusquely: 'There's no point in being secretive. We can all hear you before you even speak.'

'The war you speak of may be slow to start,' I argued.

'Well, in that case, we'll fire shots at you.'

'But I'm the dreamer.'

'Not any longer. Now we are the ones dreaming you.'"

◆

When Tsangatelo had finished dictating his nocturnal fantasies, he straightened his back as if relieved. Then he asked me to hand him the sheet of paper on which I had written, so that he could personally tear it up and cast it to the winds. And that's what he did, turning slowly and throwing the pieces of paper to the four points of the compass. Then, his eyes open wide, he stretched out his arms and faced the sun, proclaiming:

"Farewell, my dreamed beings. I'm going where I shall be the owner of my own dreams."

And he took his leave. I stood motionless, watching how Tsangatelo walked away with that shrewd ability to be no more than a shadow. Those feet furrowing through the sand were older than the earth itself. In those steps of his, all my ancestors advanced as well.

◆

My grandfather was my age when our lands were first invaded. We couldn't understand why these people considered us animals and appreciated their cattle more than they did the people they conquered. We couldn't understand why they stole our livestock, killed our people, and raped our women. They called us *tinxolo*, or "heads." That's how they saw us: we were counted as slaves, discounted as animals. With fire and brimstone, they founded an empire that was passed on from grandfather to son, from son to grandson. And it was now this grandson, Ngungunyane, who was castigating us once more.

The persistence of their aggression wrought changes among our folk. We had always lived dispersed in small groups, and occupied in minor conflicts with our nearest neighbors. But this threat had united us as one people. We became the VaChopi, "those of the bow and arrow." We resisted the invasion of the VaNguni; we maintained our language, our culture, and our gods. We paid dearly for our obstinacy. The price Tsangatelo paid was to be dislocated from his own life.

◆

A year had passed since Grandfather's departure. One morning, a messenger arrived at our house: our relative had been lost inside the mine where he was working.

"Did he die?" Grandmother asked, devoid of emotion.

No, he hadn't died. He'd just got lost. That's what the messenger answered. Or maybe "lost" wasn't the right word, he added, in sudden doubt.

"Well, so he did die, then," Grandmother concluded. "Isn't that the news you're bringing us?"

I offered the visitor a coconut shell full of nsope. The man stood there impassively, examining the drink. I don't know why, but I recalled an old song from my childhood: "How beautiful are a messenger's feet ..." And this messenger's feet gradually made their way into the song, as if they were leading me away, far from the village.

At last, the emissary raised the coconut shell to his lips. Never before had I seen anyone drink so slowly. He was worried about the news that he still had to give. In the end, he gained courage: It wasn't certain that Grandfather Tsangatelo had got lost by accident. Everything suggested that our elder had lost his bearings of his own free will.

"Of his own free will?" my grandmother mused, then immediately concluded: "It's not my husband."

Among his workmates there was only one explanation: Tsangatelo had decided to live forever in those subterranean labyrinths. Our relative had exiled himself inside the mine, wandering eternally through the darkness. The miners could sometimes hear someone digging away down in the depths. It was Tsangatelo, opening up new galleries. He had gnawed away at the belly of the earth so much that there wasn't a corner of it he hadn't reached. The danger for us was that the entire nation would sink, lacking the ground to support it.

Our grandmother laughed, neither sad nor angry. And she commented, "That miserable wretch should have returned my bride price long ago ..."

"You may not like what I'm going to say next," the visitor apologized. And he held his cup out for me to fill again.

"Go on, my friend," my grandmother encouraged him. "Tsangatelo has got lost in the bowels of the earth? You couldn't have brought me better news."

There was, however, a more serious aspect to the matter. This had been the subject of conversation in the compounds where the miners slept. There were murmurings that, from time to time, a woman went down into the galleries to take him food and water. That's how old Tsangatelo survived.

"A woman?" My grandmother asked. "Is that what you said: a woman?"

I glanced at grandmother's face, assessing the darkness of her eyes. No sign of jealousy, no surprise. Nothing. Not even a hint. The messenger wiped his trembling lips various times with the back of his hand. He wasn't cleaning them. He was plucking up enough courage to continue.

"You're not going to enjoy the rest of the story."

"The rest? What rest?"

"In fact, no one believes that the woman who goes to him is really a woman."

"So what is she, then? A spirit?"

"It's a man."

"A man?"

"A *tchipa*. One of those men who, among the miners, perform the role of a woman. The truth is this: your husband is now married to a tchipa."

Only then did my grandmother appear affected. Her look of scorn gave way to a mask of hurt and astonishment. We had all heard tell of those miners who "marry" other men and forget the wives they left behind in their homelands. But we would never have imagined Grandfather Tsangatelo becoming one of them.

With unexpected vigor, grandmother snatched the coconut shell with its nsope from the intruder's hand, threw it to the ground, and sent the messenger away. She waited until the man had disappeared and then shouted: "Tsangatelo is no longer a person! He's dead. Tsangatelo has died."

She rushed noisily into the house and straightaway set about throwing all her husband's possessions outside. Like a widow, she beat all his belongings with a rod. She was purging them of death's impurities. Then, as her stick whistled through the air, she declared, "That mole is going to rot away in the hole he's dug himself."

Her words rang out like some terrible malediction. But for me, it had the opposite effect: Grandfather was telling us there was a way out. Nkokolani was not, after all, like those tiny places where the only road out is also the way back. He had left and hadn't returned.

Even today, as I fall asleep, I can hear his long fingers digging away in the earth's belly. And that's how he is unearthing the stars next to our anthill. It is also how my mother and I buried our dream of one day returning to live by the sea again.

◆

It was noon, and it was so hot that even the flies had given up flying, from drowsiness. We were out at the back, in the shade. Aunt Rosi had come to visit us in the morning and had stayed on as if she had forgotten she lived somewhere else. She had an excuse for remaining: The paths must be on fire. At that hour, chunks of fire broke away from the sun, and no one could walk across the ground.

Mother was braiding her hair and was chuckling at the white strands her sister-in-law wanted her to hide under her new hairstyle. My father then got up and showed them a colored page he had stolen from a book in the old church. Prior to this, he had been staring at the sheet of paper as if it contained the answer to all our afflictions.

"Can you see the angels here?"

"I don't see any black angel," Rosi commented with irony. And she and my mother laughed.

"Be quiet, this is very serious. I want to ask you ladies

something. If one of these angels appeared in Nkokolani now, what would we ask for?"

"If real people don't listen to us, what's the use of asking for things from someone who doesn't exist?"

"I would ask for a husband for Imani," joked Rosi.

"If only they had oars instead of wings ...," Mother said, sighing.

I still hoped my father might want to hear my wish. But instead of that, he decided to speak on my behalf: there was no point in asking me, because he was sure of what I secretly longed for.

"Isn't that so, daughter?"

Then he adopted a rigid posture, beat his chest above the sheet of paper, and declared that, in his case, he wouldn't ask for anything. "I've been thinking," he announced, "and I have decided, as an elder of the Nsambe family, I shall speak with the spirits."

"The sun isn't even high and he's already drunk," my mother remarked.

That night, in the cemetery, there would be a ceremony to remember Tsangatelo and to ask him to bring us peace. Much more than the sympathy of the Portuguese, we must gain the goodwill of our ancestors. This cult reflected the division that dominated our family. For some, such as Grandmother and my father, our elder was dead; for others—and I was one of those others—Tsangatelo was alive and merely trudging through a long, dark tunnel. One day, he would be expelled from this tunnel, as if he were being born for a second time.

◆

The preparations for the ceremony required effort from all of us. I was charged with the task farthest away from the house: I spent the whole afternoon collecting firewood. And I gathered sticks and twigs as if they were bits of myself that I reassembled under my arm. Following the example of the other wives in Nkokolani, my mother had left large bundles of firewood burning during the night. That was what they always did. In the morning, when the houses awoke once more, the fire was already lit. In this way, the men were spared the task of lighting a new fire. In our village, lighting a flame is the exclusive responsibility of husbands.

Night had already fallen, and I hadn't finished piling up the wood in the yard. It was at this point that the church bell began ringing by itself. The birds took to their wings in alarm, and the villagers sought refuge in their houses. The local blind man, who never went out into the street, then appeared in the village square. He had returned from the war years ago without any sign of injury. But the war had invaded his head, extinguishing his sight from the inside.

The blind man listened to the fluttering of the birds' wings around him and declared: "My brothers, these are the last birds! Take a good look, because you'll never see them again."

He spun around, his arms open like wings, as if he were doing a dance on his sightless feet.

"Let us greet these birds that endow the skies with height. Let us greet them because tomorrow the only things flying in Nkokolani will be bullets."

And he went back into his house, his hands paddling the darkness. The mysterious chimes of the church bell were, for me, another kind of summons, a warning that other gods were demanding our attention. I abandoned the still-unheaped firewood and forgot about the rest of my duties. And off I went in the tenuous light that remained, toward the decaying church. It was a tiny, spartan building, in such a dilapidated state that no one ever went there. Not even God made his presence felt. People say that many a mass was once said there, and many new Christians given catechism. But ever since the last priest left for Inhambane, the building had begun to crumble, solitary and sad, like an island in the midst of an infinite sea of African spirits. It was in a tiny church, similar to this one, that I had once been taught to read letters and numbers.

◆

There is nothing like a little empty church for us to find God within us. I recalled the times when the church at Makomani was full of life and Father Rudolfo would keep saying to himself:

"Back there in Portugal, they say Negroes have no soul. But it's the opposite: these people have too much soul ..."

Maybe the priest was right. But at that moment, I didn't have a soul that could come to my aid. I knelt down and put my ear to the ground. And I heard Grandfather Tsangatelo scratching away to reach the surface. But the stone was too thick, and my grandfather's fingers were too weak and tired.

The bells started to ring again, and the owl that lived cloistered in the ruins fluttered off over my head. I advanced, stepping on the carpet of feathers as if I were walking on a patch of moonlight. There's a proverb that says that an owl's feathers are so light, they never fall to the ground. That night, the feathers spun around in a frenzy and would have risen up until they were stuck to the roofing tiles. There they would have gained flesh and wings: angels would have been born. I would have gone mad like the dogs. My howls would have caused the bravest to quiver with fear. As my mother says, for me to go mad, all I need is a little piece of the moon.

When I withdrew, the bell was still being rung by unseen hands. I returned home, now certain that it wasn't the church where Grandfather was to be found. While the others went off to carry out the ceremony to commemorate the death of someone who hadn't died, I chose another way to celebrate the life of our grandfather. I embraced the anthill as if I were hugging the whole world. That was the family's altar, our *digandelo*, where the sacred mafura tree grew. There I tied white cloths around its trunk. And there I listened to Tsangatelo as one listens to an angel beating its wings.

◆

Tsangatelo leaned against the anthill in order to narrate a tired old fable. It was night, and the gods allowed him to tell stories. This time, however, he improvised a new scenario. He stood up straight in an effort to imitate the night's vastness. And when he spoke, he seemed to be expressing himself in a new language, born from his words, as if only the gods were listening to him. This is the story Tsangatelo told:

"Somewhere, there was an ancient war, in a time before any place had a name. Preparations for battle had just begun, at that first moment when warriors are imbued with so much faith that they cannot see how weak and terrified they really are. The two armies were lining up to confront each other when a huge flash ripped through the skies. The firmament was swept by the incandescence of a star. The soldiers dropped to the ground, momentarily blinded. When they came to themselves, they had lost their memory, and no longer knew the purpose of the weapons they carried. So they laid down their lances, assegais, and shields, and looked at each other without knowing what to do until, perplexed, the enemy commanders greeted each other. After that, the soldiers embraced. And when they looked at the landscape again, they no longer saw territory to be conquered but land to be cultivated. Eventually, the men dispersed. As they returned to their homes, they heard the oldest lullaby, sung in the timeless voices of one lone woman."

10

The Sergeant's Fifth Letter

Nkokolani, April 5, 1895

Your Excellency Counselor José d'Almeida

Yesterday I went to Chicomo by way of the river. There, I took part in a meeting of officers of the Northern Column, in which we reviewed the progress and difficulties of our campaign against Gungunhane's main garrison at Manjacaze. Your Excellency will receive a detailed report of this meeting by special messenger.

The day after the meeting, I returned to Nkokolani, accompanied by Your Excellency's adjunct and envoy, our mutual friend Mariano Fragata. We journeyed the whole morning down the River Inharrime in a pirogue. At a certain point in our travels, we were stopped by a man standing on the left bank, a tall black man of a certain age, who was waving his arms to attract our attention. I gave the order for us to pause in our journey, even though the others in the boat advised to the contrary. This black man greeted me with a mixture of submissiveness and pride, and made the strangest of requests: for me to alter the date of his birth on his travel document. He needed to renew his work permit in the mines of South Africa and could not reveal his true age. He was taking the opportunity to present himself to me and asked that no one in the village of Nkokolani should be told of his appearance.

"I am Tsangatelo, the eldest of the Nsambe family. In Nkokolani, boss, you must have met my grandchildren, Mwanatu and Imani, the children of Katini and Chikazi."

He had another miner with him, who remained as discreet as a shadow, but who helped us as an interpreter during the remainder of our conversation. This other man was a Landin from Lourenço Marques, and seemed far more familiar with our customs.

"I can't tamper with your document," I began to argue.

"Who mentioned tampering?"

"You did. You were the one who asked me to change it."

"You could change it without lying. No one knows the exact day they were born. Or do they?"

"I certainly do."

"But apart from that, the Portuguese are now our parents. You, sir, are my father. How can you refuse a request from your son? From a son who is older than his own father?"

Fragata, who up until then had stayed out of the argument, climbed forward into the bow of the pirogue so as to put an end to all this talk. The elderly kaffir's eyes narrowed, and then he raised his arm. "I remember you," he exclaimed.

"I don't remember ever seeing you before."

"Boss, you're the one with the golden tooth. I'm Tsangatelo, the leader of the caravans—don't you remember? I transported weapons for your soldiers ..."

Mariano Fragata cocked his head and strained himself to peer against the light. Then he clambered out of the boat and hugged the Negro. And there, with the interpreter's help, they celebrated their reunion as if they were two companions in arms. At one point, noticing my curiosity, Fragata explained: "This fellow had never seen a white man before me. He thought the horse and I were one sole creature."

And they both laughed—the Portuguese with an austere, restrained laugh, a buttoned-up display of contentment; the African with a loud, uncontrolled guffaw, a powerful river in flood. I confess that his laughter provoked in me some boundless rage, as if I were witnessing a manifestation of the devil himself. Those sudden coarse, clumsy ways reawakened a grim suspicion I'd felt before, that, no matter how much we may teach them our language, no matter how often they kneel in front of a crucifix, the kaffirs will never cease to be savage children.

Fragata then asked that we pause and share our food and water with the two miners. Only when we were sitting in some leafy shade did the envoy begin to explain that old Negro's story. He was a former owner of caravans who, some years previously, had approached the expeditionary force, of which Fragata formed part, and offered his services to transport weapons and victuals. These services proved to be providential for the establishment of our first garrisons. At this time, Tsangatelo was a figure of authority and prestige throughout the area. His caravans had right of passage along the whole of their route, whether that lay in the State of Gaza or in Portuguese Crown Lands. Local chiefs were paid money and guaranteed their protection against armed bandits. It was this old ally, now haggard and dressed in rags, who stood before us.

"Well, now, is it really you, old Tsangatelo? And you've decided to become a miner now?"

"What about you, boss? Have you still got your gold tooth?"

Our friend Fragata seemed eager to open his lips to show the tooth, which glinted in the bright light of day. "I've still got it and shall always have it, Tsangatelo, my old friend," he declared.

As he peered at Fragata's teeth, the black man clicked his tongue and looked concerned.

"What's the matter?" I asked, noticing his anxious expression.

"It's because this tooth is only the start," the black man said.

"The start? The start of what?"

The black man replied that Fragata's entire skeleton would turn to gold. Every bone in his body, the tiniest ossicle he never knew he had, would weigh upon him. Our friend, to cut a long story short, was in the process of being transformed into a mine. With his years of experience as a miner, Tsangatelo warned: "They're going to kill you, boss. And they'll strip you as they would a seam of metal. If I were you, I'd pull that tooth out. Or do you think you'll escape because you're a white?"

We chuckled at this nonsense. And we offered him wine and some of the biscuits we had with us. He and his companion helped themselves with exaggerated stiffness. The old man wanted to know about me, and I informed him of my status as a newcomer in Africa. Then he asked the strangest of questions:

"Can I ask you something: how big is Portugal?"

"I don't understand your question."

"Do you know how big these African lands are? Even we don't know, boss. It's just that these lands of ours are so vast that we measure our journeys by the rivers we cross. You, sir, are traveling along this river. As for me, I've lost count of all the rivers I've crossed."

Then he fell silent. I wouldn't have understood him had Fragata not explained the logic of what he was saying: the black man was alerting me to the hardships I would have to face in order to cross the rivers that lay ahead of us. I couldn't begin to imagine the painful crossings, wading through treacherous riverbeds, with men, oxen, horses, guns, and baggage. "This black man is right," said Fragata. Such crossings were, my companion added, a war within a war. And the more arms we had, the less prepared we would be.

It was already late when Fragata tried to convince the kaffir to come with us to Nkokolani. Tsangatelo was adamant in his refusal. He had left the village years before, and he explained that he would not be well received. That was why he wanted to spare himself the disappointment. But why on earth would he not be welcomed? He answered in a rancorous tone: "Everyone knows the anger of those who stay, when faced with those who have had the courage to leave."

That was the end of the conversation. The old miner got to his feet, and it was only then that I fully realized how skinny he was. The man looked more like a pole than a person. But his fragility was a lie, and, like everything else in this land, either false or an illusion. Slowly, as if unhurriedness was a sign of good manners, the man began to say his farewells. He held Fragata's hands while he repeated his urgent plea that he should get rid of his gold tooth.

"Be careful, boss. If we miners go down into the tunnels, it's because we trust your gods."

This is what the old man declared. I did not understand why he was making such an assertion, which, to my ears, seemed such shameful heresy. Why was he speaking of "our" gods? Then Tsangatelo shot the following question at me, and not Fragata:

"All this gold, all those diamonds: who do you think they belong to, boss?"

"Well, they belong to whoever digs them out of there."

"On the contrary, my good sir. They belong to whoever put them there. And they were sown by the spirits of the ancestors. So I ask you whites, did you ask permission?"

"We asked your chiefs."

"Which ones?"

"Those who have authority in the area."

"Those chiefs have no authority over the earth, or what lies beneath it. That is why I say to you," the black man continued, "that it would be good if your gods protected us. For we have long ceased to be protected by our own."

The good Fragata, who will return to Inhambane in a few days, after witnessing this picturesque conversation, fell into a state of melancholy for the rest of the journey. I could but think that our compatriot had become receptive to the childish beliefs of that Negro. The truth is, even I allowed myself to be downcast because of his lassitude. What type of illness is this, esteemed counselor, that contaminates us here in these tropical domains?

I mentioned this incident because I am aware of Your Excellency's sensitivity regarding these issues. Or who knows, perhaps you feel the need to forget the farcical assertion of our feeble powers that we have displayed here throughout the centuries. The journey to Chicomo and, in particular, our crossing of the river raised in me the most agonizing doubts. What Lands of the Crown are these that have never seen the king? Has it ever dawned on King Dom Carlos that he might visit his overseas territories? And if the king ever came here, is this the Africa he would be shown? All these questions pain me, and if I share them with Your Excellency, it is because I feel that, by committing them to paper, I manage to lessen their gravity.

I remember the almost poetic way the old black man Tsangatelo alluded to the vastness of these lands compared with those of Portugal. The words of that African native lead me to ask another question: Can such extensive territories really be ours? Can lands that cannot be contained in one map really belong to Portugal?

The English in South Africa already accuse us of compromising the prestige of the white race. And they went as far as proposing the enlistment of Boer mercenaries to put down the rebellion of the Landins and deal with Gungunhane's disobedience. Maybe we would do well to accept mercenaries in our ranks. If we shamefully accepted the British Ultimatum, it would be better to forfeit some territory and by so doing save our dignity where we maintain an effective presence.

P.S. Your Excellency urged me to use a less formal tone in our correspondence. You told me you were tired of dealing with official documents, as tired of them as you were of sleeping away from home. You asked me to compose letters rather than reports and to write as if I were a friend. Your broad-mindedness is a true blessing as far as I am concerned. And so, dear counselor, I shall use a more familiar tone from now on.

For this reason, and confiding in you as a friend, I shall tell you what happened last night. I fell asleep as if far removed from myself, or as if my body were more boundless than the African veld. And I slept fitfully, aware that a river was flowing through my slumber. When I awoke, the old miner Tsangatelo was sitting at the end of the bed. He looked like a black swan and was gliding silently along while the sound of lapping water filled the room. I realized at this point that the bed was a canoe, which the miner was paddling. I held out my arm to him and pleaded: "Teach me to laugh, Tsangatelo! Teach me to laugh!"

The heat of African nights induces the strangest of dreams. The truth is that these ravings have taken up all my time. I keep recalling my childhood house, in a cold village up in the north of Portugal. In that first home of mine, laughter was left outside, as if joy were something that had to be wiped clean from our feet on a threadbare mat by the front door. My father, stern and serious, wore black, as if we were mourning all the dead in this world. In the darkness of night, when the whole household slept, my mother would tiptoe to my room so that my father wouldn't hear, in order to say good night. "Your father won't let me kiss you," she would murmur. And she added in a whisper, "Your father is afraid that I will belong to him less if I am too much of a mother." In a hushed voice, she would tell me stories. They were simple fables, some to provoke laughter, others tears. But by that time, I had already learned to hold back my tears and swallow my laughter.

I was born and lived among shadows. My home had the smell and the silence of an orphanage. I had everything I needed to be a good soldier.

11

The Sin of the Moths

He who plans acts of revenge is convinced he is anticipating the future. It is an illusion: The avenger lives only in a time that has passed. The avenger does not act only in the name of whoever has died. He himself has died. He has been killed by the past.

We could tell our father had woken up from the loud smack of his lips. The noise could be heard throughout the village. The residents would all comment: Katini's surfaced. They were joking, but at the same time issuing a warning. As he awoke, he returned from his dreams, and there was a need for caution: the man had the dust of the gods on his feet.

That morning, our father awoke without making any noise. Carrying a large bag, he left the house nervously, and passed by the barracks where his younger son was living. He abruptly ordered him to come with him. Then he set off toward the river, and as he went, he recruited the young men he encountered along the way. He asked them all to bring their hoes with them on the trip. He crossed the rice fields and paused to contemplate the valley in all its width. These seed crops were an expression of disobedience that filled Uncle Musisi with such pride. The VaNguni invaders had prohibited us from growing rice; they claimed it was "white man's food." But those were only words. The real reason was that these little grains were of no use for brewing liquor. The invaders could steal more and better things from us if we sowed corn.

At the river, the scene changed: the fields all contained corn. The rice fields we had left behind were merely a temporary transgression. As for the rest, we had abandoned our own food crops—sorghum and millet. Musisi was right: we were imitating the invaders. And we were doing so in the most intimate fashion—we ate what they ate.

Father clambered up onto a termite mound, examined his little army, and then looked up into the heavens until his eyes filled with light. When he climbed back down, he seemed stunned, and stumbled around, gathering the hoes of those present and piling them up clumsily. Then he filled cans with kerosene and ordered them to set fire to the heap of tools.

"We don't need them anymore," he said. "When we need to dig, we'll use this bone." He brandished an elephant rib he was carrying in his bag, as if it were a spear. Then he bellowed more orders: after the first blaze, we would burn the crops until there wasn't a patch of green left in the meadowlands.

The young men stepped back, horrified. In the face of everyone's confusion, Katini reacted even more furiously: "Do what I tell you. I'm not mad—obey me!"

The youths fled, terrified. Only father and son were left amid a sea of smoke and flames. It wasn't long before the whole village turned up, carrying leafy branches with which to beat the flames. A group of men ran forward to hurl insults at my old father and assault him. Mwanatu even intervened in his ridiculous uniform, proclaiming, "In the name of the Portuguese Crown, leave this kaffir alone!"

They dragged Katini away, shouting all the while, "Tie him up, lash him!" They were looking for tree trunks with holes in them, used for immobilizing the feet and hands of bandits. Fortunately for Katini, all the tree trunks were being consumed by fire.

With his face swollen and covered in blood, Father gathered his strength and berated them: "You ignorant, brutish blacks, don't you realize I'm saving your lives?"

As far as he was concerned, it was obvious: The soldiers invading from the north were starving. They weren't guided by hatred. It was hunger. If they found out about our cultivated fields, they would attack us for sure. That was what he was trying to avoid. Our indigence was our best defense against aggressors. No one mounts an attack on those who have nothing.

The villagers returned home, throwing me the sort of look reserved for orphans. Behind me, my father scraped at the ground with the elephant rib. For a moment, I thought he was digging his grave.

◆

At home, my mother pretended she knew nothing of what had happened that afternoon. Sitting on the elephant bone, my father waited in vain for her to pay him some attention. Kneeling in front of a huge clay pot, Mother was busy, rinsing her hands in water and meticulously rubbing her fingers. The episode with the soldiers still upset her. There was a trace of blood that she couldn't get off her skin, and a smell of fish she couldn't forget.

Finally, she sat down on the ground, elbows on her knees, as if she needed support to keep her limbs from collapsing.

"Why don't you go indoors, Mother?"

She shook her head. You're even less protected "indoors." Envy had chosen our place to take up residence. Although it was made of wattle and daub, our house was unique in the village. The walls were painted with lime, and the doors had brightly colored patterns. There was ample space inside, several rooms. It was rectangular in shape, and had a huge veranda at the front. All this made us different.

In the other homes, the traditional mafura-oil lamps had long been extinguished. In the porch of our house, two gas lanterns displayed the privileged status of our family, the Nsambe clan. The moths danced blindly around these sources of light. They seemed to emerge from the walls, flakes of lime wash that stood out against the background as they fluttered frantically. My father said that in previous lives these moths had been daytime butterflies who had fallen in love with their own beauty. As a punishment for their vanity, they had been banished from the light of day. Their yearning for the sun caused them to commit suicide by throwing themselves at the lanterns. The glass in these lamps was their final mirror.

For me, the moths were relatives of Grandmother Layeluane: Struck by the brilliance of a spark, they plummeted to the ground with the levity of light. Nothing caused them suffering. In each fallen insect, Grandmother was born and died again.

All of a sudden, when the night seemed consumed by this sacrifice of their wings, my father raised his arm and alerted us: "I can hear the clank of metal. Guess who it is?"

"Husband, please ..."

"That slow grating of iron bolts can only mean it's your brother Musisi."

"Please, husband, don't get into an argument with him. We're family, we all depend on each other to live."

◆

The hatred Katini Nsambe felt toward his brother-in-law Musisi was timeless and without cure. It had begun with trivial envy. The truth was that my father had never served as a soldier. He lacked this proof of complete manhood.

In one of the battles from which he was conspicuously absent, the VaChopi and the Portuguese fought together against the forces of Ngungunyane. During the confrontation, his brother-in-law was wounded by someone in his own ranks. For Katini, the incident merely confirmed his certainty: the shot that kills us comes from within rather than from outside. As he put it: "This man Musisi goes around all covered in glory, displaying his valor ... It wasn't bravery at all, it was an accident."

This is what had happened: A Portuguese soldier had confused Musisi with the enemy. The man firing the shot was pardoned in advance. For the Portuguese, the Africans, whether enemies or allies, were an indistinct mass—black by day, dark by night. The bullet lodged in Musisi's spine and remained there, apparently without risk or consequence. Within his body, however, the bullet came to life, and his vertebrae turned into metal, one by one. They became projectiles, as lethal as the original bullet itself. When his brother-in-law moved, the grinding of rusty hinges could be heard by all. Musisi would never get over the incident. Wherever he went, he carried the war inside him.

Mother laughed at this unresolved jealousy. Men go to war to be awaited. Whether victor or vanquished, the soldier must appear greater when he returns than when he departed. The warrior returns from battle in order to exhibit his wounds and look forward to the supreme solace of his beloved's arms. At the same time, it is not love's consolation that the soldier yearns for most. He seeks to forget, to erase his consciousness. Katini required neither consolation nor oblivion. Music is where he found self-expression, and where he waged war against himself. Music was his kingdom. Drink was his throne.

As for Aunt Rosi, she had a different explanation for the stormy relationship between the brothers-in-law. What divided them was a dispute over power. With the absence of Grandfather Tsangatelo, Katini exercised his authority over the whole Nsambe family. Musisi found this unacceptable.

For me, the explanation for their rivalry was something else. In fact, that fateful shot contained two twin bullets. The first hit Uncle Musisi. The other hit my poor father's soul. That is why not a night goes by without his waking up in a panic as he listens to a bullet whistle past. He sits up, breathless, on his sleeping mat and sees an iron bird whiz through the air so fast that he doesn't even have enough time to awaken from his slumber. He pulls the blanket over his head to shelter from this messenger of doom. The worst thing about the past is what is still to come.

◆

In the darkness of that night, we got proof that my father was right in foreseeing the arrival of a visitor. What he had heard might not have been exactly the clank of metal, but a resonant clapping of hands announced the arrival of Uncle Musisi. He was in an agitated state of mind, following the news that enemy soldiers had been seen in the vicinity.

"We know," I said. "We know they're out there somewhere."

"We know nothing!" his sister promptly corrected me.

And she repeated the sentence slowly, stressing each syllable: "We-know-no-thing." Her eyes undermined the audacity of our words. She didn't want anyone to find out about our encounters with the VaNguni soldiers.

Uncle Musisi repeated what he had heard from the sentinels charged with looking out over the plain: Ngungunyane's troops were spread out as far as the eye could see on the plains of the Inharrime. They were advancing like red ants. The emperor of Gaza was moving the capital of his kingdom from Mossurize to Manjankhazi.

"I can guarantee you one thing: there have never been so many people marching together in this world."

I didn't understand the silence that ensued. It was as if we were mourning our anticipated death. I was only a girl the first time we had been invaded. For that reason, the tension being generated at that moment was beyond my comprehension.

"Where are Dubula and Mwanatu?" Uncle asked, breaking the silence.

"You know very well that your nephews no longer live in this house."

"Stay by the door and keep a lookout." Then he looked at me and added: "I don't want them here while we discuss these matters. We can't trust either of your brothers."

Uncle sat down closer to the fire, and the cuts in his face glowed brightly in the light of the flames. Each cut corresponded to the death of an adversary. In my father's view, those tattoos were all false. Musisi had never dared kill anyone. At least he, Katini, had fathered children, some of whom were alive, others dead. Musisi's children had never got as far as being born. As far as I could see, his situation was like my own: that of a barren tree.

◆

"The food is ready!"

With a solemn expression, Mother ordered us to take our seats. She told me to pass a basin of water around among the men, so that they could wash their hands. The *ushua* was served in an earthenware pan, and next to it there was a dish of dried fish curry. Fingers came and went in a well-practiced dance, and for some time all that could be heard was the sound of chewing. Only after they had satisfied their initial hunger did Uncle Musisi raise his flour-coated fingers and stammer: "Now the war is going to begin again."

His fingers, suddenly whitened, danced in the darkness as if gaining a life of their own, detached from his body.

My father decided to intervene in his usual complacent manner, casting a balm on the world and its bitterness: "We are having our dinner, dear brother-in-law."

"So what?"

"There are things one shouldn't talk about while eating. Besides, wars never begin. When we awaken to them, we realize they started long ago."

He was playing for time, brooding over his choice of words. As far as he was concerned, all conflicts in this world belong to the same, timeless war.

"Shall we alert the Portuguese?" Mother asked, ignoring her husband's enigmatic discourse.

"Never!" Uncle answered abruptly. "This is our business alone. The Portuguese have interfered enough in our lives. I'm not like your husband, who no longer knows who he is or where he's from."

"I'm a Chopi to the core. Just like you, my dear brother-in-law."

"Don't call me Chopi! The term was invented by the invaders. As far as I am concerned, I belong to the VaLengue, which is our older name. I come from those who use the bow and arrow, I like fish, and I don't use oxen in my ceremonies."

"You, my dear brother-in-law, are no more faithful to our ancestors than I am."

Mother raised her arms into the air, as if she were trying to stop the heavens from collapsing, and exclaimed: "Enough, enough! We've got the enemy at the gates, and you people are arguing? We don't have a choice. Tomorrow let's go and see the Portuguese, just as we've always done."

"You don't understand, dear sister. The Portuguese have abandoned us. We've been left to our own fate."

"If you don't want to, I'll go and see them myself," Mother argued.

"Where will you go?" my father asked.

"I'll go and speak to the sergeant."

"You're not leaving here, woman," my father replied, animated by a sudden sense of pride. "I'm the man of this house, and I'm the one who'll go."

And he went on repeating, at least ten times, "I'm the one who'll go and see the sergeant." We knew, when we heard him, that it was an empty promise.

As he left, Uncle Musisi peered around and asked: "By the way, my dear brother-in-law, where's the rifle I left with you?"

My father shrugged his shoulders. "What rifle?" he asked offhandedly. It wasn't hard to picture what had happened: out of the barrel of the gun, Father had made a pipe for his still. For him, the value of weapons was just this: to be dismantled and turned into other, more productive objects. And is there anything of greater worth than a still?

"I'm the one who'll go and speak to the Portuguese."

"As long as you keep your sons away from all this," Musisi warned.

"I've already said," my mother declared, "no one talks about other people's children in this house."

When Uncle had left, Mother called me, pointing at the bushes that surrounded the house. "See how they're covered in locusts? War won't be far behind."

12

The Sergeant's Sixth Letter

Nkokolani, May 12, 1895

Your Excellency Counselor José d'Almeida

Today I took stock of the arms held at this post. Just as this building cannot be called a barracks, neither can we call the rusty pile of junk here weaponry. It was because they were worthless that they escaped the late Sardinha's lust for profit. The situation is as follows: with the exception of the rifles that I myself brought, there isn't a single firearm of any use to us. The natives are convinced that there is a powerful arsenal here. Let them go on believing. This lie is the only purpose our outpost here possesses.

I have heard it said that not far from here, in the village of Nhagondel, there is a military post in exactly the same situation. The ruins and the state of abandonment are identical to this one. The only difference is that there they appointed a poor black as sergeant. In view of this other case, I appreciate the respect shown me. If it weren't for the letters I write you, Excellency, my solitude would be unbearable. God forgive me, but I would have preferred a thousand times to have stayed in prison in Porto than face this harrowing exile. Your Excellency may not read my missives. You may never honor them with a reply. But I shall persevere with these manuscripts just as a drowning man obstinately keeps surfacing. Only when I am writing do I feel alive and capable of dreaming.

Do you know one of my rare sources of entertainment here? It is to inspect the munitions held at this post. They may be old and obsolete, but when I touch them, I rediscover a passion I felt during my years at military school. And among the old papers left here, I have found literature on the wars between the English and the Zulus. From my reading, it has become clear that one of the greatest disadvantages for the Europeans was the time it took for them to reload their rifles. The time it took was more than a delay; it was deadly.

I have to confess that I was astounded by our decision to buy an Austrian repeat-action rifle known as a Kropatschek. Not because of the gun itself, but because we made such a decision. We are the first to use the Kropatschek in Africa. Let me explain myself better, before Your Excellency loses his patience and stops reading. It is just that when we made our choice we won an unexpected victory. But you know who were the first to be defeated? It was we Portuguese. If I tell you this rifle defeated us, it is because it overcame our provincial tendency to imitate the English in everything. Forgive the petulance of my conclusion, but this is how any war is won: by causing us, first and foremost, to defeat ourselves.

As Your Excellency knows only too well, in Portugal there are increasing protests against the expense incurred by the war in Africa. The irony is that there is no war at all here. And if there is to be one, we shall be massacred mercilessly, and there will not be a single Kropatschek to save us.

I admit that my pessimism may be the result of the dramatic events I have witnessed. The storekeeper Sardinha's suicide perturbed me far more than one might have thought. I cannot forget that a compatriot of mine lies buried in my backyard without a headstone or a coffin. He may have been the target of the most serious accusations, but he was a Portuguese who was not given the chance to defend himself. The finger that pulled the trigger was his, but the indictment I read him was mine. Though Sardinha's bones are no burden to the soil, they are a burden I have to bear during my sleepless nights.

I know what I am talking about, for, like Sardinha, I was summarily convicted, and there is no distance in this world that will make me forget the unjust exile I have been subjected to. It might be different if I were totally immersed in Africa. The fact is, part of me remained in a Porto square with my own army's gunfire brushing past my skin and grazing my very existence. More than the revolt of January 31, I cannot get out of my head the memory of that day when they took me and the other mutineers from the jail to a ship. We marched down the streets and through the port of Leixões under a strong military escort. We were not the ones they feared. What scared them was the reaction of the crowds who filled the city. For the first time, I felt pride in the uniform I was wearing. But this feeling faded away immediately when we boarded the ship to face the court-martial that would judge us. Great was the cowardice of those who governed us. It was not enough for us to be concealed from the eyes of others. The absurdity of the verdict had to be delivered hidden by the sea mists. The ship I boarded was coincidentally called the *Mozambique*. Little did I know that the military tribunal would elect to deport me to the colony of the same name.

What I went through on that ship, awaiting my judgment, is impossible to describe. We were made to wait for days on end, suffered storm after storm; weakened by hunger and seasickness, we were so exhausted when we were brought before the court that we lacked the discernment to answer even the simplest questions. In truth, any acuity we might have had would have been of little use: we were condemned from the start. Whether we were civilians or soldiers, innocent or guilty, there wasn't even a pretense of justice.

One of the detainees, an elderly teacher, recalled a curious episode from the history of France. Knowing that Protestant leaders had come to the city, the Catholic king ordered his army to round them up and kill them all. The officer who received the order asked how, once they had arrived in the area, they would be able to distinguish between the Protestant leaders and the rest of the population. To which the king answered: "Kill them all. God will recognize his own."

I certainly wished to forget the tribulations that had led to my exile. But they all came flooding back when I was part of a firing squad in the wake of the skirmishes in Lourenço Marques. In our sights was a group of black rebels who had been captured the previous day. As was the custom, the firing squad consisted only of Portuguese.

The condemned men were lined up before us. They were all adolescents, little more than children. None of them had had a trial; no one had heard them, in Portuguese or in their native language. Those who were about to die had no voice. At that moment, some kind of emotional upheaval, motivated possibly by fear or by guilty conscience, convinced me that those who were going to die bore within them sufficient liability from birth:

their race, the gods they did not have. But there followed a curious mishap. The trigger of my gun jammed. At that precise moment, I sensed that this wasn't merely a technical fault but a sad omen. I pressed the trigger again, and there was a sudden crack, a flash, and a scorch mark. The bullet had exploded inside the rifle.

It wasn't the lesion that shocked me, for that was slight and a passing phenomenon. For me, the root cause of the incident was imponderable. It was a message from that other inferno, where not even the demons dwell. The bullet had detonated not inside the rifle but in the depths of my being. And the gunpowder would seep from my hands like burning lava for the rest of my life.

I am haunted continually by the thought that those young blacks, so far removed from me because of their color and features, were in the end like me. Just as they had rebelled, so had I. Like them, I too had dared to point my gun at the powerful. Perhaps that was why my gun had jammed and the bullet discharged inside the chamber. That bullet continues to explode inside me. If I were a bird, I would have long ago plummeted to the ground, stoned.

13

Between Oaths and Promises

War is a midwife: from the insides of the world, it
causes another world to emerge. It doesn't do it out
of anger or any feeling whatsoever. It does it because
that is its profession: it plunges its hands into time,
with the arrogance of a fish convinced the sea
exists because of it.

I set off along the streets of Nkokolani, and walked down
the one lined with orange trees. They had just blos-
somed, and their sweet perfume spread through the village. The orange trees might not keep monsters at bay,
but they conjured up the spirit of distant geographies.
The roots of these trees, according to Tsangatelo, lie in
another continent.

I was so intoxicated by the powerful scent that I almost
forgot where I was going, which was, inevitably, to the
Portuguese garrison. I changed direction and started
walking purposefully. I needed to get the better of my relatives. It wouldn't be long before they paid Germano de
Melo a visit. They would request protection against the
forces of Ngungunyane heading southward en masse.

Sergeant Germano de Melo was at the door, with a
look of panic on his face.

"Come quickly, Imani!"

"What's wrong, Sergeant?"

"It's my goddamned hands! My goddamned hands
have gone. See here, look: I've lost my hands again."

He wandered, horrified, through the house. One certainty drove him forward: his hands had disappeared. He staggered sightlessly, with his arms stretched out in front of him shaking more than his voice. "I've lost them," he repeated, in despair.

He had become a victim of such episodes with increasing frequency: He lost feeling in his hands. On such occasions, he would become helpless and dependent, like a child. This is what had happened shortly before my visit: his hands had become ever less visible, ever more transparent, until they had disappeared, weightless and without any memory of ever having belonged to him.

"Sit down, Sergeant Germano. I'll heat some water and wash your hands."

"But what hands, if I haven't got any?"

"I'll wash your arms and rub your wrists. Your hands will come back—you'll see."

These outbreaks of intense fear were the result of an accident he had had when handling a gun. He never told me the details of what had happened. I never asked him. Dark memories are like an abyss: no one should lean too far over them.

"I'm very ill, Imani. They say Africa transmits diseases. But I have fallen sick from Africa, the whole of it."

◆

Old Katini would surely be angry at my having anticipated his visit to the sergeant. He would want to be the first, before all others, to present a request for protection against the VaNguni soldiers. But no one was more capable than I of conveying our people's fears in fluent Portuguese.

This is what I thought as I entered the garrison. The moment I got used to the half-light, I realized that nothing had changed. The old building was still a strange mixture of grocery store and military base. In some ways, it had even deteriorated further: weapons and merchandise, uniforms and rolls of cotton fabric, military reports and account books, everything there was jumbled up together. The grandiose plans for building the military post had long been shelved. Defensive fortifications were awaited; soldiers were awaited. From the other side of the continent, the promised Angolan platoon would never get there.

A bogus garrison and nonexistent troops: this was the void that Germano commanded. It was little wonder that he was contemplating his arms as if he had never seen them before.

"So, where is your guard, my brother Mwanatu? I didn't see him when I arrived."

"I gave him the day off."

Then I noticed that the sergeant's knee was bleeding. He had hurt himself on the edge of a crate. The flies were already buzzing around the wound.

"We'd better clean that cut," I told him, waving a damp piece of cloth at him.

"You can certainly clean it, but you'll never get rid of the flies."

"And why is that?"

"Those flies were inside me. They're flying out of me. I'm rotten, Imani."

I went over to the wall, took down the rifle that was hanging there, and placed it on Germano's lap.

"Go on, take hold of the gun."

"I can't. I haven't got enough feeling in my hands yet."

◆

So, the Portuguese complained that he didn't recognize his hands? Well, I didn't feel my soul. I hadn't felt it since I found out my grandmother had died without leaving any remains for the earth to take in its arms. My mother would die in the same way, and I would return to my initial name of Ash: without hands, without a body, without a soul.

This is what occupied my thoughts as I knelt at the sergeant's feet. The delays and despairing had so upset Germano de Melo that he had become unrecognizable. This white man, who had presented himself a matter of months ago with such an elegant bearing and such an impeccable uniform, sat there now, beaten and submissive, surrendering to the care of a black girl.

At that moment, I prayed that none of my family would walk through the door and catch me washing his arms in warm water. It would be of little use for me to argue that this white man was a special creature. I would be no more than a witch in everyone's eyes. And I would be condemned to death. There's no other fate in Nkokolani for those they call *valoii*.

◆

"Go on, take hold of the rifle," I insisted. "Hold it with your hands. They're yours ..."

Slowly, the white man's fingers felt their way around the rifle, as tentatively as those of a blind man. To my surprise, he raised the gun and leaned it against his ear. He sat there for some time with his face against the butt of the gun, as if he were peering through the silence.

"In my country, this is the way we know how many people the gun has killed. Do you know what we do? We listen to the cries of those who died by pressing our ear to the rifle butt. Why are you laughing? In my country we also have beliefs, just as you do here."

"And has this gun ever killed anyone?"

"No. This gun is still waiting to make its debut. It's a Martini-Henry. Brand-new."

He placed the gun on my lap and got up to go get another gun from the cabinet. I asked him to take the gun away. He reacted, offended and surprised: "Are you scared? Raise your arm. There, like that. Now, this arm is a weapon, the most reliable of weapons. This rifle is merely an extension of your arm, your hand, your will."

And the sergeant's hand ran up my arm, across my shoulders, up my neck. "You're trembling. Are you afraid?" he asked. It wasn't out of fear that I was trembling. Fortunately, the sergeant stepped away and became distant once more. He was lost in thought. Then he spoke: "That devil Gungunhane has got one just like this, and do you know who gave it to him? The queen of England herself! They're well suited to each other ... But this other rifle"—and he bent down to pick up the second gun—"this one I really love ... Take a good look at it, Imani, because this is the gun that's going to defeat Gungunhane."

"I'm sorry. But the way to say his name is Ngungunyane, Sergeant, sir. If you can't say it, you can always call him Mudungazi. But it's important that we call our enemies by their correct names ..."

"Is that so? Well, then, listen: this gun is a Kropatschek. Now say 'Kropatschek,' go on, see if you can ..."

The difference was that I would never have to call a gun by its name, and Germano would have to utter the name of the African emperor every day. That's what I should have told him. But I held back submissively.

At that point, we heard the distant tones of a marimba.

It was my father, trying out a new composition. Independent of my will, my body began to sway, something that the sergeant noticed immediately. He took a step back and exclaimed: "At last, I can see you're African! For a moment, I was convinced you were Portuguese."

I was surprised to see how still Germano de Melo remained, so removed from the allure of the xylophone. The Portuguese man's body was unhearing. Something had died inside him, even before he was born.

◆

At last, the sergeant succumbed to fatigue. His ravings tired him out, and when he came to his senses, he looked like a mat that had been thoroughly beaten and turned upside down. He was but a shadow of the man who had stepped ashore from the River Inharrime a matter of months before. Sprawled in a big old armchair, he fell asleep after muttering:

"I'll be back in a while, Imani. I won't be long."

I saw myself in a situation that I could never have imagined: sitting in a chair like a wife, next to a white man who had given in to sleep, and with a rifle weighing heavily across my knees.

Gingerly, I lifted the gun, sluggishly and reluctantly, as if I were picking up a snake by its tail. However, I gradually became familiar with the rifle, to the point where I squeezed it against my breast, carefully, like someone cuddling a child. I peered at the barrel, fearing that the screams of those who had killed might emerge from it, along with the groans of those who had died. I allowed my finger gently to exert pressure on the trigger.

And I thought to myself: a millimeter, one tiny millimeter, was all that separated life from death. That was when I heard a voice. At first, I thought it was the Portuguese talking in his sleep. Then I realized the voice was coming from inside the gun, and I began to recognize it. It was asking for help. The intensity of the noise grew until I could bear it no longer. At that point, I shouted out in despair:

"Dubula! My brother Dubula!"

The Portuguese awoke and came over to calm me down. I dodged him like a caged animal.

"Don't touch me! Please, don't touch me!"

"I'm not touching you."

"Yes, you are! And don't look at me, because I'm all dirty."

How could I explain to him that I was dirty from a death that was half mine? But Germano de Melo wasn't waiting for an explanation. It was his turn to placate me. "It's a good thing I got my hands back," he said as he placed a capulana around my shoulders.

"Your trembling will pass; you're just nervous ..."

It wasn't my nerves. Neither mine nor his. It was that house, and its invisible inhabitants competing for cracks in the roof tiles: owls, moths, and bats.

"You should leave this house, Sergeant, sir. Go and live somewhere else, anywhere except here."

"It seems impossible that you should believe in witchcraft, Imani, a girl like you ..."

"I have to go, but I can't do so without telling you the reason for my visit. We are all alarmed here in Nkokolani. Do you know that large numbers of Ngungunyane's soldiers have been spotted?"

"Yes, I know about that, they told me. Mudungazi is moving his capital from north to south. He's marching south with thousands and thousands of Ndau people."

"Tomorrow my father will come to see you. He will ask you to defend us ..."

"And you will have our support, you may be sure. Tomorrow I shall send a message to Inhambane. You can rest assured: our army will help you. You can tell your people."

"My people? I have no people …"

"I mean your family."

"I'm sorry, Sergeant, sir, but there are those in my family who think that 'ask' isn't the right term. We pay tribute, that's what they say. We have the right to be protected."

"And that right will be respected."

"Pardon me once again, but people also ask: Where are the troops you are going to protect us with?"

"They will send troops from Inhambane. As for weapons, I've got them here."

As I was leaving, he came to me with a piece of paper, waving it in front of his face. "You can tell your father I've received guarantees from the highest order that the VaNguni won't disturb you. You can see that this letter has come from António Enes himself. Come back inside; sit down and write a copy in your own hand."

I sat at the table in the living room, my back straight, elbow propped securely, just as I had learned to do at the Mission School. In a leisurely tone, the sergeant slowly dictated each paragraph:

My Dear Gungunhane:
I, great king of the Province of Mozambique, beholden to King Dom Carlos I to assess the situation regarding the war and to send for forces from Lisbon (this being at last necessary), dispatch my envoy with this letter in order that we may engage in some honest talking, and that we may know once and for all whether you are a true son of the king of Portugal.

You need no reminding of what the king has done for you, because you know only too well that if the king had not given your father, Muzila, weapons to overcome Mahueva, you would not now be the ruler of Gaza. You remain powerful because of the king's great friendship and his constant gifts, which show that you are a true son to him. My great leader told me you asked permission to fight the Guambas and the Zavala. He has forbidden it, and I confirm this. I do not give you permission to fight them, and if you do so, you will regret it. I want to ensure the rule of law, and if they harm you I shall punish them, if necessary by sending them to Guinea.

Signed: The Royal Commissioner

Standing behind my chair, Germano surveyed the manuscript, his hand on my shoulder. I begged the gods that no tremor of mine might signal to him how much I was disturbed by this contact.

"Have you copied it all? Well, now go to your family and read them what you have just written down ..."

As I left, I could still feel the touch of his hand. I asked him if he could smell the orange blossom. He answered that he had long ago forgotten the perfumes of this world. And his words saddened me.

◆

"Royal commissioner?" asked Musisi.

Among the crowd of relatives and friends assembled in our yard to hear about my visit, there were some who laughed. In the middle of this circle of people was Uncle Musisi, who was ready to disbelieve both the messengers, me and the sergeant. Farther back, Mother was busy, bustling around a fire. She was making salt. She had been occupied with this task ever since morning, when she had set off for the mudflats bordering the lagoons. With a snail's shell, she had scraped the saltpeter that had accumulated on the wide patches of sand. At that moment, she was washing off the dirt in a pan of boiling water. In due course, the water would evaporate and the salt would appear like a white towel in the dark bottom of the pan. While she toiled, she sang: "... *sand is yearning, salt is forgetting* ..." My mother made salt so as to forget.

"Be careful, mind you don't burn yourself, woman," my father warned.

She stifled a mischievous smile. Uncle Musisi persisted: he wanted to know who this royal commissioner was and what credit he merited that made him so different from all the other whites, whom we viewed with such distrust.

"His name is António Enes," I explained. "He's the representative of the king of Portugal. He's the one who gives the orders in the Lands of the Crown."

"And did he write that piece of paper?"

"Yes, it's a copy that I wrote in my own hand. The commissioner sent that same letter to Ngungunyane. It's written here that we can stop worrying about the threats by Ngungunyane's soldiers. I'll read it and translate it for you."

◆

When I had finished reading, the letter hung from my fingertips. It was as if that piece of paper had gained some unexpected weight in the face of my family's reticence. One of the neighbors broke the silence:

"Where's Guinea? Is it before or after Inhambane?"

"Be quiet, all of you," Musisi ordered. "As far as I'm concerned, this letter just proves how they treat us like children."

"Sometimes it's nice to have a great father," my mother retorted.

"Speak for yourself, sister. Do you want to know what I say to these promises? I laugh. That's what I do: laugh. And do you know what I'm going to do? I'm going to ask one of our own for help. Tomorrow I'm going to speak to Binguane."

"Is Binguane a Chopi?" my father asked.

"At least it'll be among us blacks."

Binguane lived in the vicinity of Nkokolani. He was a feared military leader who fiercely opposed the VaNguni hosts. I had already seen him. He was a tall, powerful man in spite of his age. Like me, he was of mixed Makwakwa and VaChopi descent.

My father warned: "That's a very bad idea. Ngungunyane will be even more enraged at us. There's no one in the world the emperor hates more than Binguane and his son, Xiperenyane."

There was more than an element of truth in Katini's words. When still a child, Xiperenyane had been kidnapped by Muzila, Ngungunyane's father. This was common practice in the Empire of Gaza: the children of eminent families were kidnapped. The quickest way of ensuring loyalty is through blackmail.

Xiperenyane grew up in the bosom of the royal family, and it was said that he beat Ngungunyane in all games and competitions. As soon as he fled the court, he became the leader of a formidable group of rebels. What Katini said was really true: there was no one Ngungunyane hated more.

"You're giving the wizard his witchcraft," my father said, renewing his warning.

Musisi, who had withdrawn into himself, now returned to the fray in a different tone of voice: "While Imani was reading the letter, I began to have an idea. And this idea has to be discussed now, because tomorrow I'm going off to war, and I don't know whether I'll come back."

"Don't talk like that—it will bring bad luck," my mother reminded him.

"For me, this tale of the unfinished garrison is nothing but a pack of lies. It's no more than a store disguised as a military post. The real garrison always was in Chicomo, and they never intended to build another one."

"So what's this white man doing here?"

"Ask yourself that question, brother-in-law. This man's here to spy on us. That's why, my dear brother-in-law, we're going to spy on the spy."

"You're out of your mind, Musisi."

"And do you know how we're going to spy? Through your children."

"That's enough, Musisi," said my mother. "I don't want my children mixed up in these matters."

"No? But your children, dearest sister, are already very much mixed up in it. Let's spy on the Portuguese through the letters that the sergeant sends and receives, like this one your daughter has just read to us. These papers can be our eyes and ears."

"I beg you, dear brother: don't involve my daughter in something like that," my mother insisted. "My elder daughters died; my sons are sleeping goodness knows where. This daughter is all I have left to make my life worth living."

Then she grabbed my hand more firmly than ever before. And in those fingers of hers, I felt the extension of my own body.

14

The Sergeant's Seventh Letter

Nkokolani, May 25, 1895

Your Excellency Counselor José d'Almeida

Some days ago, I listened to the xylophone orchestra of which Imani's father is a worthy maestro, even when he is completely intoxicated. On this occasion, I was the one who felt intoxicated, while delighting in the harmonious notes the Negroes managed to draw out of the keys.

It suddenly dawned on me. Music is a boat, and in it I complete the one journey I have yet to make. "Can I play?" I asked. And I tried to reproduce the melodies with which my mother used to lull me to sleep. It didn't go well for me, but I realized that my tunes and those of the Africans had one thing in common: they both brought order to a frightening, chaotic world.

I couldn't help recalling the beautiful letter that Ayres de Ornelas wrote to his mother, recounting his first visit to the court of Gungunhane. I have with me a copy of the missive, which, like so much of our correspondence, was intercepted and reproduced. A friend in Lourenço Marques copied it by hand and kindly gave it to me. If I forward it to you now, it is because the document sheds some light on the feelings people in Lourenço Marques harbor toward our Lieutenant Ornelas. A soldier of that rank is not expected to hold the art of the Negroes in such high esteem. How can a lieutenant, in time of war, confess to have so much respect for those we are convinced have no soul?

For the singularity of the feelings expressed, I am transcribing here part of the letter Ornelas sent to his mother:

When the king of Gaza appeared, Gungunhane's regiments intoned his war chant. Nothing in the world can convey the grandeur of that hymn. The harmony of the anthem, whose sonorous, majestic notes, enthusiastically rendered by more than six thousand voices, made us quiver to our very core. What majesty, what energy there was in that music, now slow and drawn out, almost moribund, then resurgent, triumphant, ardent, and pulsating, a blazing explosion of passion! And as the regiments, which we here call mangas, drew farther away, the solemn notes predominated over a wide area, rebounding from the hillsides and among the forest trees of Manjacaze! Who could have been the anonymous composer of such a marvelous work? What spirit he must have had, he who was able to capture the African war with the raw crudity of his poetry, in just three or four movements? Even today, I can still hear, booming in my ears, the echo of that terrible Vátua war chant, so often hearkened to by the Chopi sentinel, riven with terror, lost among the thickets of these bushlands where I have been living for the last month.

I imagine that Your Excellency Counselor José d'Almeida will share this sensitivity toward the beauty blacks are capable of producing. Such beauty, let me respectfully suggest, has become part of your life. Your Excellency has never confided in me on the matter of your marriage to a native woman—and, indeed, why should you? This fact has proved the subject of much malicious comment in the places I have passed through. But I can appreciate it ever more intensely, my dear counselor. I have to admit feeling a certain attraction for Imani, the girl who is a frequent visitor to our post here. And it is not just a carnal feeling. It is something deeper, more total, something I have never felt for a white woman. I confess that this impulse may be the consequence of the solitude that has been imposed upon me. Or it may be a prisoner's delirium. But the truth is that this girl has insinuated herself in the most submissive and subtle fashion, and has gradually wormed her way into my soul, so much so that I can dream of no one but her.

Yesterday, for example, Imani gave me a lesson on the *chicuembos*, the spirits to whom the natives pray and give offerings. And she explained that, for the Chopi, there are various kinds of spirits. The one that appealed to me most was the spirit they called Majuta.

It had such an effect on me, I ended up dreaming I was one of these ghosts on that very same night. I was dressed for the part, following the precepts of these particular souls: I wore a long, full white gown, of the type worn by Muslims, and carried a rifle slung across my back. I could have been an Arab slave trader, in my big military boots. However, the laces were undone, and I marched along with my legs wide apart so as not to trip on them. I approached Imani, who was sitting, half clothed, on a chair at the entrance to the barracks. I tried to take my boots off, but was unable to. I begged her in a low voice: "Help me, Imani. My laces, can't you see? They're snakes. I've got snakes on my legs."

She knelt down and once again massaged my back with her warm hands. But, despite all her attentions, I couldn't help lamenting: "They say Africa is a slaughter-house. I wish it was, Imani, I wish it was. I would rather have died than be obliged to live like this."

As she crouched next to me, her capulana slipped open, revealing her firm breasts. And, unable to control myself, I caressed her bosom, while murmuring: "I'm losing my mind, Imani. Allow me to at least believe I'm still a man."

My white gown falling, endlessly falling—that was how my dream ended. And I'll say no more, for fear of appearing ridiculous.

Please forgive the audacity of these personal confessions. In truth, it took Imani some time to risk touching my body. Even when I was in the thick of my hallucinations, she remained distant, while declaiming a strange litany, which went literally as follows: "There's a shadow in the Portuguese, there's a shadow in his eyes, there's a shadow leaving his face, traveling over his body and stealing his hands. Let's make this shadow go back in and die in the light of his eyes." It might have been a mere suggestion, but that ditty calmed me, and I gradually regained my clarity of thought.

P.S. As a minor item of news, I should tell you I received a letter from the Italian woman Dona Bianca (do you remember, the proprietress of the boarding house in Lourenço Marques?). Well, she told me of her wish to travel to Inhambane to visit the botanist, Fornasini, and his family. She wants to be with someone from her country, of her language. Do you see how powerful is the appeal of one's origins?

15

A King Made Dust

There are people who transform the sun into a simple yellow spot, but there are also those who create the sun itself out of a simple yellow spot.

—PABLO PICASSO

Everyone in this world lives in one unique place and one unrepeatable time. Everyone except us in Nkokolani. Like the bats in the legend, we lived at a crossroads between worlds. An invisible, unbreachable frontier traversed our souls.

This duplicity would manifest itself on the morning Uncle Musisi woke up earlier than usual, tied the most formal of cloths around his waist, and adjusted the coat his father had sent him from the mines over his bare torso.

His body was thus assuming the trappings of two worlds. In his goatskin satchel, he put a handful of mafura fruit, and left without saying goodbye to his wife. He was going to visit Binguane, intending to request what he had refused to request from the Portuguese: protection against Ngungunyane's warriors.

◆

On his way there, Musisi recalled the last time he had been in Binguane's domains. On that occasion, he was accompanying Grandfather Tsangatelo, who was visiting the great *nkosi* to ask for his support in getting back his wife, Layeluane. The matter was a delicate one and needed a widely respected negotiator to deal with the Crown authorities. Tsangatelo had left to join the Portuguese military forces who were facing rebellion in the vicinity of Lourenço Marques. He thought he would be away for a month or two; he was away for nearly a year. The *indunas*, or officials, from Inhambane turned up to collect taxes. Layeluane was unable to pay and explained to the collectors the reasons for her husband's absence. They didn't believe her. They arrested her and took her away as a guarantee of payment. She was what the Portuguese termed "taxes in arrears." When the men were absent and families couldn't pay, the women and their children were taken away until their husbands turned up to pay their ransom. The moment he arrived from the battlefront, Tsangatelo paid what he owed, but no one in the Portuguese administration knew of his wife's whereabouts. Grandfather was hopeful that Binguane might use his influence.

Musisi recalled Tsangatelo's deference when presenting himself to the chief, Binguane. At the entrance, there were large straw baskets known as *xirundzo*, which showed how good the harvest had been and, above all, revealed how the country folk had been generous with their gifts. While waiting to be seated, Grandfather stood there on tiptoe. It was said the chief hated short people. "I want men capable of seeing beyond the plains," he proclaimed.

Opening his arms over the great baskets, the chief commented with pride: "This year, we'll dance the *ngalanga*."

Then he closed his eyes and remained like that, as if he had suddenly fallen asleep. Grandfather realized he needed to explain the reason for his visit without further delay. When he had finished, Binguane assured him that he would not only intervene by contacting the Portuguese personally but would also send his men to question the indunas who had taken her away. "Don't worry—your wife will be here within a couple of days. Let us talk about another matter. I've been told that you are negotiating with the Portuguese military to furnish them with a caravan of porters."

"I was also going to ask you whether I should trust them, after what they did to Layeluane. Tell me, nkosi, do you think I can trust these Portuguese?"

"Do you trust your own race?"

"How can I? Look at the case of the VaNguni ..."

"And do you trust those in your own household?"

"You know only too well I can't. I can't even trust this son-in-law of mine who has come with me."

"Do you know why I trust you? Because you are pretending to be taller than you really are. You want to please me. This was why I spread the rumor that I hate small men, so I can assess their willingness to please me, rather than concern over their size. You can stop stretching yourself, my friend."

"I am grateful, Binguane."

"I trust you enough to tell you this: I want you to treat the Portuguese well. We haven't got any other, more useful allies. Ask them to pay me in guns. And let them leave these guns here in our village. I'll settle up with you afterward."

Tsangatelo took his leave, but Musisi lingered behind. Taking the opportunity to satisfy a long-felt curiosity, he addressed the chief:

"Tell me, Binguane. You have just visited Ngungunyane. I've always wanted to know what he's like. What is Umundungazi like?"

"And what's the point of knowing about him?"

"People say he's a bad man, and that his top teeth appeared before his bottom ones. That was why he was given his name. Do you know what Umundungazi means in their language?"

"I've already said there's no point. You give this man too much importance. That is how an enemy gains greater stature."

They both knew: Umundungazi means "the destroyer of the nation." That was why the elders of the court had changed his name. For Binguane, the change could have been avoided: the original name could have given us a good reason to like him. Who knows, maybe he would have helped us destroy his own nation?

◆

This conversation was still clear in Musisi's memory. But he had a doubt: would Binguane still recall it? At this point, he heard a violent roll of thunder that caused the ground to shake. The sky was clear, and Uncle wondered what the reasons were for that roar tearing through the firmament. He even paused for a minute in his plan, but then resumed his journey. When he was halfway there, he was startled by a loud uproar. He caught a glimpse of various Nguni regiments marching back from battle. From the thicket of ironwood trees, he had a clear view of the soldiers marching in line. They wore a white feather on their foreheads, a sign that they had killed enemies. And they whooped like animals in heat. Grandfather Tsangatelo was right when he said: "Soldiers must be encouraged to shout. Their shouts prevent them from paying heed to their own fear."

In the thick foliage where he was hiding, Musisi feared

for his life; even the sound of his breathing seemed too loud. If they noticed his presence, the tattoos on his face would reveal his identity straightaway, and he would be summarily executed. He was one of those whom the invaders called "the ones with cut faces," not even considered a person. He would be killed like an animal, without pity, without burial.

The soldiers disappeared into the distance, and Musisi continued his journey stealthily toward Binguane's village. When he got there, he dropped to his knees as if his legs had lost their ability to support him: the village was in flames, the ground littered with corpses. A group of women was gathering the wounded and covering the dead with mats and sheets of cloth.

"Where is Binguane?"

"There's nothing left of him," they replied.

"Where is his body?"

"There's nothing left, we've already told you."

This is what had happened: In despair at the weight of his defeat, Binguane took down the Portuguese ensign from its flagpole. He gazed lingeringly at the golden crown in its center. It was said that this crown symbolized gold. But what he saw was a blazing sun, and he waited while its glow flooded his eyes. Then he tore the cloth in half and rolled himself in the blue half. Having covered himself in this way, he sat on a barrel of gunpowder, in an effort to blow himself up.

A mishap sullied the nobility of his act. Before he could set fire to the barrel, it fell over because of Binguane's weight. The gray powder that leaked from it took away the breath of those who wanted to help. Binguane didn't give up. He set fire to the cloth wrapped around him, and then hugged the barrel as if it were his most cherished wife. It was then that the most deafening explosion occurred. And night fell, both within Binguane and outside him.

◆

I awoke with a start at the distant roar of thunder. The same things had happened to me that would happen in my father's nightmares: I remembered the iron birds swooping across the heavens. Day was breaking. I peeped through the curtain. There was a faraway glint that looked as if it might be the red flame of a bushfire. I went through the house to make sure the windows were closed. A strong wind had blown during the night, and the floor was covered with dark specks. For sure, it was the soot from the fires, and I swept the floor with a broom. I contemplated the burnt cinders, black and twisted, as if I recognized the same matter I was made of. Powder and ash. And I reverted to my original name.

◆

Within hours of his death, Binguane had become a legend. At night, when stories can be told, the old recounted the true reason for the great warrior's death to their young listeners. And this is how the story went:

There was once a king who didn't believe in the existence of clouds. He argued that clouds only existed in our eyes.

"I can only believe in what I am able to touch." This is what he said. And he ordered a ladder to be built that would be tall enough for him to climb up to the cloudy altitudes. It took years to build the ladder. When the king was summoned to see it, he looked up at the top and was unable to make out all the rungs.

"I am going to climb it," he announced.

He climbed and climbed, and grew ever more tired. Swallows would stream past, puzzled at such clumsy company. When the king was already dizzy and gasping for air, he saw that he was surrounded by clouds. He stretched out his arms to touch them, but his fingers passed among those billowing vapors as if they were rays of light penetrating water. And he smiled, happy. He had, after all, been right all along.

As he descended, he announced: "I didn't touch them. They don't exist."

As he climbed down, he noticed he was becoming lighter and lighter. By the time he was near the ground, he was having to hold on tightly. The slightest breeze caused him to flutter like a flag. When his feet touched the ground, the king had turned into a cloud. All that was left of him was the ladder that takes the unbelievers up into the heavens.

◆

People say that, on that very night, Binguane returned to collect his ashes. But some of them had already been blown away by the wind. He could therefore put only half of himself together again. This is why he wanders through time, incomplete and riddled with holes: half warrior, half Chopi, half hero, half vanquished. It is also said that our great-grandchildren will have forgotten this half of their past. And they will conceal their names for fear of being made to shoulder the burden of other people's defilement.

And things will remain so until another Binguane comes forth. And he will be a new kind of warrior, for he will teach us to overcome the boundaries that have divided us. Then we shall be able to visit the two halves of time known to our ancestors.

16

The Sergeant's Eighth Letter

Nkokolani, June 5, 1895

Your Excellency Counselor José d'Almeida

Being here, alone and abandoned, I feel myself gradually turning into another Sardinha: more wedded to these folk, nearer to these Negroes, than to my own compatriots. Your Excellency is my only friend, the only bridge that still links me to Portugal.

This week, I felt as if I were once more taking up my sense of mission. The kaffirs brought me a Vátua prisoner. And this act of deference, this subordination, eventually gave me back my tarnished military pride.

Despite his mistreatment, Gungunhane's soldier maintained an enviable air of dignity. He asked permission to speak, and I was led to understand, with the help of Imani's mother, that his people viewed the Chopi with the same sense of superiority as we do in relation to all blacks. What is more, the prisoner claimed that those lands belonged to them by divine right and that the natives there needed someone to civilize them. I ordered the prisoner to keep quiet. I hated him not for what he said about those who had been defeated, but because, in all his haughtiness, he was beginning to sound like those who had sent me to Africa.

The news reaching me over the next few days confirmed the Nguni soldier's hatred of the villagers. I received continuous complaints from the Chopi concerning atrocities committed by Gungunhane's troops. And the complaints were so many that I became not merely insensitive to them but more and more removed from the victims and at odds with what was rational and just. It even occurred to me that the Vátua prisoner was right: From his point of view and that of his nation, they are not committing a crime. On the contrary, they are heroically building an empire. When one thinks about it, what they are doing is not so different from what we ourselves are doing, with all due respect, and bearing in mind cultural difference. We are also defending an empire, authorized to do so by God and our natural superiority. We also adorn the history of this empire with pomp and splendor. If the Vátuas win this war, the fate of this nation of ours will be fulfilled without our being either avowed or disavowed. No one will have any memory of António Enes. And the valiant Mouzinho de Albuquerque will be a lackluster loser. The State of Gaza will survive intact, with all its glorious history. Gungunhane will survive, the one great hero. This Negro will shine, just as Caesar, Alexander the Great, Napoleon, Afonso de Albuquerque once shone. And the statue of the African king will one day feature in the sacred village of Chaimite, in honor of his victory.

I recognize, Excellency, the audacity of these thoughts of mine, which I could never share with anyone but you. And I confess that these ideas have haunted me throughout these last few days. So much so that they made me recall an episode that I thought had faded from memory. Once, on a day off from school in Lisbon, I saw a man standing in the middle of Rossio Square. He pointed upward and announced, in an eerily familiar tone, "They are all the same."

I didn't understand.

The man repeated himself: "They are all the same, wherever they are." He was talking about statues. He pointed toward the monument to King Pedro IV. And the strange fellow then declared that the figure represented there was not our king. He was, in fact, Maximilian I, the "emperor" of Mexico. An unknown Portuguese had bought the statue, which was on sale in Paris, given that the aspiring emperor had been shot even before he was crowned. They had saved costs and gained luster. And the man reiterated that statues, like imperial narratives, were no different one from another. "This king is walking. But if he was riding a horse, you would see for yourself that even the horse is the same!"

For the rest, these recent weeks have gone by as if time were standing still. I can, however, tell you a more personal story, though it is one that gives me pleasure to share. Some days ago, Imani's father came to visit me. For a minute, I feared he was coming to get even with me over my attempted advances on his only daughter. This was why I greeted him with such bonhomie: "Good day to you, Katini Nsambe!"

"You are a soldier, sir, and you shouldn't call me by my name. Soldiers aren't interested in anyone's name."

"So what are you doing here?"

"I've come to give you a litter. One I made myself."

"And what would I want with a litter?"

"Why, to journey through the bush, of course, just as all the Europeans do."

"But I'm not like all the Europeans. I've got my legs, and I like to tire them out."

"You are a good man, sir. But be careful, boss, for, here

in Nkokolani, goodness and weakness speak the same tongue."

Then he revealed that, while he was walking through the forest, he thought of giving me a tree. An entire tree, complete with roots, trunk, branches, and leaves. With such a gift, he would be offering me the sky, the earth, and time. But since he couldn't do this, and, besides, given that I had refused the litter, he would offer me a hen.

"A hen?"

I had no time to show any misgivings, for he began dragging over a rough wooden cage with a well-fed brown-feathered chicken inside it.

"Where you see a hen, sir, I see eggs. And when there are no more eggs, meat. Meat for a week's worth of curry."

I took the hen out of the cage, and she wasn't at all frightened. Nor did she scamper off. Rather, she nestled by my feet like a cat.

"I'm going to give her a name," I announced, moved by the creature's gentility.

"Please don't do that," the poor black fellow begged in alarm. "If you do that, this hen will never again think she's a hen. And she'll invade your dreams, just as you, boss, will invade hers ..."

Ever since then, I have shared the intimacy of my home with a hen. Contrary to the advice I had received, I named her Chestnut. During the day, I leave her in the backyard. During the night, I shelter her inside the house, to keep her from being devoured by genets. In the half-light of my room, under the flickering light of the oil lamp, Chestnut looks at me with gratitude and then hides her head under her wing. I recall her former owner's warning, and am amused by the thought that the hen is dreaming, in Portuguese, my own dreams. I hope that, in exchange, I have the same dreams as hers, which are no doubt less oppressive.

Yesterday Katini knocked at my door once again. I peered through the window and saw him standing in the yard, clutching a huge xylophone. This time, he hadn't brought the product of his craftsmanship as a present. Knowing that I was unwell, he offered to play in order to alleviate my suffering. Music, he said, is capable of chasing away illnesses and ghosts. I waited for him to sit down in the yard, eyes closed, the sticks pointing vertically, up into the heavens. He played a few loose notes as if he were plucking up courage. At last, he spoke in a slow, labored Portuguese: "I am going to play the music of the Portuguese ..."

"The music of the Portuguese?"

"A song the priest taught me. He told me it was the anthem of Portugal." He immediately started to chortle the words, badly pronounced, but in perfect tune:

The truth shall not be eclipsed,
The king shall not be deceived, no,
Let us proclaim ...

I interrupted him gently. I smiled sadly in anticipation of his disappointment at what I was about to say.

"That anthem," I explained, "isn't my anthem."

"Aren't you Portuguese?" he asked.

I didn't reply. In these circumstances, it would be better to let the poor man fulfill his generous intentions. And, full of feeling, the man played a curious version of the Portuguese anthem. At first, I was puzzled. But I confess that, after a while, I found it moving. That composition of his began to soothe me. And night fell in Nkokolani with a white man drinking nsope and a black man playing the Portuguese national anthem.

I have at last discovered, my dear counselor, a humanity that I didn't know existed within me, out here in these backlands. These seemingly remote folk have given me lessons I would never have learned anywhere else. Some weeks ago, for instance, a native of Nkokolani appeared before me who had been summoned to the administration at Zavala, charged with tax evasion. The administrator ordered a sepoy to whip him. It was not the act of disobedience that needed to be punished. What was beyond pardon was a Negro's pride in fearlessly contesting Portuguese power. This was the impression that remained with me from the unfortunate kaffir's story, related without lament or complaint.

I understood the logic behind the thinking of our authorities. It was necessary to humiliate him, to do to him what they do to elephants in India when they want to tame them: smash their knees so that their feet will forfeit their dreams. The administrator ordered that he should first be lashed with a cat-o'-nine-tails. At this point, the black proceeded to correct him politely: There were no cats there, whether with one tail or nine. Moreover, that dried-up appendage belonged to an animal known as an *mpfufu*. If we didn't have a suitable name for it in the Portuguese language, he suggested we could borrow the term from his own tongue.

It didn't occur to the administrator that our language already possessed the word "hippopotamus." And he took these declarations as proof of yet greater insolence. If there wasn't an appropriate name for a cat-o'-nine-tails, then let him be beaten with an old wooden bat.

I should tell you, by way of a brief aside, that while the kaffir was relating what had happened his face became contorted, and tears filled his eyes. He found it more painful to recall the incident than it had been to suffer the punishment—at the very time when the wood was lacerating his flesh, he remained impassive. Not one single complaint during the thirty strokes. The sepoy charged with administering his flogging was denied such a trophy, and the victim withdrew from the room with his hands turned upward, as if he were asking God to bear witness to the unbearable pain he was suffering. He bade a polite farewell to the sepoy who had beaten him, but he didn't leave. Rather, he knocked on the door of the administrator's office and asked, "I would like to ask you a favor, Lordship."

"A favor?"

"I would like you to beat me."

"Haven't you had enough?"

"I want people to see that I am not just anyone. I want to go back to my village and say out loud that, when it was my turn, it was a white man who delivered the beating."

Later, when I spoke to the administrator, he confirmed the story. And he made it clear that he had refused the presumptuous kaffir's request. "That's exactly what he wanted," he insisted. "These blacks are like big children, and they see in us a father figure charged with punishment and absolution." I am not sure that his interpretation is correct. In my view, the black man's motive was different: to prove the cowardice of those who order people to be punished but are incapable of personally delivering the punishment.

I reproduce apparently mundane episodes such as this in order to highlight our stubbornness in not realizing that the human reality here is far more complex than is presumed in Lisbon. When I was included in that firing squad in Lourenço Marques, I was unable to guess the age of the youths we were to shoot. They could have been children, they could have been adults. As Sanches de Miranda rightly says, these creatures are impossible to read. And this increases our anger at them.

And it is a pity that we are content to remain so ignorant. For it is this ignorance that ensures we come out losers, not only in our ability to govern well, but also in our capacity to intervene militarily. An understanding of the most fundamental issues escapes us, and we consider it right to support certain local rulers unconditionally. These instances of support are, however, precarious and based on fragile, temporary consensus. Only today, with the help of a translator, I witnessed a curious conversation between two chiefs who offered to resolve a quarrel among local blacks. I shall reproduce their colorful exchanges as faithfully as possible. They were debating whether there had been a betrayal in the surrender of land to the Vátua invaders. And they argued the matter in the following terms:

"We gave them those lands," one said, "but we didn't surrender our gods, who are the only owners of the land."

"Words. Those are just words," the other retorted. "We surrendered everything to them."

"Are we not the ones who still command the sacred rites?"

"Let me ask you this, then: What language do our *ngangas* speak in these rites? Do they speak in our language? Or isn't it true that we now speak to our gods in the language of the invaders?

17

A Lightning Flash from the Soil

All generals know that protection from their own army is
more important than defense against the enemy.

Early in the morning, I was told that Katini and Musisi
would go and seek an audience at the garrison. Without
waiting, I set off. Some days before, I myself had
informed the Portuguese of my family's intentions.
Even so, it would be better if I went ahead on the day of
their visit. After Binguane's death, the atmosphere was
tense, and it was important that the sergeant should be
left in no doubt as to the urgency of what would be asked
of him. It was with this in mind that I walked through
the streets, which were still shrouded in a fog; I took this
for a village mist at first, but then I saw that it was in fact
a thick cloud of smoke. The smoke emanated from afar,
from where Binguane had embraced death.

My brother Mwanatu had become even more vigilant
while on sentry duty at the entrance to the garrison.
Whereas before he had sported a false weapon, he now
had a new piece of equipment: he wore a pair of white
gloves. "Come in quickly, sister; we're on full alert," he
whispered to me, with a flurry of his fingers.

Germano was leaning over a map spread right across
the table. Without looking up, he asked: "Do you know
what's happened?"

"The whole village knows."

"And do you know who's just been here? It was Binguane's son, Xiperenyane."

"Xiperenyane was here?"

"He came to ask me to intercede in order to save his granddaughter. During yesterday's attack, the little girl was abducted by the Vátuas. And the story's going around that she's already been killed, devoured by Ngungunyane's witch doctors."

The Portuguese was perturbed. It was clear from the hoarseness of his voice. He paused, staring at me with his blue eyes, and then addressed me in an almost aggressive fashion: "Have you come because of the classes? Well, the classes are over."

"Over?"

"You can go on visiting me, but don't teach me anything. I came to this world's end in order to forget that there are such things as languages. To forget that there are people, forget that I've got a name ..."

And he stretched his arms over the table as if to hug the map. Draped over it in this fashion, he repeated: "What I want is to forget."

I took a few steps forward and murmured fearfully: "Can I ask something?"

"What is it you want?"

"Can I touch your hair?"

He smiled and inclined his head toward me. My hand ceased being mine and supported itself first on his shoulder before sinking into his thick mass of hair. The Portuguese must have misunderstood my request. I was impelled only by my curiosity to feel that hair of his, which was so different from ours. His reaction was to raise his arms and cup my breasts in his hands. While this was happening, the buttons of my blouse burst and rolled crazily across the floor. Then each button twisted and shrank as if it were melting before some invisible fire.

The Portuguese persisted in his carnal efforts. I wanted to resist, to bite him on the arm, attack him with all the fury I could muster. But I let myself just stand there, submissive, like the woman I had been brought up to be. At that moment, I have to admit, I was overcome by a strange torpor: for the first time, I felt my heart beating in another body. The sergeant's fingers caressed my nipples as if they were buttons made of flesh. And I lingered, delaying any attempt to get away.

"My father will be here at any minute. I just came to warn you."

The Portuguese came to his senses abruptly and withdrew in silence. I remained there alone, my blouse half undone. And I contemplated my breasts as if I had never seen them before. Where we come from, it's the size of breasts that transforms girls into women. This pair of curves proclaims our ability to bear another life. At that moment, my breasts merely suggested I had a great deal of life left to live.

◆

I was desperate to get out of there. Even so, I hesitated before picking up my buttons. Maybe I should leave them there, all shrunken and twisted on the floor. Maybe I was being punished: no other woman in Nkokolani had ever had buttons for her clothes before. When my sense of urgency eventually prevailed, my hand brushed the floor and I realized the buttons were burning like embers. In spite of this, I held them in my left hand while I tidied my clothes and hair.

Then I went to wait by the front door for my family to arrive. When they came, I leaned against the doorpost to allow them to pass. My brother Mwanatu blocked their way, conscious of his obligations as a sentry.

"Stop these crazy games, Mwanatu," said my uncle. "That rifle is in a worse state of repair than your head."

My father shrugged his shoulders in disapproval. As he passed his son, he straightened Mwanatu's collar. It was a discreet way of expressing his joy at his European bearing.

"How is our *kabweni*, our little corporal?" he asked, unable to conceal his pride.

"I'm not a kabweni, Father," my brother corrected him. "I'm a lance corporal in the infantry."

He smiled at me and then resumed his statuesque pose, as if his only occupation were contemplating infinity. My intentions were very different: to get out of there as quickly as possible. But I was hampered in my efforts by my father's arm.

"You're coming in with us. Who can better translate for us?"

"There's no need—you speak so well, Father."

"I don't have enough Portuguese for what we've come here to talk about," my old father argued.

"I haven't come to say anything at all," Uncle countered. "I'm here only to control what your father is going to say."

The sergeant was excessively attentive in the way he received us. He had put on his uniform, to show that he was fulfilling official functions. His agreeable manner was, however, more for my benefit than for my relatives. He opened a bottle of wine to greet the visitors. His goodwill notwithstanding, our host was ignorant of our etiquette: Among us, it's the dead who drink first. In the name of our dear departed, we spill the first few drops on the ground. This is followed by a moment's reflection, to show how these false absentees still hold sway over time. After that, the women are served—not out of any deference, but because the men suspect the drink might have been poisoned. Only after all this are the men and guests served. Such is our accepted etiquette.

The soldier was the first to drink. He did so directly from the bottle, still wearing his hat. The wine dribbled abundantly over his chin and down his neck. He seemed to want to bathe in it rather than drink. After listening to my father's fears, he adopted a formal tone and set about placating us:

"I have already told you that you will not be disturbed. These guarantees were given me by my superiors, who are also those who command you and who command Gungunhane. There was no need for you to come here with your request ..."

"Request?" My uncle was indignant and spoke in Txitxope. Then, turning to me: "Translate this, niece. I want to tell this white one or two things."

"Go ahead, Uncle, but mind how you talk. We don't go to someone else's house to abuse them."

"Be quiet, Imani. Binguane has just died. And we'll all die if these bosses of yours don't take this seriously."

"Very well, Uncle. Now let's speak in Portuguese, so that he doesn't get suspicious about what we're saying."

"Ask your boss the following: Who do we pay tribute to? Isn't it to the Portuguese? We are subjects of the Crown. We are Portuguese—isn't that what they say? If this is the case, Portugal has the duty to defend us. Or am I wrong?"

My father, anxious, hastened to soften his brother-in-law's intervention. And he made use of his clumsy Portuguese. "Don't mind him, boss. My kinsman's just worried ..."

"There's no need to translate. I can understand that

your brother-in-law is angry. I've known for a long time what he thinks of the Portuguese. Let's talk to one another like human beings—I mean, like civilized folk. And you, Imani, you know where everything is here, go to the kitchen and get me another bottle like this one." With the modest step of a servant, I went to the kitchen, where I saw two bottles of brandy on the table. Under them was a telegram sent in the name of the royal commissioner. It was dated two weeks before, and directed to the military high command in Inhambane. I couldn't resist taking a look at it. As I read through the text, a bitter taste welled up in my mouth. This is what it said:

We cannot, under any circumstances, exchange urgent support for the Chopi for our need to defend Lourenço Marques. We cannot expedite any reinforcements to Inhambane under pain of leaving our southern territories exposed. It is possible that Gungunhane will be unable to resist his thirst for revenge against the Chopi, the people who have offered him such resistance. But this is damage that we have to ignore. In fact, we should consider this: the Chopi themselves should be blamed for any punishment they receive. The Vátuas streaming south with their troops are not intent on wreaking vengeance on us Portuguese—their natural enemies—but on those who are black like themselves. It is for this effrontery that they now intend to punish them. It is not appropriate for us to intervene. These are our orders, then: let things take their course.

I returned to the room, my ears buzzing so much I couldn't listen to what was being said. I only realized from the gestures the Portuguese made that he was asking about the bottle I had forgotten to bring.

"I've read the telegram," I announced as I made for the door.

"What telegram?" the Portuguese asked, astonished.

I waved the piece of paper I was carrying, opened the front door, and, in a firm tone of voice, asked my relatives to leave with me. When I saw the flight of steps, it seemed endless. I was descending into the depths of hell. The Portuguese had lied. And the hurt caused by such a lie was a measure of how fond of him I had become.

◆

The following morning, I made my way barefoot to the River Inharrime. I waded into the bed of the river until the water was up to my chest. It wasn't that I was trying to kill myself by drowning. Quite the opposite: I wanted the river to impregnate me. Such a fruitful liaison had been successful with other women. For them, the secret had been to remain calm until their souls were indistinguishable from the dead leaves floating downstream.

This is what I wanted at that moment. For of one thing I had no doubt: no man was going to possess me. What I had left was the river, the river of my birth. Its waters were already flowing inside me when I hit the bank once more, helpless like some old tree trunk bobbing along at the mercy of the current. And there I remained until I had gathered enough strength to go back home. It was then that my feet sank in the mud. Rather than trying to struggle against the absent ground, I freed myself of my clothes and, stark naked, abandoned myself to the silt's slimy embrace. For a moment, I allowed myself to be possessed by the pleasure of feeling my skin covered by another skin. It was then that I understood the delight animals take in a mud bath. That's what I yearned to be: a wild animal devoid of beliefs, without any hopes.

Covered from head to foot in sludge, I walked back along the path to the village. Under the embittered gaze of the women, I made my way to the sergeant's house. When Mwanatu saw me, he fled from his guard post. The Portuguese was sitting on the veranda, and didn't recognize me until I had spoken:

"Would you like to see me naked, Germano? Well, then, throw water over my body. No one will ever undress me like that."

In a daze, the Portuguese asked me inside. He closed the door and crept around the edge of the room like a hunter fearing his prey. He left and returned with a cloth and a pail of water.

"Now it's my turn to wash the bad omens from you," he declared.

He moved his hands over my arms, shoulders, and back. Then he threw the cloth aside and splashed the water over my body. When the Portuguese saw me undressed and defenseless, he went mad. He hurriedly took off his clothes, his fingers shaking, his chin covered in drool. And as he held my waist, I let him lick my breasts until I felt my skin pulsating with his blood. Then the man lay down on the floor. He patted the ground, inviting me to lie down next to him. I declined. Instead, I looked down at him in drawn-out, queenly contemplation. In taking my time with carrying out his punishment, I felt the perverse thrill that a lioness feels before delivering the final blow. I tossed the telegram of the previous day onto the ground, placed a foot on his chest, spat in his face, and, in the gentlest voice, insulted him in my own language: "You lying white! You'll slither away like a snake."

The Portuguese was still wallowing on the floor when he saw me leave, wrapped in a piece of white material that I had taken from a shelf. More than the insult itself, I had taken the greatest delight in addressing him in Txitxope. It was possible that no other black person had such a command of Portuguese. But the hatred I felt toward him could be expressed only in my mother tongue. I was doomed: I was destined to be born and to die in my own language.

◆

Back home, I called the family together to reveal how dishonest Germano de Melo had been in his promises. "Is the Portuguese lying?" my father asked incredulously. "You must have misread it, daughter. You are mistaken." And he repeated: "You are mistaken." Musisi kept quiet, holding back the satisfaction he felt that his original suspicions had been proved true.

Without getting an answer from me, my father opened a bottle of wine and served himself generously. When the bottle was as empty as he was, Katini sat down in front of his xylophone. By this time, the floor was no longer enough to serve as a seat: his intoxication multiplied whatever he looked at, including the instrument's keys, which disobeyed him and slipped from his control. He looked up as if he were invoking the spirits. And in this position he shouted for his wife: "Come and dance, Chikazi. I want to see you dance."

Like a ghost, his wife crept into the center of the floor space, and stood there without moving.

"Let's celebrate, woman. Didn't you hear the pledges of our Portuguese friends? The war will never reach us here! Is there a better reason to dance?"

Father attacked the keyboard furiously, as if he were punishing the instrument he himself had made. And his wife stood still, her gaze fixed at the floor.

"There's no need to move about if you prefer not to. You, my dearest Chikazi, you dance even standing still."

It occurred to me that I should take mother's place to save her from humiliation. However, I had one more task to fulfill, conferred upon me by the indignation still burning in my heart. I hurried off along the footpath that led to the village. I could still hear the uneven notes of the xylophone as I made my way furiously through the bush. I entered the old church, where my brother Dubula was waiting for me.

"I got your message," he said without greeting me. "What do you want?"

The floor of the church was covered in owls' feathers. I took my shoes off. And the stone felt as smooth as a cloud. Water dribbled down the walls like those wounds that time tears open in a cave. I was summoning up the courage to tell him my reasons for being there. I dug my nails into a damp crack in the stone and spoke: "You know, Dubula, my body has never learned to be a woman."

"I don't know what you're talking about, sister."

"Yes, you do. You know very well. Mother never allowed me to go through the initiation rites. I've come here so that you can teach me how a woman can be aroused by a man."

"Don't say such things, Imani. We are brother and sister, and we can't even talk about such matters."

"You can; you always acted as if we could."

"What did I do?"

"You always took a peep when I was having a bath in the backyard."

Dubula denied this vehemently. I was lying. But it was half a lie. For while he had always taken a look, he had never been able to see. When I revealed my body, Dubula was blinded. This temporary blindness wasn't the result of some defect in his vision, but of excessive desire.

"Today I bathed in the river. I washed myself with water and mud."

"Why?" Dubula asked, puzzled.

I didn't answer. But my brother knew: It was the others who took their bath in the river. We didn't. Our family did the same as the Europeans: we would assemble basins and buckets in the yard, and I would linger in my bath, possibly because I was aware of Dubula's furtive presence. My brother was the reason for a display of choreography in which I concealed and revealed myself. Water splashed onto the stone, and the noise the water made was exactly like rain falling. The drops glinted, lit up on my breasts; water trickled over my buttocks. It was like a dance: I bathed merely in order to be caressed.

"There's going to be a war, dear brother. That's why I recalled the past. Because I fear for the future."

And I told Dubula what had happened at the garrison. When I told him about the loathsome telegram, he got to his feet, tense and in a hurry to leave the church.

"I've got to go," he whispered. He opened the door and peered out to see if it was safe for him to leave.

Before he could disappear, I asked: "Dubula, tell me something. Do you not have a woman in your life?"

"I'm a soldier. Women soften one's heart. Just look at what's happening to that sergeant of yours."

"I don't want you to speak of that man."

"I know you, Imani. All the time we've been here, you weren't talking to me. You were talking to your Portuguese."

"That's a lie, brother. A lie!"

"Do you know what's going to happen? The thing that's going to happen is what our father always dreamed of: the Portuguese will go back to where he came from, and he'll take you with him."

"Never!"

"If I were you, sister, I'd go straight to his house. And I'd ask him to take you away with him. Do that if you like him. For when I return to Nkokolani along with the VaNguni, we'll put an end to that garrison once and for all."

"Aren't you going to bid me farewell?"

He wasn't going to do that, he murmured. One takes one's leave only if one hopes to meet again. He didn't want to see me ever again.

◆

I went back home as if I were dragging my shoulders along the ground. Our elders say: He who walks alone seeks the shelter of his own shadow. Well, I didn't even have a shadow.

Mother was awaiting me in the backyard. She told me her friend had just left, the mother of Ndzila, my best friend from childhood. We had attended the Mission School together.

"Is Ndzila here?" I asked eagerly.

She took her time in answering. She chose her words carefully, in order not to hurt me.

"She arrived yesterday. But her father sent her straight back to Chicomo. He doesn't want her here."

"Because of me?"

"He says you're a bad influence. As far as this village is concerned, dear daughter, you are worthy of much suspicion. Your fate is to remain alone, unmarried and childless. You have your father to thank for that."

It was the price paid for having been delivered up to the world of the Portuguese. The possibility of seeing Ndzila again brought into focus something I always attempted to ignore. I had no friends in Nkokolani, neither male nor female. What was still more serious: I didn't even have a desire for friends.

Mother understood my sadness and sat down next to me. She didn't touch me or look at me. As if she were talking to herself, she began by saying that I was a woman, and that the women of Nkokolani are supposed to belong to someone in order to cease being no one. That is why a single girl is termed *lamu*, which means "she who hopes." It's a way of saying that we shall be people only once we become wives.

"Don't lose hope, daughter. You haven't stopped being a lamu yet."

The certainty of such condemnation was the best encouragement my mother could offer me.

18

The Sergeant's Ninth Letter

Nkokolani, June 9, 1895

Your Excellency Counselor José d'Almeida

This week, offended by my having lied to her, Imani turned against me and humiliated me in an elaborate fashion. I shall spare you the details of the scene she caused at the military post. It was fortunate that the place was shielded from the rabble's curiosity and prying eyes.

But there is something I must confess: When Imani mistreated me, I felt as if I were being crucified on the floor of the house. As I bore the brunt of her fury, I realized how she was my only reason for living. Now that I have squandered the chance to conquer her, what is left for me in this world?

I do not know, sir, how I shall be able to continue my mission. In truth, I have forgotten what that mission was, if indeed it ever existed. I recall having read a letter from King Affonso of the Congo, addressed to the king of Portugal. I cite here, without any claim to precision, the words of this black monarch: "In our disputes with other nations, we take captives and we can kill. But nothing will work as efficiently as our seductive women." King Affonso was right. In the end, I too fell victim to this power of seduction. I am one of the vanquished. I was defeated in a battle that never was.

I do not know how to get through the days, and I am terrified of the nights. You cannot imagine the bad dreams that assail me.

One nightmare is more repetitive than moths circling a lamp. In this nightmare, I see thousands of kaffirs dressed in our uniforms, seated in a circle. And we, the Portuguese, dance around a fire dressed in the animal skins and loincloths worn by natives. Everything inverted, upside-down.

Gungunhane appears, riding a white horse, in order to review his troops. Then, with an emperor's vanity, he dismounts and takes his place on a throne. On closer inspection, one can see that the kaffir has a small mustache, clipped in the fashion of our officials. He orders us to stop our dancing, which he finds too noisy and lewd. Then he tells us to sit down and open our mouths, and keep them open until he has finished speaking. In impeccable Portuguese, the Negro declares: "You wanted our land? Well, it's all yours."

And, with brute force, he pours sand down our gullets. Soon, when we are stuffed full, the chief summons one of his queens, who comes over bearing a huge ivory tusk.

"Were you dreaming of ivory? Well, here you have it."

Using the ivory as a pestle, the queen grinds the soil that has accumulated inside our mouths until we are completely asphyxiated. And so we die, sitting with our faces turned to the sun, rivulets of sand flowing over our chins. This is the nightmare that makes me wake up with a start and grab the first bottle I find on my bedside table. I drink eagerly, and as I put the bottle down, I read the old label on it: "Black Man's Wine."

Forgive this discourse on intimate matters. You may attribute my audacity in this to the abandonment in which I find myself, far from everything and everyone. I have been feeling so depressed over last few days that I have resorted to frequenting the village's dilapidated church. If it had a priest, I wouldn't set foot inside it. But, perhaps because it is in such an abandoned state, I let myself linger there in silent, wordless prayer. And do you know whom I pray for in this way? Well, I ask God to protect these poor natives. And I beg him to spare them the ravages of the Vátuas.

Every time, I ask for more, but with less faith. Once, in the peace of that ruined church, I ended up falling asleep. And when I awoke, I sensed that the building was swaying, as if rocked by the waters of a river. The church was a boat, and in it traveled an uncle of mine, Maurício, who had become a priest. This uncle appeared to me now with his head attached to his body by one strip of flesh. And he was entreating me, in a voice that was as ruptured as his throat: "Write me down and put me in a letter, nephew. Send me back to my country inside an envelope."

Maurício had abandoned the church, disillusioned with the priesthood. He married and became the father of an adorable child. However, he remained an austere, taciturn man. Wishing to put an end to his own life, he killed his wife first, and then his son. He wanted to paint the walls with his victims' blood. But the walls rejected his paint. The house was alive. It escaped from its foundations. The man found himself out in the open air, with only the night for a roof. The following morning, he awoke without knowing where he was. Then he saw his wife and child floating above him, each of them holding a knife. His body was never found, and whatever blood there was had left no stain or sign of coagulation. Once

Maurício departed, no one remembered he had ever had a body. He who had abandoned God found no direction to give his soul.

After this terrifying vision, I never visited the church again, for fear that the ghost of Uncle Maurício dwelt there. But I followed the advice of my freakish relative. The endless letters I have written (most of them without an address or addressee) have been a means for me to bring order to the frenzied visions that forever assail me, and send them on their way.

I have written so many letters that I fear I have fulfilled my old mother's prophecy. She said she had known a man who had done nothing except write ever since he was a child. His right hand had become deformed, and his eyes had narrowed. And he wouldn't stop writing. All his infinite scribbling was, in the end, no more than one sole tract: it was a letter to the Messiah. In this missive, the man enunciated the world's evils. He could not omit any of humanity's failings under pain of missing the final act of redemption.

He spent years writing; there wasn't a single day when he didn't fill page after page. The Messiah died before he had finished his lengthy dispatch. Even so, the man continued to compose, in the belief that his document would be ready for the successor to the Savior of the World. He grew old surrounded by piles of paper, heaped up until they reached the ceiling. There came a day when the man no longer knew where the door and windows were. His was now but an inner world. At this time, he decided he should end his long epistle. He signed his name at the end of the last paragraph and lay down with the sheet of paper on his chest. It was then that he realized his infinite letter had been addressed to himself. He was the Messiah. And he was dead.

19

White Horses, Black Ants

The most dangerous enemies are not those who have always hated you. The ones you should fear most are those who, for a time, were close, and viewed you with fascination.

Clouds hemmed us in throughout the morning. They grew furrowed and black until the sky was ripped apart like a piece of old cloth from Musaradina's store. The villagers shut themselves in, alarmed. Only I braved the rain. Nkokolani is dominated by a terror of lightning, and during storms, everyone takes shelter under the thatch of their huts. I was completely alone under the thick ceiling of clouds; in order to expose myself even more, I climbed to the top of a dune. And from that solitary hilltop, I was confronted by an unexpected sight that filled the entire horizon: a mass of humans was advancing in an infinite wave. It was an ocean of people, so huge that not even God could have imagined it so vast. On either side of the column marched soldiers, carrying all manner of weaponry.

It was like looking at rain: a sight not limited by one's range of vision. At first, I was horrified. However, my panic gradually gave way to a strange feeling of resignation. And I had the urge to go and join that human wave. And to get far away from Nkokolani. To get far away from myself.

◆

The march of that multitude would extend over days on end. There was an endless parade of rifles and javelins. The ground shook with the passage of carts, and the landscape bowed under the weight of the ox caravans.

In an instant, all the inhabitants of our village assembled at our vantage point to watch this apocalyptic scene, terrified. Next to me, my mother commented: "There's more gunpowder in that multitude than there is sand in the whole world."

"The next time it rains," Aunt Rosi added, "bullets will fall instead of raindrops."

The vast majority of those on the march were country folk, who staggered along as if they were already dead. According to Musisi's sources, they were VaNdaus, forced to abandon their lands in the north, where Ngungunyane's capital had been located.

Our uncle proclaimed out loud what we already knew: The Portuguese kept Angolans because they were blacks who had been torn away from their native land, with no family or hope of return. The VaNguni now had their own Angolans in the form of the VaNdaus. The VaNguni had forced them on this journey southward because their troops in Gaza offered them no guarantees of loyalty. And these troops, both old and new, were beginning to wonder whether it was worth sacrificing themselves for a king who caused them to suffer such torment. This was why they were deserting, dying of hunger and thirst. Musisi stopped talking. Once again we listened to that long line of people advancing, as if we were listening to an endless line of ants.

Every so often, from among the mass of civilians appeared groups of uniformed soldiers. These were the emperor's guards. Keeping to a devilish rhythm, they stamped their feet in unison, and a rumbling, volcanic sound erupted from the soil. I feared Grandfather Tsangatelo would get a fright and emerge from the bowels of the earth, throwing the sinister procession into chaos.

My father's anguish was of a different kind. In a subdued tone, he muttered with a sigh: "This will be the end of us! A curse on the VaNguni!"

◆

The endless procession was far from over, and in the village, relatives and neighbors had already begun to dig holes near their houses and wells.

At first, I thought they were digging over the soil for planting. But the holes got deeper, to the point where entire households could be accommodated. The men climbed down into the holes and raised their arms above their heads to verify the depth. And then they went on digging.

The following morning, a delegation went to assess the state of the fortifications around the village. While this was happening, my father summoned us and ordered us to climb down to the bottom of the holes. Mother brought provisions, and neighbors and aunts stocked the trenches with large pots of water, which they covered with wooden lids.

At that point, my brother Mwanatu appeared on this strange scene. Our relatives were astonished, and commented on his visit. He hadn't put in an appearance at our home for months. He seemed even more of a simpleton than usual, and I was afraid he might fall into one of the freshly dug trenches.

"The sergeant sent me to ask what you're doing," Mwanatu declared.

"We're sowing ourselves," I answered impatiently. My tone of voice was so harsh that I scarcely recognized myself. "Go and tell your boss that. Tell him this is how people are born: at the right season, their seeds are cast into the soil. Honestly, Mwanatu, how can you be so stupid?"

"Actually," he replied in all candor, "I thought we were digging to try and find our grandfather under the ground."

And since no one paid him any attention, he turned on his heel and returned to the barracks. As I watched him walking away, I thought: We are not buried when we die. We are buried right after we are born.

◆

The following day, enemy troops entered our village. It would be a lie to say they were VaNguni soldiers. Most of them were from other tribes, other nations. Some were VaNdau, others were Makwakwa, others Bila, and others still were, well, just others. And there were even some of ours, bearing our names. These people, who had come from nearly everywhere, surrounded the village and made for the trenches where we were hiding. Furious, they shouted insults at us, as if our antlike labors somehow diminished their status as warriors.

Standing on the edge of my trench, an Nguni chief ordered us out of our hiding places. He watched me climb out like someone contemplating an animal emerging from its lair. When we were lined up on the open ground, the invaders grabbed sticks and shovels and began to fill in the trenches. I felt the thud of the sand in my heart. Those clumps of soil weren't just covering the holes but taking my breath away. At each swing of a shovel, my body faded away. I was gradually extinguished, buried.

At that moment, my long-held suspicions were confirmed: There is nothing in this world that isn't within me. Rocks, trees, all dwell under my skin. There is no outside, no far away: everything is flesh, nerves, and bone. Maybe I wouldn't need to get pregnant. My body gave shelter to the entire world.

◆

The enemy soldiers withdrew, but not before setting fire to the houses on the edge of the village and seizing boys and women as they came in from working in the fields. Plantations were devastated, and many folk were left without any crops. My father was right in his apocalyptic ravings: it would have been better if we had destroyed our own cultivations.

Like all the other houses in the center of the village, ours was spared, but despite that, we were no less anxious. The problem was that the hours went by without our knowing what had happened to my father. For a while, we thought he might have been abducted. But, no, that hadn't happened. He reappeared in the sacred wood that belonged to our family. There he was, sitting on an old mortar, his fingers clutching the handle of an ax. With his hand suddenly emboldened, he seemed to have rediscovered, godlike, the origin of the world. Next to him lay a coconut tree that he had just felled. Pointing at the trunk, he declared: "This is only the first. I'm going to cut down many more."

There were no longer many coconut palms in our plantation, but Mother avoided commenting on this reverie of his. Her man might know about everything except the business of living. Without our coconut trees, we would be consumed by hardship. But Katini's convictions were those of someone guided solely by the spirits. Due respect was therefore required.

And so this was why the neighbors began to collaborate in felling the coconut trees and transporting the timber. My old father assembled the trunks and sawed them. But most of the time, he contemplated the material in a daze. Standing there, motionless, he behaved as he always had: as if, by dreaming his task, he had already completed it.

No one ever questioned the purpose of such an enterprise. We imagined that a new khokholo was being prepared to surround our village. Faced now with the threat of another attack, these palisades were more than justified.

One day, however, we noticed that my dear old father, during the course of his lumbering, had juxtaposed the trunks end to end. Then, once they had been fixed together, he raised a mighty mast, so tall that it brushed against the sky.

Mother steeled herself and interrupted her man's mysterious undertaking: "What's that thing there for?"

"It's a mast."

"I don't understand—are you making a boat?"

There was a glint in Chikazi's eyes. But her husband didn't answer. He reacted as if making boats were the most mundane of occupations. So Mother bade me: "Go and speak to your father. Gently, in a leisurely way—don't frighten him. Sometimes your father finds words very daunting."

However, once in his presence, I didn't have an opportunity to speak, for he suddenly confronted me: "Do you know where I can find your other brother?"

I shrugged my shoulders. I didn't like the fact that my brother had lost his name, as if he were dead. Dubula was the "Other" just as I had once been the "Live Girl."

Father summoned us together—the "ongoing family," as he put it. Uncle Musisi and Aunt Rosi came, along with our cousins and nearest neighbors, and we sat ourselves on the trunks scattered around the clearing and waited for Katini to speak. He made the most of our respectful display of good manners, and was in no hurry to begin his address. Eventually, he pointed toward the huge mast and declared:

"It looks like a boat, but it isn't one. What I'm making is an island. It's an island that will save us all."

Not the slightest shadow or the least doubt clouded our gaze. We were giving the mysteries time to unravel right there, by themselves. Some even thought Katini was referring to the houses on stilts that our brothers had built in Chidenguele, where they and their families took refuge every time they were attacked on land. Musisi was the only one who showed any sign of impatience. He blatantly signaled to me to serve the drinks.

Father raised his voice in order to impose his authority: "This war can only be won by not fighting a war."

We VaChopi were few. In order to win the battle, he predicted, we had to ally ourselves with ghosts, and not with people. It's those souls that control fear, and no one has greater power than fear. These ghosts had greater influence than the most renowned military commanders, men like Maguiguane, a Shangaan in the emperor's service. The VaNguni, my father continued, are strong only on land, where they can leave their footprints: "On the water, they lose their body."

Mother smiled, thinking of the sea. And her shoulders swayed as if they were waves. Her arms danced, and her body turned to water. Her very rhythm contained all the hours she had spent waiting for the river to turn into the ocean, sitting on the banks of the Inharrime.

She now focused her thoughts on such times in the past. That past when, as they both sat on the beach, old Tsangatelo would ask, "What do you see when you look at the ocean?" And Chikazi didn't know what to reply. Each wave brought people, life after life reaching the coast and dispersed by the surf. Generation upon generation of the most diverse people had flowed out onto the beach. Their dead caressed her feet when she walked along the wet strand. That was what made Mother smile as she listened to her husband talking of oceans and islands.

"On the water, they lose their body," Katini repeated.

One of the older neighbors got up and placed his hand on the shoulder of our inventor of islands. He was gaining courage to address us all. Finally, he spoke and said that there was no point in nurturing our illusions. Ngungunyane's troops were now very different. Most of his soldiers were VaNdau. And they weren't scared of the sea. Whether we fled to the ocean or escaped to the lagoons, we would be as vulnerable as on land. Those who had been enslaved by the VaNguni would be even crueler than their masters. Unfortunately, that is the way of the world: those who have suffered want others to suffer. We would be more harshly treated by the slaves of the VaNguni than by the VaNguni themselves. We would suffer so much at the hands of the blacks that we would forget how much we had suffered under the whites.

When he finished speaking, a long silence ensued, until my old father intervened once more: "All this is just talk, my brothers. Enemies are not for killing. If we kill them, they'll return in bigger numbers. All we have to do is tire them out. Imagine them gone, pretend they never existed."

This is what our father said. But he wasn't even listening to his own words anymore. He was just pretending he existed.

◆

To what sea was it that our mother would never return? I'll never find the answer. In fact, I had difficulty in remembering my childhood village on the coast. For years, we lived alongside the fishermen on the coast, to the north of the estuary of the Inharrime. It was Grandfather Tsangatelo who decided we should go into exile inland. Our relatives were puzzled. We were protected by the sea. When enemy troops approached, we would run to our fishing rafts and sail away over the waves of the Indian Ocean. Our assailants were horrified by the ocean, which, for them, was a nameless domain forbidden by the gods. The most they could do was to scale the dunes and then limit themselves to contemplating our colorful craft, impotently. Out on the swell, we were safe from the invading hordes.

It was by accident that Grandfather discovered this vulnerability among our enemies. On one occasion, he was fleeing across the sands with me in his arms. Behind us came the timbissi, the emperor of Gaza's execution squad. In his headlong rush, Grandfather ended up stumbling over the moorings of an old boat. In despair, he made use of the craft and rowed out beyond the breakers. It was then that he realized that the sea was a frontier: the bravery of those elite guards sank into the wet sands of the beach. In later incidents, his suspicion was confirmed: the VaNguni never dared enter the sea. They were scared not of the waters as such, but of the spirits that dwelt in them.

In the end, Mother was right in her anguished doubts: Can one escape one's own salvation? What was Tsangatelo's reason for tearing us away from that protected shore and leading us away across dunes, rivers, and marshlands?

◆

That afternoon, Aunt Rosi summoned me outside. She was seated on her usual mat, sifting rice. I remarked on her tired air, as if her sifter was a burden to her. Rosi spoke without looking at me:

"The dead give us the most work just before they die."

She had come from the neighboring village, where her mother lay dying, in the final stages of an illness. For months, my aunt had been leaving first thing in the morning and returning in the afternoon, and exhaustion was now etched into the curvature of her spine. Once before, she had nursed Grandmother, whose prolonged demise continued for years on end. In every family, there is someone who silently assumes the responsibility of looking after those who are bidding us farewell.

"I'm not complaining," Auntie declared. "I want to tell you about a dream that afflicted me last night."

She had had a dream about blind horses. The animals had crashed against trees and stumbled over rocks until their legs were broken. And she stared into their eyes, which were pools of dark water, and suddenly her foot slipped and she sank into the despair of these great animals. This had been her dream, and her chest was heaving by the time she finished relating it. Auntie was a soothsayer, and she asked me whether my family and I could decipher the meaning of her fantasy.

"In the books you've got at home, I want you to find a drawing of a horse. If you find one, bring it to me."

"I'll go and see what I can do."

"Whatever you can do, please, do it quickly. I've got a bad feeling. I'm going to tell you something, girl: those horses were people. The Portuguese give them names, just as we do our children. That's what you told me, didn't you?"

"I did indeed," I confirmed.

◆

The horses that gave Aunt Rosi nightmares were an auspicious promise for me. If only my nights were filled with the clatter of hooves. And I blessed the dreams I had that made me lose my sense of place and proportion. Dreams were my drug, my drink.

It was my father who pulled me up from the mat where I had been dozing. He passed his hand over his head before asking: "Has your aunt been here? Did she tell you about her nightmares?"

"Yes."

"These dreams she has worry me a lot."

He stood in deep thought for a moment, a blade of grass between his teeth, while he gazed at the ground. All of a sudden, he blurted out decisively: "Go to the garrison, Imani. Go and take a look at the white men's papers and see if they mention horses ..."

"Auntie asked me almost the same thing."

"I am worried about something else. I want news of Mouzinho and his cavalry. He should already be here with his horses, fighting alongside Xiperenyane. Something has happened."

◆

Father was right: the report was there, at the sergeant's house, amid details of accounts and expenses. This is what it said:

When Mouzinho de Albuquerque's cavalry regiment disembarked in Lourenço Marques and paraded down the Avenue of March Seventh as far as Ponta Vermelha, the elegance and loftiness of our troops produced the same reaction in all those watching: "What magnificent troops!" A flurry of excitement filled those exhausted residents of the city with enthusiasm. Captain Mouzinho had been promised that he would encounter the necessary facilities to get his plan of action under way. But by the following day, the captain was already feeling disillusioned: the mounts waiting for him were totally unprepared for any type of service requiring horsemanship, let alone for warfare. He even gave orders to have training intensified and to augment the feeding regimen. But what happened during the following week surpassed even the most pessimistic predictions. The condition of the animals grew strangely worse: some of them woke up sick, no use even for pulling carts, and others turned into wild beasts that proved impossible to break in. Mouzinho still hoped that the horses sent up from Durban would compensate for the group of old nags and hacks that he currently had to work with. Mouzinho struggled against the skepticism of his officers, who insisted that cavalry could not be used in war out in the African bush. He obstinately wished to prove the contrary, but to do that, he desperately needed animals in peak condition.

When the horses arrived from Durban, his disappointment could not have been greater. Most of them were pack horses, defective, arthritic, and worn out from pulling carts for the English. The vendor in Durban had provided certificates to the effect that the animals had left the port in good health, and this was confirmed by the Portuguese military official who had handled the purchase. What had happened on the journey by ship to cause the health of the horses to deteriorate like this? What mysteries have conspired to hamper the patriotic intentions of our gallant captain?

◆

I returned home determined to tell a lie: that there was no report whatsoever, no letter, no reference to horses. Aunt Rosi might well dream, but the reasons for her nightmares were personal and bore no relation to what was happening in the world. There was no reason to suspect any wizardry. My brothers were therefore safe from any suspicion of trafficking reports and passing them on to the enemy. Everything was as it should be, and it wouldn't be long before Mouzinho arrived at the head of his messianic cavalry.

The following day, it was our turn to visit Aunt Rosi. The occasion was propitious, for Musisi had gone out hunting and the soothsayer was at our disposal. Even without the proof of papers, my father's doubts had deprived her of sleep. There was some sinister reason behind the delay in the arrival of the horses and their riders.

"Today, he cried all day long," the soothsayer announced as soon as she saw us coming.

"Uncle Musisi crying?"

"No. The one crying was my son. The one waiting inside me."

Rosi had never been a mother. She had miscarried every time she had become pregnant. Her babies had "turned back," which is what they say when they talk of miscarriages. Auntie was destined not to leave any descendants. In the past, she had resorted to the spider test to find out who was the cause of her sterility. Next to a cobweb, she had left two pieces of material, one cut from an item of her husband's clothing, another from her own. The cloth chosen by the spider would belong to the infertile spouse. In the end, the test proved inconclusive. The spider walked past both pieces of cloth without touching either.

And now there she was, arching her back to give her skinny belly a bump.

"You must look after it well," my mother insisted. "All children must be well looked after."

And that is how Chikazi continued their conversation, as if her sister-in-law's words contained an unquestionable truth. At the time, I was unaware that all the women in the world form a single womb. Each one of us gets pregnant with all the babies conceived. Those that are born and those who turn back.

◆

My father must have been used to Rosi's recurrent fits of delirium. At those moments when our relative declared she was pregnant, her belly would grow round. All false, all true: even her hands, her mouth, and her nose gained the curves that came from a piece of good news.

This time, however, Rosi was more convincing than ever as her hands caressed her voluminous abdomen. I looked at my father to try to ascertain whether there was any point in our sticking to the purpose of our visit.

Aunt Rosi understood our silent hesitation and put us at ease: "You can relax; this child isn't going to be born today. He's been like this, waiting to be born, for some years. We are both biding our time for when there's no war."

Our mother led her sister-in-law to a patch of shade, and both of them busied themselves with the same rice sifter. They separated the grains together, their fingers touching and entangling, until Rosi asked me: "Have you seen Mwenua anywhere, niece? And the other one, Munyia, have you by any chance seen that lazybones?"

I shook my head. I pretended it all made sense. Aunt Rosi was the *nkosikazi*—literally the "big wife"—and the principal woman of her household. Uncle Musisi had married two more, much younger women. It was she, the first wife, who had chosen the other ones: Mwenua and Munyia. The whole village knew that these two women had been raped and killed by the VaNguni. The whole village except for Aunt Rosi.

"Did you hear my question?"

My eyes remained glazed, as if everything around us were in darkness. My father had disappeared in the shadows.

"I'll see if I can find the other aunts," I declared, as I left.

I moved away, but not far. At the back of the house, I found my old father, smoking. His eyebrows furrowed conspiratorially as he saw me and said: "It's sad. So sad. I'll go back, I can't leave your mother alone with her."

He stubbed his cigarette out in the sand and crept back across the yard to join the two women. I peered from afar. Auntie had spread the papers she had received from Father on the ground. When she saw him approaching, Rosi asked: "Explain to me how you do it."

"Do what?"

"How can someone read? I'd so like to know ..."

"It takes time to learn, Rosi."

"I've seen how you do it. You pass your finger along the lines and move your lips. I've done the same, but I can't hear anything. Explain the secret to me. I'm a fast learner."

Father looked down and passed his hands over the sheets of paper lying in the dust.

"In order to read these papers, Rosi, you need to stay still. Absolutely still—your eyes, your body, your soul. Stay like that for some time, like a hunter lying in wait for his prey."

If she remained still for a while, the opposite of what she expected would happen: The letters would start looking at her. And they would whisper stories to her. All that you see on the page looks like drawings, but within the letters there are voices. Each page is a bottomless chest of voices. As we read, we are not the eyes, we are the ears. That is what Katini Nsambe told her.

Rosi knelt in front of the papers and remained motionless, waiting for the letters to speak to her.

20

The Sergeant's Tenth Letter

Nkokolani, June 28, 1895

Your Excellency Counselor José d'Almeida

The feeling of guilt from which I suffer defies description, Excellency. Yesterday Nkokolani was attacked by the frightful Vátuas (I do not know why I persist in calling them by this name, for they refer to themselves as VaNgunis). These monsters killed, burned, raped. Before the attack, I sent Mwanatu to find out why the locals were digging enormous trenches. These were not defenses for combatants. They were hiding places, which the locals hoped would render them invisible. The strategy failed. Those wretched folk were taken by surprise and were helpless against the cowardly brutality of Gungunhane's soldiers.

After the invasion, I visited the village and its agricultural lands, but I did not have the courage to do anything but glance briefly at that desolate expanse of prairie covered in ashes, which would occasionally flutter up and away in no particular direction. Then I returned to the barracks, never for a moment imagining how this ruined outpost had protected me so effectively. I sat down with Chestnut on my lap, and returned to the only task that still made any sense: writing.

I don't know how I can step outside the house, such is my remorse. I've been here too long, I've forged ties and been lulled into a feeling of empathy; Ornelas found it in music, but I find it in the simplest details of these humble folks' lives.

Tired of writing, I took off my army fatigues and placed them on a hanger. I sat gazing at the uniform as if it were me hanging there, crumpled, lifeless, and devoid of substance. This was a strange feeling for someone who had never really been a soldier. But the problem—permit my audacity, Your Excellency—is that I have never been anything at all. I am the empty uniform, up on its hanger, which is only ever put on and taken off by a shadow.

I confess, Excellency, that it often occurs to me to give it all up and set off through the bush toward Inhambane, and from there escape to the north, to the capital of the colony, Mozambique Island. I wouldn't just be going to an island. I would be an island. Take me away from here, I beg you.

I have been losing my sanity over a long period here, but after what I saw yesterday of the massacres in Nkokolani, my state of mind has descended to depths from which there is no return. I awoke in the morning completely paralyzed. All I could do was move my lips. At this point, and without anyone to help me, I thought I was going to die. Even that simpleton, the boy who carries messages for me, would be of little use, for he never enters my quarters without permission. I was unable to call him. Fortunately, Imani dropped by to visit me. Alarmed by my silence, she entered the building and found me in that wretched state of torpor. I communicated with her by blinking. The girl hesitated for a moment. She seemed to want to leave me there, defenseless and on the point of death. But then she did what she always did when faced with such afflictions: she massaged my chest and arms. Slowly, I regained my strength.

I remember she told me this: Our eyelids are wings left over from a previous age, when we were birds. And our eyelashes are the surviving plumage. This is what her folk, who have survived on absurd superstitions, believe. And as I returned to my normal state, she even told me of other beliefs. She said, for example, that in the language of the Zulus, the same verb is used for "to fly" and "to dream." I hope so, I thought to myself. I hope our bullets hit those cursed Vátuas when they are in full flight.

The young black girl's intervention helped but didn't cure me, for the illness from which I suffer has no bodily origin. It began before me; it began in the history of my people, doomed because of the smallmindedness of their leaders. I recall Tsangatelo asking me how big my country was. Little did he know of our small size, which comes not from our geography but from an innate spiritual state in which yearning for the past coexists with a fatalistic attitude toward the future.

All this asphyxia could be compensated for by Africa's infinite geography. But these vast distances produce the inverse effect: Everything here becomes nearer. The horizon is at the touch of one's fingertips. And I imagine the endless trajectory of these letters as they cross the African veld. As I think about this, I scribble these words as if they were horses, as if they were ships conquering distance. I don't know whether this is the feeling you have. Nor do I know the reason for my confiding these confused emotions to you.

Last week, I went out to have a taste of this sense of a journey. And I went down to the banks of the Inharrime, guided only by Mwanatu. I wanted to witness the advance of our troops commanded by Colonel Eduardo Galhardo. I wanted to find a Portuguese military column moving forward, thus proving the inexorable progress of our troops coming from the north to encircle the perfidious Vátua chief. The journey, I thought, would be good for my ruminations and fevers. It would have been better if I hadn't done it. I went in the hope of receiving some new momentum, but what I saw left me in even greater despair. No one can fully appreciate the titanic effort required to cross rivers with those wagons, guns, and people.

The colonel called me to one side and told me, "It's good that you should see the difficulties we face and that you should report all this to António Enes, so that he may know how hard we are struggling to advance over the terrain." Galhardo wanted a messenger, an ally in his quarrel with the authorities in Lourenço Marques. This was why he kept repeating, "António Enes doesn't believe me, he thinks I'm afraid, that I'm inventing excuses." The colonel was right, and unhappy in his certainty.

I walked down the slope to contemplate the entire wagon train. I watched closely the young soldiers buried in mud up to their hips, and it was as if they were being devoured by these African backlands. At this point, one of my hallucinatory episodes got the better of me. All of a sudden, what I saw weren't crates of ammunition but coffins; instead of rifles, I saw the crosses of Christ; instead of Colonel Galhardo, I caught sight of a priest wearing a cassock. And in the blink of an eye, that whole caravan turned into a funeral cortege. I was at a funeral. And among the numerous caskets there was the coffin containing Francelino Sardinha. My blood-covered hands worked ceaselessly to open up a grave in the stony soil.

I already had reason enough not to sleep, but I now had an additional motive to remain vigilant: the noise of a shovel scraping the soil. Night, they say, is the doorway to hell. The worms that before wriggled at the bottom of the grave now seethe at the doorway itself. Huge worms, the color of flesh, fill my slumber with terror.

At this precise moment, I am gripped by a fit of nostalgia that renders me paralyzed. And that is why I am lying down while I write this, and why my much-praised calligraphy has turned into this clumsy scrawl. It is this apathy, Excellency, that has incapacitated me for a mission I did not understand at the outset and now suspect never existed. This is what I discovered: The spiders that I watched on my tabletop on that very first day had always been inside me. And inside me they spun a web that hinders not only my movement but my whole life.

The bundles of sisal, the lengths of old cloth, the walls of the house—I made my web out of all these things. And I was imprisoned in the hope that this false garrison might be mine, might be Portuguese, my home. But I was impotent. A far greater creature devoured the spider and its web. This creature's name is Africa. No wall, no fortress could stop it. And there it was, infiltrating through the cracks in the sound of the marimbas and in the wailing of the children. There it turned into roots, which spread among the gaps in the bricks. There it was, dwelling in my dreams, invading my life in the shape of a woman. Imani.

21

A Brother Fashioned from Ash

I know the Europeans' ploy. First they send traders and missionaries; then ambassadors; then guns. They might as well begin with the guns.

—EMPEROR TEWODROS II OF ETHIOPIA

I was summoned to the door. A stranger had brought something for me and wanted to give it to me personally. He had come from afar, from lands that have a name only in other tongues. I peeped at the door, suspicious and undecided. A family's generosity is measured by the way it welcomes guests. But it is also true that, where we come from, no man turns up at another person's house in order to speak to an unmarried woman. Good manners dictate that he approach her parents and wait as long as necessary for his intentions to be established. But we Nsambe were different, less attached to tradition. For this reason, I agreed to go to open the door. A man of a certain age waved a sheaf of papers and, in a hoarse voice, announced:

"These are letters I've brought from the mines."

"We don't know anybody in the mines."

"Yes, you do."

"Who?"

"You remember only too well."

The papers were all crumpled, and so dirty that the words were illegible. In spite of this, the messenger's stubby fingers straightened the sheets of paper with a woman's delicate touch. I was confused by a flurry of doubts: Was Grandfather really alive? And had he written those letters, he who couldn't read a word?

"Tsangatelo dictated them, I wrote them down," the messenger confirmed, as if he were reading my thoughts.

I recognized him. He was the same miner who, many years before, had brought us news of Grandfather. At the outset, I had been assailed by a suspicion. I was now certain that this man was his companion, his tchipa, who looked after him down in the depths of the earth.

If I was unable to decipher the handwriting, I was also unable to understand a word the stranger said. Specks of something that looked like soot flew out of his mouth and stuck to his lower lip, which drooped under the weight of his blackened saliva. Grandfather's emissary coughed more than he spoke.

Eventually, the visitor made himself understood. Old Tsangatelo was asking us to tell my mother that she would never again see the ocean. None of us in Nkokolani would return to our lands on the coast. The tchipa repeated the prophecy with certainty: "We never return, no one ever returns."

I examined the messenger's face and realized that he was harboring secrets and maybe even answers to some of our old questions.

"I'm not going to ask you your name. But I would like you to help us understand what made Grandfather stay so far away from the ocean."

"Tsangatelo taught me one should never say anything to anyone who may be unable to forget."

"It's not for me. It's for my mother's sake, so that she may not suffer the illusion of one day returning."

"I'll tell you the story," the messenger said.

◆

It all began one magnificent morning during the rainy season of 1882. Up until then, Tsangatelo had never seen a white man. The first European he had ever seen appeared mounted on a horse, which was an animal unknown to him. The horse was white, much paler than the rider. Horse and rider combined to form one silhouette, so that Grandfather thought they were one creature. And it was with horror that he watched the man try to separate himself from his lower half. When the rider dismounted, Tsangatelo Nsambe heard flesh tear and bones splinter. He shut his eyes in order not to see blood pouring as if from the neck of a chicken. A question addressed to him in Portuguese brought him back to reality:

"Are you the man they call Tsangatelo? Are you the *pombeiro* in this region?"

Grandfather didn't speak a word of Portuguese. He guessed more than he actually discerned what the foreigner was asking, and nodded in answer to the first question. But neither he nor anyone else in the village understood the word *pombeiro*. The term had been brought from Angola and designated the traders who organized expeditions into the African interior.

"I am Tsangatelo Nsambe, son of Zulumeri, who is the son of Masakula, the son of Mindwane, who is the son of ..."

The Portuguese raised his arm to halt this interminable introduction. In truth, there was scarcely an interruption: as he progressed through the list of his ancestors, the tone of Grandfather's voice grew ever lower. He didn't want to make himself too conspicuous, always a fatal risk in such a tiny, poverty-stricken environment.

His care proved fruitless. Within a few seconds, a whole sea of people surrounded the visitor. Fearful of being swallowed up by the crowd, the foreigner climbed back onto his saddle. He wanted to be viewed from below, as if he were a god: against the light, his silhouette standing out against the sky. From high up on his horse, the Portuguese cast a condescending, haughty glance around him, as if he were thinking: So many folk here, but not a single person.

Along with the rider, there were two more Portuguese, also on horseback. The animals were diverse, different in color and in size. But the whites were all the same: their faces shielded by their widebrimmed hats, their mustaches long and turned up, and their eyes restless and furtive. One of them, the shortest, said something in a kind of hybrid tongue that, with some effort and creativity, Tsangatelo Nsambe translated as follows: "We need your services."

Grandfather was the owner of caravans of porters. It was he who organized the transport of cargo over long distances. In those days, there were no roads. The only tracks were those made by travelers' feet. The porters were the highway, the railroads, the sea, and the rivers. For centuries, the produce of wretchedness and fortune, glory and betrayal, was carried on their backs.

Tsangatelo was hardly popular for the way he treated his porters. Countless times, he had ordered those who were tired or sick to be beheaded, on the grounds that they were indolent. He himself told the story of a woman who, tied by ropes to other women, insisted on carrying in her arms a baby who had died of hunger days before. He had to order her killed. It was not done out of malice, Tsangatelo defended himself. She was a bad example to the others. These people are rascals, he would say. Life has taught them to lie, to feign grief and sickness.

It was therefore natural that Tsangatelo Nsambe should be hated for all those years of mistreatment. But the greatest hatred derived from the fact that he had become prominent, richer and more lordly than anyone else in the village. In a poverty-stricken place, it is a crime to stop being poor. In our village, wealth is never born unsullied.

A feeling of apprehension ran through Tsangatelo when he sat down with the Portuguese who spoke the hybrid language. It was a first meeting, a "mouth opener," as we call it here. The foreigners merely wanted to announce their arrival and organize a formal business meeting for the following day.

That night, Grandfather found it difficult to sleep. He was on his guard: elsewhere, the transport-and-porterage business had been usurped by white and mixed-race traders. For that reason, he rose early and got himself prepared to make an impression on the Portuguese delegation. He did not want them to take him for a worthless peasant. He asked his elder brother to lend him European clothes. All his brother had was a jacket and a pair of spectacles he had found at the entrance to the village. Wearing the jacket over a skirt made of cowhide, and with the glasses perched on the end of his nose, Tsangatelo appeared, vain and full of self-confidence. Let there be no doubt: nobody in the entire region provided better services than he did.

"And what's more, I only pay the porters who manage to complete the whole journey."

But he didn't pay in money. He paid in slaves that were captured along the way. That's life, he was wont to philosophize: Those who are someone's property today will be the owners of others tomorrow. All of us in this world are descendants of slaves or of the slave owners.

The Portuguese took a huge pistol out of his holster, and the gleam of metal blinded Tsangatelo. He looked down and pretended to shake his callused feet. Waving the gun as if it were a fan, the European said: "The cargo we shall be consigning to you is highly sensitive."

"I've carried a lot of ivory for both the Portuguese and the English. My caravans go as far as Inhambane, and even farther, to Lourenço Marques."

"This time it's different. I'll be frank with you: it's arms."

Grandfather rolled down the sleeves of his coat, which had ridden up as far as his elbows. He pushed his glasses up to the bridge of his nose and shook his capulana to clean it of some imaginary dust. Then, for the first time, he looked the European squarely in the eyes. "You bosses are from elsewhere. The only distance you know is that of the ocean. On land, distance can have a huge advantage."

"And what might that advantage be?"

"Distance may offer a thousand ways to escape. But it's the biggest prison there is. No porter dares to flee."

"Very well, let's get to the matter in hand. Are you willing to transport these arms?"

"Where are the arms coming from, and where are they going?"

"Someone will bring them from Lourenço Marques to the River Limpopo. From there, you will transport them as far as Chicomo."

As he returned to his house, Grandfather was beset by a strange feeling. Arms, he thought, don't move from place to place. They have always been where they are today. They are born and reborn like weeds, for no reason and without intention.

◆

Tsangatelo went home along the beach. Darkness had fallen, and the paths through the bush were full of danger. His wife was awaiting him in the front yard; she listened in silence to the account of his meeting with the Portuguese.

"Arms?" she wondered.

She remained silent for a time. She contemplated the sea, which is a way of not looking at anything. Then she got up, her hands on her lower back, as if to counterbalance her body. With the serenity of one harboring a great certainty, she declared: "Learn this, husband: a weapon cannot be regarded as business. If you accept this assignment, I shall leave this house, I shall run away from this village. And you'll never see me again."

"But these weapons, wife, are for expelling our enemies."

"When these enemies leave us, the rifles won't go to sleep. And we shall be massacred by the same arms we carry across our shoulders."

"I don't know why I told you about it. I've got my business activities— they're men's things."

His wife's objections made Grandfather uneasy and disturbed his night's sleep. The following morning, having slept badly and woken up even worse, Tsangatelo saw one of his porters standing outside the door. At his feet was a bundle of ivory and animal pelts. The man bowed respectfully, and took advantage of being bent over to place his hands under the bundle. When he raised his load, something happened that Tsangatelo was never able to describe: along with the bundle, he lifted all the ground around it. As if it were a towel, the surrounding earth was raised, and a cloud of dust hung suspended in the air. All around the porter, a bottomless abyss opened up. With apparent ease, the man hoisted the surrounding terrain above him. Then he deposited the world on his head. Without moving, his feet straddling this suddenly created island, the slave issued his warning: "No one will ever walk again! The caravans have died, they have died forever."

The owner of the porters, the powerful Tsangatelo, shook from his head to his feet. He was the target of a curse. Somewhere, in some unknown pot, his sinister fate was being cooked.

That very same day, Grandfather Tsangatelo decided to leave the village by the seashore. This is the reason, concealed from us for years, why we had abandoned the place where we had once been happy.

◆

Tsangatelo's messenger made off without even leaving a footprint in the smooth sand around our house. I was supposed to go and tell my mother the news brought to us from the depths of the earth. But I didn't. I stayed at home the whole day, respecting the leisurely pace at which messages travel through our homeland. I would speak to my mother the following day.

But I didn't do so. For, in the early hours, we received news of a ghostly creature who had invaded the village, dashing frantically along the streets. This bogeyman— this *txigono*, as we call them— pillaged houses and broke into corrals, leaving behind a vast trail of panic and chaos.

In an instant, it was our turn to witness the truth of these rumors: a monstrous figure broke into our backyard after vaulting the fence, and spread terror among the women and children.

At a first glance, it looked like the ugliest, most terrifying of wild animals. But then I detected a certain familiarity. Monsters are all the more frightening the more they resemble a human figure. Such was the case with this apparition. On the txigono's head swayed three ostrich feathers, on a kind of bonnet made of animal skins and tied behind by a ribbon, which made the head look all the more bulky. Around his neck, he wore a dark cowhide strip we call a *tinkosho*. His legs, belly, and arms were adorned with leather ribbons. Around his waist, he had tied the skin of a wildcat. At first, he bellowed more like an animal than a person. But little by little, we noticed he was shouting in Xizulu, the language of the occupiers. And our fears intensified with that realization.

Once they had recovered from their surprise, some of the men plucked up courage and jumped on him, overcoming him by force. They were already mistreating him when my father interfered: "Let's see who this miserable wretch is."

They stripped him of his ornamental disguise. I don't know whether I was surprised: the person hiding behind that mask was none other than my brother Dubula. I helped him up from the ground while my father went about getting our furious neighbors off the premises. Eventually, when we were on our own, Katini gazed at his son at length, and then asked: "Why?"

Dubula, who was busy gathering up the adornments that had scattered across the ground, did not reply.

"Why did you dress like that?" my father once again pressed him.

"I didn't dress like a warrior. I am an Nguni warrior."

"Have you gone mad?"

"I've never been more lucid."

Our father spun around, his hands clutching his head. What would Germano de Melo say when he found out that someone from our family had made such a sad exhibition of himself?

Mother knelt in front of her son and put her hand on his head before gently pleading: "Leave, before your uncle gets here. If my brother sees you dressed up like that, he'll drive a spear through you."

"I came here precisely for my uncle to see me."

"Are you trying to challenge him?"

"On the contrary, I'm doing this out of respect for him."

"I don't understand, son."

"Uncle Musisi is the only man in this family. I'm proud to have him as an enemy. I hope to face him one day in hand-to-hand combat."

◆

A brother is our other half. But Dubula was more than a half of me. He was me in another body. Although he was my brother and our mother's favorite son, life had removed him from our home. My dear elder brother belonged to that minority who viewed the Nguni presence sympathetically. For him, the biggest enemy, and the one upon whom we should all concentrate our fury, whether now or in the future, was Portuguese dominion.

Before the invasions, we were not aware of Dubula's devotion to the VaNguni. We would see him scale the highest hill in the early evening. It was a dune stripped of vegetation, white enough to hurt one's eyes as one looked at it. Up there on its crest, which faced south, he sat there, vigilant. The village believed he was looking out for the VaNguni. But it wasn't fear that moved him. It was a desire to see them arrive.

Later, I would climb the path to give him a shake and insist he return home.

"This can't go on, Dubula. We want you to come back and ask for your father's forgiveness."

He never answered. He was waiting for the barbarians as if he were waiting for himself. He wanted to be invaded. He wanted to be conquered, occupied from head to foot, to the point of forgetting who he had been before the invasion.

"Better Ngungunyane than any Portuguese."

And he would explain: The Nguni monarch was an emperor who no longer had an empire; the whites were an empire without an emperor. The emperor is finished when he dies; an empire installs itself inside our head and remains alive even after it has disappeared. We needed to defend ourselves from hell rather than from the devil.

Time after time, we begged Dubula to step back from his avowed sympathy for the occupier. Uncle Musisi would never accept his ranting and raving. My dear father, by now at the end of his rope, pressed him by asking: "And what if the VaNguni emerge winners at the end of this war? What difference will it make to us?"

"If the VaNguni win, I shall always be able to be someone. What people will we be if the Portuguese win?"

We should look, he said, at the example of Maguiguane, Ngungunyane's military chief. He wasn't an Nguni, but he had been accepted and promoted. And he challenged us further: In the Portuguese army, was there a single black commander? Thousands of blacks had died fighting on the Portuguese side. Had we ever seen any tribute, any reward, given to the Africans who had fallen? Only our brother Mwanatu, who was retarded from birth, believed he had gained the respect of whites. My brother Dubula said all this with such passion.

When a father and a son argue over something, the true reason for their dispute is inevitably different, a quarrel that is older than words. I already knew the outcome of the arguments from both sides. And it was always my father who brought the issue to a close, saying: "As far as I'm concerned, the color of the snake doesn't matter. The poison that kills us is always the same."

◆

On the eve of the decisive battle, which would be fought on the plains of Madzimuyni, the warrior Xiperenyane visited our village. His bearing filled everyone with confidence. The Chopi commander benefited from the support of the Portuguese. However, he appeared not to need protectors. The son and successor of Binguane was supremely confident of his own power.

All the villages in the area had furnished men to swell Xiperenyane's army, which would face the VaNguni. Every family except for mine was busy with preparations for the great showdown.

On the night before, my father invited his brother-in-law Musisi to smoke *mbangue* together with him. "Smoking together" was the term used for any situation supposed to mark the end of a disagreement. But Father didn't smoke. Only Musisi inhaled the soothing smoke and retained it in his chest. My old father limited himself to occasionally cleaning the horn that served as a pipe. Every time he bent over, he would complain with a wince: "The ground is getting lower and lower."

They allowed time to billow out before broaching the

real subject of their meeting. My father was the one to reveal himself first: "Today I'm going to unearth my javelin."

He filled his hand with sand and blew firmly onto his closed fist, to show that he was making a pledge.

"I don't understand," Musisi commented. "What are you going to unearth?"

"Tomorrow I'm going with you to the battlefield."

"Did you have a drink before smoking?"

"I've made up my mind: tomorrow I'm going to fight the vultures."

Musisi replied with a burst of laughter. The invitation to the smoking ceremony was supposed to signal harmony, but it could not have produced greater discord. As he left, Uncle took care not to look back. He was defending himself against an ill omen.

Musisi's scorn merely reinforced my old father's decision. During the evening, he presented himself to his wife solemnly and fully armed. "I was mistaken; I have no more illusions," he declared. And he added somberly: "Tomorrow I shall be a soldier, I shall go with your brother."

Chikazi dropped the rice she was sifting. Her husband's announcement caused her spirit to sink, a grain among the grains of rice. And she became even more worried when her husband dragged a sleeping mat out into the yard. He was going to spend the night out in the open to show how determined he was to wage war. On the eve of battle, a warrior sleeps far from his beloved.

◆

That night, the square was filled with men and boys. Musisi climbed up on an old tree trunk and addressed the crowd:

"What do you think, my brothers? Do we wait for the Portuguese?"

A vibrant *no* echoed through the village. Then, once again, Uncle made the gathering pulsate: "Do we wait for the Portuguese, who never turn up?"

He was talking about the Portuguese, but he was referring to my father, Katini Nsambe, who was nowhere to be seen. The Portuguese army had received orders not to intervene. Lying drowsily in his bed, my father was obeying the orders of alcohol, of which he had consumed a copious amount.

The local *nyanga*, or witch doctor, took my uncle's place on the improvised platform in order to spread his powerful message. In a tone of voice that recalled song rather than speech, he assured those men that they could advance without fear, for the remedies he had prescribed inoculated them against the enemy weapons.

And the throng moved off in a disorganized march, singing and whooping raucously. Seeing those folk spreading out along the road, I thought how much we resemble our enemies.

◆

When our men came back, it was clear that they weren't soldiers. They were peasants and fishermen, totally unprepared for warfare. At heart, they were no more soldiers than Mwanatu was a sentry. It didn't matter who they were; in that ragged procession, they bore with them the sadness and shame of defeat. They passed through the square, their heads bowed, their spears dragging along the ground. My father stood beside me, witnessing this depressing scene. I had never before seen his eyes so devoid of life. Katini pretended he could see and feigned tears.

The vanquished disappeared into the shadows of their homes. All of them had returned, except for Dubula.

◆

Two days passed without news of my elder brother. We knew he had set off for the battle of Madzimuyni and that he had joined the ranks of the aggressors. But no more was known. On the days that followed, no one spoke of his absence, but a dark cloud hung over our house.

On the third day, Chikazi decided to visit her brother. I went with her, without being asked. She didn't get as far as sitting down in Musisi's yard. Her anxious hands crossed and uncrossed on her breast, and then she cast them forward as if she wanted to hurl them along with her accusing words: "Dubula hasn't returned yet. Musisi, you killed my son."

"Who told you that?"

"I was told in a dream. We are brother and sister; we are visited by the same ancestors."

"I didn't see Dubula. I didn't see him either before or after the battle."

"You didn't see him because in war my son became someone else. You killed him, Musisi. So listen carefully to what I'm going to tell you: you're never going to have a peaceful night's sleep again."

◆

That same morning, I made my way alone to the cursed lowlands of Madzimuyni, which had already become known as "the plain of the dead." I wanted to look for my brother, in the vague hope he might still be alive. As I was walking away from the village, some country folk accosted me, bewildered:

"Where are you going? This path is closed off."

When I told them where I was going, a shudder of alarm ran through their gaze. And they pleaded with me not to go any farther. Faced with my determination, they shook their heads and hurried away from me, as one does with lepers or the insane.

Before setting off along the vaguest of tracks, I found myself screaming: "Are you frightened of me? Well, you should be. For I am leaving as a woman, and I shall return as a ghost."

I started unhurriedly to descend the slope that led to the plain. As I progressed, I ruminated. My brother had joined the battle in the certainty that he knew his enemy. In my case, it was the other way around: I did not know who to hate. I had no one to die for. Which also meant that I did not know who to love. And I envied him for having found a reason to die, after losing the meaning of life.

Dubula and I were united in the fear we inspired in others. People were frightened of him because he was so disobedient. Men and women feared me. Men feared me because I was a woman. Married women feared me because I was young and beautiful: I could be what they had once been. Single women envied me for belonging to the world of the whites: I was what they could never be.

Absorbed in these thoughts, I did not realize that I had arrived at the scene of the tragedy. I took off my sandals before stepping onto the battlefield, as if I were entering some stranger's house. I crossed the field among corpses, groans, and death rattles. There were so many dead that for a few moments I was unable to see. I was blind, unable to move or even to volunteer a gesture. Amid so many bodies, only mine existed. When I regained my sight, I noticed that my feet were red. It was then that I realized that all the soil was bleeding, as if some subterranean belly had been torn open.

◆

The cruelty of a war isn't measured by the number of graves in a cemetery. It is measured by the number of bodies denied burial. This is what I thought while I picked my way between dismembered people, jackals, and scavenging birds.

The greatest wound war can inflict is making us search for the bodies of those we love. Who would have said I'd be one of those women, condemned to journey through life amid ashes and ruins?

While I moved forward across the wilderness, I called out my brother's name, in the vain hope that he might answer.

"Dubula!"

◆

The corpses looked as if they had been sown by some drunken god: scattered erratically, but here and there in sudden heaps. Had someone brought them there? Or had they, in some final, gregarious urge, dragged themselves toward a particular place, fearful that death might come upon them while they were alone and defenseless?

And once again, my cry wafted over this desolate terrain:

"Dubula, my brother!"

Suddenly, I heard someone answering. In front of me,

a warrior, still in full military regalia, twisted and groaned. He was lying on his back, his face concealed behind his war mask, and he appeared to be very badly wounded. He kept repeating in a lugubrious tone: "Sister? I'm here, sister. Help me!"

At first, I thought his voice strange—he had been so badly injured that even his voice had become distorted. From under the plumes covering his face, he murmured: "I'm here, sister!"

My tears hampered my vision. I uttered the most senseless question: "Dubula, are you alive?"

I got no other answer than the sound of my own sobbing. The person I was looking for was there. Maybe it was too late to save him, but at least Dubula would come back home in the company of someone who loved him. And I thought of my mother's happiness when she saw us staggering home, each supporting the other as if we were one and the same shadow.

"Come, dear brother. I'll help you."

I avoided looking him in the face. In the eyes of the dying, we see our own death. When I touched his hands, I was assailed by a sudden doubt. Those weren't my brother's hands. That young man was someone else, who, in his death throes, took me for a relative. I got to my feet and walked around the body, ready to leave. It was then that the dying man whispered: "I knew you would come. That's why I waited ..."

With some effort, I helped him up. I offered him my support to walk, and together, arm in arm like a pair of newlyweds, we set off toward the village.

"Come, brother. Let's go home."

The soldier took a couple of steps and then fell on top of me. A gush of blood soaked my body, and his arms lost all their strength. Even so, I managed to raise that lifeless weight again and crept forward with great difficulty until the youth collapsed once more, defenseless, on his final stretch of ground. Kneeling, I tidied his clothes, just as I always did with my brother when, overcome by drink, he lay down to sleep at the entrance to the house.

That was when I was aware of a noise. Someone was approaching. At first, it was no more than a shape. It was wearing a black cape, which gave it the appearance of a bird of prey. When it got nearer, I realized it was one of those miserable wretches who make a living off the spoils of war. He skipped among the bodies with the ridiculous prance of a vulture. On his back, he carried a gunnysack full of clothes and weapons. In the weakest of voices, I begged him: "Help me, please!"

He came up to me as if I were just one more piece of war booty to swell his already bulging sack. I stepped back, alarmed. Then, the man asked: "Where are you from? I've never seen you before."

"I'm from here."

"Are you reaping a harvest as well? I haven't seen such a good one for many a year, praise be to the gods."

In my silence the man recognized the strongest expression of disapproval. His raised arm was the black wing of a bird of prey.

"I only steal from the dead to save them from being robbed by their own families. Those jackals will be here before long ... And you, what are you doing here?"

"I'm looking for someone. A brother."

"I'm not referring to this cemetery here. I'm asking why you are in Nkokolani."

The man had the smell of a creature of the wild, and when he came near, his breath was like that of a hyena. He bent over the body that lay in my arms and spat before speaking. "That man no longer contains a person."

He was about to walk off when he thought better of it, and, dragging his sack noisily behind him, he circled me for a while before asking, "What's your name?"

"Me? I don't have a name," I replied.

It was as if I'd dealt him a blow. He let go of his sack, and its contents rolled out onto the ground. He advanced toward me, his arm raised. "Never say that again. Do you want to know how to really kill someone? You don't need to slit his throat or stick a knife in his heart. All you have to do is steal his name. That's what kills the living and the dead. That, my girl, is why you must never again say you don't have a name."

As he crouched down to put the stolen objects back in his gunnysack, he went on talking quietly, almost as if it were a family confession. He told me he could teach me the skills required of his occupation, a craft in which there was always plenty of work. He said he had already robbed the graves of whites in cemeteries in Inhambane and Lourenço Marques. And he had noticed that Europeans write the names of those they had buried on a stone. It's their way of resuscitating them, he said.

"Was the one you're looking for a military chief?"

"No, he was a soldier like anyone else."

"So much the better for him. Do you know what Ngungunyane does with the bodies of his most powerful enemies? He cuts out their hearts and backbones and grinds them into a powder, which he then feeds to his soldiers. That's how they eat up our strength."

And off he went, humming to himself and dragging his dusty gunnysack behind him. His gentle voice contrasted with his sinister figure. I waited for him to disappear, and then I removed my own clothes to cover the lifeless body of the man who, for a moment, had been my brother. I left him there lying on his stomach, without a grave or gravestone, but covered out of respect for the Creator.

I entered the village stark naked, and it was as if I had come to the wrong place. Nkokolani was deserted. More than deserted, it gave the impression of never having been lived in. I screamed, I wept, I ranted and raved.

Little by little, the women began to rush toward me. "Why are you screaming, daughter?" they asked. I didn't know how to answer. Most of the time, we shout in order not to listen to ourselves. "Why are you crying so much?" they asked again. And, once again, they received no reply. When you return from the dead, you have no words.

"Let's take you home."

That is what war does: People never come home again. The home that was once ours—that home dies, no one was ever born there. And there's no bed, no womb, there isn't even a ruin to anchor our memories in some ground.

◆

The following day, I decided to visit the witch doctor who had blessed the troops and promised to protect their bodies against bullets. His house was situated on a bend in the river, where no one else dared to live.

The nyanga was seated next to a fire that was still lit. That was where he had cooked the medicine he had given my brother to drink. I picked up a handful of still-burning ashes with the intention of throwing them at the witch doctor's face. My desire was to burn his eyes, to blind him for good. But I stood there, gestureless, the ashes burning my hands.

"It wasn't my fault," the man defended himself. "When your brother left here, his body no longer had substance," he said.

Perhaps that was true. Maybe Dubula was an angel, and a bullet had torn through his wings. That is how heavenly beings fall to the ground. To emphasize what he was saying, the witch doctor, barefoot, kicked up a cloud of ashes. Then he forced me to spread my fingers to let the embers slip through.

"Can't you feel the burning?" he asked.

I walked off without saying goodbye and wandered along the banks of the Inharrime. At a certain point, I waded into its sluggish waters and allowed myself to be carried along, facedown, like a dead leaf. Rain washes the dead. The river washes the living.

While I floated in the slow current, I realized that it wasn't enough to leave Nkokolani. I wanted to escape from life itself. Grandma Layeluane had died in the heavenly fire. Grandpa Tsangatelo had disappeared into the depths of the earth. I would dissolve in the water's embrace.

"Dubula!" I called.

A dark shape appeared on the riverbank and waved at me casually. In gesture and dress, he was the man who, but a short time before, had been scavenging on the field of battle. But it wasn't him. It was the blind villager who was approaching, sniffing his way along like a dog. He asked me to keep talking to him so that he could locate me. I told him who I was. And he waved his arms in an empty embrace: "Come back to dry land, Imani. The river is a place to be born."

When he felt my body, he pulled me by the arms as if he were rescuing me. "How did you know I was here?" I asked. And he replied that mine was a noisy sadness, and that I walked like Tsangatelo in the mines: my fingers scratching the soil in search of a way out.

"Your way out is this river, girl. There's no other road. And take your father with you. For old Katini is as blind as I am."

In a world of gunfire and death, my father had ears only for music. I should take him away, the blind man pleaded.

22

The Sergeant's Eleventh Letter

Nkokolani, July 10, 1895

Your Excellency Counselor José d'Almeida

Imani appeared at the post this morning, enraged. There was no need for her to speak. I realized that I should follow her. I accompanied her down lengthy trails, and as we went, I glanced sidelong at her and saw she was all the more beautiful for being furious.

"May I know where you are taking me?"

She did not answer. We headed out into the scrub at a swift, determined pace, until I smelled rotting flesh and was faced with the most oppressive sight: a vast plain covered with bodies. I wanted to turn back, but Imani took my hand and patted my arm with a gesture that almost resembled a caress. Her voice concealed a caustic tone: "See, Sergeant Germano, look at this huge cemetery, and tell me where I may find my brother Dubula among so many dead ..."

And she went on to say, in a cool, controlled voice, that my lie was as bad as that of the witch doctor who had guaranteed immunity from enemy weapons. Where, she asked, were the Portuguese forces I had promised?

"Do you remember your promise to help us? So how are you going to help us now, Mr. Sergeant?"

I shook myself free of her grip violently and ran back home. I rushed along paths full of thorns, ignoring any direction other than the one that would lead me away from that nauseating stench.

I must have passed out. All that I remember next is waking up in the yard of my house. But a few feet from my face, Chestnut, the hen, was fixing me with her myopic, empty look. And I could hear the notes of a xylophone in the distance. And then I heard the distant song of a woman. I told Chestnut: The other side of the ocean, there's a woman who sings. She has no name. I call her "Mother." My mother sings in an undertone, in order not to be heard by my father. These ancient songs are mine now, but who will I sing them to? To you, my darling hen.

While I was giving free rein to my delirium, Chestnut fell asleep instantly. There was no one else in the house, but I behaved as if I feared waking someone up. I was still a prisoner of that man who, during my childhood, watched over the night.

Having at last regained some clarity of thought, I staggered into the house, heated up some leftover tea, and set about going through the correspondence I had left untended when Imani came looking for me. I have been taking a look at your most recent complaints, my dear counselor. I can judge for myself how great an offense you must take at the ridiculous mistrust expressed by our mutual superiors. Our royal commissioner can only be receiving false information regarding your good self.

The accusations leveled at Your Excellency are not only without foundation, but hugely unjust. To expect negotiations with Gungunhane to be concluded in just a few days is to fly in the face of the notion of time that rules the lives of these natives. For my part, I acknowledge that I should be gaining the confidence of the local chief. But throughout this period of time, I have been unable to decide whether my interlocutor should be Imani's father or uncle. They both quarrel over which of them should command the villagers. I should choose the uncle, who, though not sympathetic to us, is closer to the court of Binguane. However, I am entangled in favors done me by Katini, Imani's father.

In any case, it is impossible to understand the order you have received to withdraw immediately from Manjacaze and await new instructions in Chicomo! What will Your Excellency do in Chicomo, apart from waiting for no reason at all? My dear counselor, they are giving you the same thing they gave me: a prison sentence. The result of their arbitrary decisions will be catastrophic to our presence in southern Mozambique.

I am tempted to agree with Your Excellency when you say the treatment you have received is due to the fact that you are living with a Negro woman. What you do possess—forgive my candor, Your Excellency—is fame and recognition. I have neither of these. Come to Nkokolani, my dear counselor. There is space in abundance to give you and your Negro spouse shelter.

Please do not take the audacity of this invitation seriously, my dear counselor. Now that I have reread what I wrote, I notice how the tone of my correspondence has gradually changed. These letters are, to use a term of comparison, the balcony where the women in our native land escape their solitude. I sit on this balcony as if I were contemplating some street in Lisbon. Unfortunately, it couldn't be a street in my village. For there I had no sibling. I had no childhood.

You will be puzzled by all my outpouring, Excellency.

Maybe I am far more of a poet than a soldier. Indeed, the most precious things I brought with me were two books of poetry that I read and reread over and over. One is by Antero de Quental. The other by Guerra Junqueiro. The latter poet could only be referring to this outpost when, in his book *Finis Patriae*, he writes:

Of hewn rock those battlements prevailed,
Over giant condors.
Now those mutilated stones
Are crushed
Into gravel for roads.

And I have been looking at these verses again in such a state of mind that, one sunlit afternoon, I was assailed by a strange dream. I had been drinking, and I lay down dizzily on my back, my face exposed to the sun. Suddenly, I felt a rock move underneath me. I sat up, alarmed. And I saw that I was in a clearing covered with stones of a considerable size. In the middle of my delirium, I realized that one of these stones was talking.

"Don't be frightened, we are stones," the rock said.

"That's not true," another rock challenged. "We are people. We pretend to be stones in order not to be taken onto ships as slaves."

"And who takes you?"

"They all do. Blacks take us. Whites take us."

The figure of Mouzinho de Albuquerque appeared in this dream. He was an experienced soldier. He could tell which stone was false and which was true. Riding along on horseback, the warrior scraped the rocks with the blade of his sword, thus lighting fires that devoured the paths behind them. Then horse and rider turned around and crossed that sea of flames unharmed. With his eagle's eye, Mouzinho assessed the authenticity of those rocks. Upon the live stones, the horseman unleashed vigorous blows. Pieces of flesh flew in all directions, blood and fire mingling in one single red sheet.

Just imagine all this nonsense. Which is why I say: enough of poorly written verses and poorly lived dreams. Enough of me. In your last letter, Your Excellency asks me to describe my everyday routine, engulfed as you are in arid political matters. I fear, dear counselor, that we shall continue in the same sterile monotony. For my day-to-day is, let us call it, a day-without-day. However, I cannot complain. On the contrary, the routine is good for me. I must never forget that I am a prisoner. And, like any prisoner, I must invent routines in order to overcome the monotony of time.

In the early morning, Mwanatu brings me water and buckets for my morning ablutions. Imani arrives later with food prepared by her mother. She laughs as I take the pan from her: "You're now my mother's husband; I don't know how my father takes it." Her smile, always awaited but always sudden, does me good. The girl no longer insists on my lessons. She gets on with other duties: tidying, cleaning, washing clothes. I should not have allowed her to tidy my room. It is risky, for the girl can read and might go through my papers. But the damage, if indeed it exists, has already been done. And not a day goes by when Imani doesn't ask me to lend her paper, ink, and a pen to write with. She sits in the kitchen and scribbles away at manuscripts on goodness knows what. I have to admit, that is the only moment when her presence gives me no pleasure. In the end, I offered her a pen, a pot of ink, and a ream of paper, on condition that she go and write far from here, where I could not see her. I do not know why I get such an uncomfortable feeling at seeing a black person writing. I am pleased when they speak our language correctly and without an accent, but I fear the power they may acquire from writing, as if it were an invasion.

So this, Excellency, is my routine here in Nkokolani. As you can see, it is something that can be described in half a dozen lines. And all the better, for it is getting late, and one can hear the hyenas and jackals outside. It is dark, insects flutter around the lamp, and with my pen nib I fish out bugs that have fallen into the inkpot. They are still alive, and I let them walk across the paper. Behind them, they leave a trail of ink as if they had written a secret message.

There is something I have not yet told you about my daily life, my dear counselor. It concerns a routine that I observe most religiously. Tomorrow, before ordering Mwanatu to deliver my correspondence, I shall ask him to sit in the armchair and listen to me. For the thousandth time, I shall tell him about the trial of the rebels of January 31. This is what I do every day. Mwanatu, retarded as he is, is the perfect audience for an obsessive narrator: he understands what is being said, but he is incapable of understanding what one is trying to tell him. The lad is a stone with ears. No matter how many hours I take, he never seems to be bored or tired.

What I have related countless times to Mwanatu, I shall now have to tell you. I would like you to know what happened in that trial, which sentenced not only me but the whole country. You, dear counselor, were also condemned in that court-martial. What happened was as follows. We were kept waiting for days in dormitories on the *Mozambique*—civilians and soldiers together, sergeants and captains, journalists and politicians.

Every time we were led out by our guards to exercise

on deck, we had to witness the sad sight of relatives and friends sorrowing on the quayside. They wept and cried out for their husbands, sons, and brothers. And some women, in their despair, threw themselves at the ship's mooring cables. On each occasion, I looked carefully to see whether, by any chance, my dear mother was among them. I never saw her. No doubt she was in our distant village, unaware of my perilous situation.

My companions were summoned one at a time to the cabin where the court-martial was taking place. There they were summarily tried. When my turn came, a terrible storm arrived, and huge waves caused us to roll so much that we were continually thrown from one bulkhead to another. Holding on to a hatch with his left arm, the clerk of the court, on his face a ghostly pallor, proceeded to read the sentence. The customary gravitas of the judges was turned on its head. Swaying and staggering like drunkards, those issuing the sentences were as fragile as those being sentenced.

Again and again, nausea forced the clerk to interrupt his solemn reading. On the point of puking, he reached the final words of the sentence: "... and, for all these reasons, the defendant Germano de Melo is sentenced ... is sentenced to ..." Unable to finish, he was overtaken by an uncontrollable attack of vomiting. The other magistrates hurriedly rushed to the deck, each one holding on to another so as not to be swept away by the waves.

Some days later, after the storm had abated, we were once again assembled to hear the sentences yet to be read. The same clerk of the court announced the names of the accused, and as he read each name, a defendant got to his feet and was led off the ship. We then realized that the list concerned those to be freed. When their names were announced, soldiers would stand up and, as they scuttled off, remove the caps and tunics that identified them as soldiers. The list was only half read, and the room was already almost empty. In my anxiety, I glanced at a journalist sitting next to me, who had been listening quietly throughout the whole process. "And you," he asked me, "are you so anxious because you're going to be sentenced?" I replied that I had faith in our defense attorney's speech. When the session opened, I had jotted down passages from his breathtaking statement. I unfolded the piece of paper and read an excerpt from my defense, for my companion's appreciation:

> And what shall I tell you of the popular acclaim for those who are now presented to you as criminals? Are you not, by any chance, aware? Have the reverberations of such enthusiasm not reached my lord judges' ears? Is it not true that the streets and windows filled with folk cheering the parade of the rebel soldiers? Is it not true that Dom Pedro Square welcomed them like a celebratory new dawn, in which the greatest joy reigned supreme on everyone's face?

I paused in my reading to look at the journalist's mocking face. And he asked, "Have you finished?" I answered no, that I still wanted to read the final part of that brilliant speech. I felt like getting up from the bench in order to give the right luster to the attorney's words:

> Considering all these circumstances, you must show due mercy to so many unfortunate men. And what reason is there for you not to show it, gentlemen? You are the judges, but history will judge you ...

The journalist gave me an intense look. His playful air had given way to a paternal tone when he spoke. "Do you know how I console myself? We, the losers of January 31, will be happier than our judges at the court-martial."

At that point, the *Mozambique* started unexpectedly to move. At first, we thought it an illusion, or that this was just a maneuver to adjust the ship's position in the face of the fierce waves. But then, perplexed, we noticed that the ship was leaving Leixões and passing Matosinhos. And the *Mozambique* plowed through the choppy seas until it reached the sheltered waters of the Tagus estuary. There the ship dropped anchor. In these tranquil waters, I regained a kind of harmony that had been interrupted, a mixture of tension and hope that preceded the announcement of misfortune. For it was then that I was sentenced to exile in Africa.

23

A Wingless Bat

This is how we bury our dead: We take them to the granary, and we gather the grain with which to fill their cold hands. Then we tell them: Go now with your seeds!

Early in the morning, a group of women burst into the house where the Portuguese lived, disturbing his sleep. They made so much noise that the sergeant could not understand what they were all shouting about. Finally, he managed to understand the woman who was gesticulating the most:

"We have just seen the Virgin."

"The virgin? What virgin?"

"We don't know. Besides, how many are there?"

Germano stumbled about as he got dressed and then skipped around the yard while trying to get his feet into his shoes. The group headed off in the direction of our house. It was dark, and the Portuguese guided himself by the bulky figures in front of him. The woman leading the throng pointed at the ground and declared in a mixture of Portuguese and Txitxope: "See here, sir? Here are her footprints."

"Are they hers?"

"No. These are the footprints of an angel."

"What angel?"

"The angel who came with her."

The sergeant stopped to remove some sand from his shoes. He felt like putting a stop to this tomfoolery and going back home, but he feared being misunderstood.

The sun wasn't yet up, but the heat was searing.

"Is it far from here?"

"We're nearly there; it's not far."

That's what they always say, the sergeant thought: "We're nearly there." Why can't these people measure distances? And once again, he expressed his doubt about the supposed apparition. At that hour, it was so dark, could they not have made a mistake? To which one of the women retorted: "When we get there, you'll see, sir: it's a Virgin just like the one that was in the church."

"It's most probably her twin sister," another woman replied.

"And this one also has her hands stuck together," a third woman added.

"Hands stuck together?" the sergeant asked, surprised.

"The priest always called her the Virgin of the Stuck Hands, because her hands were always together."

The Portuguese was in no mood to correct her. It was difficult enough to understand what those women were babbling about. The oldest of the peasant women from time to time translated the jumbled speech of her companions. What the sergeant needed was someone to translate his own thoughts. And he imagined himself unsticking the Immaculate Virgin's hands with a lover's tenderness. Then he fancied he felt those hands, grateful and free, caressing his body. Damned heat that makes us sin, he thought as he wiped the sweat from his face.

That was when he heard the sound of a shot coming from the barracks. Then, just afterward, another shot. And then another. The women saw the Portuguese rush back to his house in a panic.

◆

After my brother Dubula died, the birds no longer crossed the skies over our village. The few that did fell to the ground, helpless, like shreds torn from clouds. As they fell, their feathers broke loose and the wind made them spin around, each one in its fanciful flight. These apparitions became more and more scarce. Soon the inhabitants of Nkokolani lost the habit of looking up into the heavens.

While on guard duty that morning, Mwanatu didn't stop looking at the skies. That was when he heard women's voices behind the barracks. Then he saw the sergeant going out into the darkness, following a line of women. He even thought of following the unruly band, but he couldn't abandon his duties as a sentry. At that moment, a huge fish flew over the roof. The creature landed on the trunk of the mango tree, but because it was difficult for it to remain on its perch, it took off again into the skies, moving its fins as if still swimming. Mwanatu raised his gun and fired. Once, twice, three times. The fish struggled through the air and seemed likely to collapse, but then, with a sudden series of lunges, it managed to regain height, revealing nevertheless that it was a novice in the use of wings.

The guard rushed out into the street, impatient to announce what he had just seen. Peasants gathered to listen to him, with a mixture of enthrallment and disbelief. Conflicting opinions emerged: The gods were confused and exchanging water for sky, some affirmed; it was the final punishment, others insisted; the more optimistic proclaimed that the disaster that had been announced would fall not upon our people but on the VaNguni. If the sky had turned into the sea, then the invaders, a people who disliked water, would be condemned to die. And the enemies of our nation, cursed, would sink beneath the swirling waters.

At that moment, the sergeant appeared, out of breath. Alarmed by the gunshots, he didn't have the courage to deal with the news of the flying fish. The Portuguese crossed himself, shook his head, and looked up into the heavens to plead for help.

"In this land of yours, my dear Mwanatu, Jesus would be out of a job: here there isn't a soul who can't work miracles."

My brother walked away with his head held high, and his finger erect to emphasize his judgment: "There are angels around. I've already shot at a few."

◆

What was driving us crazy was the smell. That fetid odor coming from the fields of Madzimuyni was a declaration that the vultures and hyenas hadn't yet turned all the bodies into mere piles of bones. It wasn't the corpses that were rotting but the earth itself.

The smell clung to the walls of our house, stuck to the clothes Mother had worn ever since she was told of her son's death. And even when my father arrived, yelling, Mother remained motionless and absent. Katini's face was covered in blood. Like the other men, he made a great fuss of exhibiting his minor wound: "I'm going to go blind!" I helped him sit down, and he sat staring at my mother, waiting for her to pay him some attention.

"Who gave you a scratch like that, husband?" she asked at last. "What woman has such sharp nails?"

"It was a tree! It was a tree that clawed me," he declared as we washed his face.

While out looking for materials for his marimbas, our old father would place his ear next to tree trunks. He was checking to see if the trees were pregnant. And this is what he had done that day, to choose wood for his very last marimba. However, someone was poisoning his tastes and gestures.

"That damned tree had claws. I saw its claws pulling me down into hell."

He was talking in a loud voice to impress his spouse. To no avail. The sky was vast, and Chikazi's gaze tempered its infinitude. My old father closed his eyelids so that the water might flow down his face. And with his eyes closed, he listened to his wife:

"The white hen—why did you kill her?"

"Because I was hungry."

"It was being kept for special ceremonies."

"What ceremonies? No one has died."

"Yes, they have. Your son, your first son has died. Don't lie to yourself, Katini Nsambe."

And she went on, getting her worries off her chest in one go: "The other boy migrated from his own head. And this daughter of yours has already left us. We're alone, my dear husband."

"Imani, are you going to abandon us?" my mother asked me.

And without waiting for an answer, she continued: "I was already absent, inventing visits from messengers as if Grandfather were still alive. And I made all these things up because I was scared. I was alone, without friends, without suitors." That's what my mother said. She added that it was my father's fault.

"Are you accusing me of being a bad father? For wanting my daughter to leave this wretched place, for wanting her to go somewhere better?"

"She's running away from her own self."

And Chikazi got up, her hands pressed against her

lower back, in the same posture as pregnant women. After a long pause, she added:

"The white hen was for our son. And he died."

"Have we seen his body?" my father asked. "Answer me, Chikazi, don't turn your back on me. Has anyone seen his body?"

I was filled with a desire to tell them Dubula had died in my arms, but I remained quiet. The one whose life has ended in my arms was still on his way to becoming my brother.

◆

A week had gone by since Dubula's death, and not a single bird had returned to our skies. Early on Sunday morning, our mother was found hanging from the great zebrawood tree. She looked like a dried fruit, a dark, shriveled bat. We went and called our father, who approached cautiously, dragging his feet. Under the tree's wide canopy, he sat down to contemplate the body as if he were waiting for leaves to spring from it.

"She isn't dead. Your mother has just got be-treed."

Every now and then, the breeze caused the corpse to sway. It was like a dance, of the type she had regaled us with so often.

When night fell, I asked: "Are we going to leave her there? The wild animals will eat her."

It was dark, and I didn't notice the sergeant arriving. He immediately exclaimed, horrified: "Take that body down! Right now!"

As always, Mwanatu ran forward to obey. My old father, however, raised his arm and proclaimed: "No one's going to do anything. That is not a body. That is Chikazi, my wife."

The sergeant walked around the tree, at a loss. He repeatedly tried to approach me, in a clumsy attempt to offer solace. During one of these approaches, he got as far as suggesting we pray together. But he immediately corrected himself: "No, not pray, for no one prays for someone who has committed suicide." To which he added, with sudden conviction: "For the love of God, Imani, ask your father to take her to the church."

"Take her to the church?" my old father retorted. "But she's already in a church. Our church is that tree."

This was a puzzling observation, coming as it did from my father. The reaction of the Portuguese was one of incredulity. Wasn't Katini a converted kaffir? Germano shook his head in an effort to expel his bafflement. What guarantee could one have of a black man's fidelity if even such a respected head of family could skip from one belief to another with such ease? The sergeant crossed himself discreetly and muttered between his teeth: "They don't feel the burden of guilt, nor do they know the meaning of shame. How can we expect them to be good Christians?"

◆

So the body stayed there until the following day, suspended like a bat in the dark. I approached it early in the morning, fearful of seeing the person who had always seemed to me to be immortal suffering the effects of time. But there were no signs of degradation, no smells, no flies or ravens. And in the cloudless sky there was no sign of vultures. I sat down next to Father, who had sat there the whole night. His eyes were fixed on his deceased wife. At one point, he said:

"She's so pretty!"

He was right. Even shriveled as she was, Mother retained the grace of a living creature, perhaps because her body was soaked by the rain that had fallen in the early hours. Drops fell from her feet, feeding a tiny, sad puddle. "That's how she should be," my father said, nodding slowly. "The dead should be washed by the rain."

"Do you want me to climb the tree, Father?" I asked after a long silence.

"Let's leave her where she chose to be."

◆

Gradually, the same rope that had strangled our mother began to suffocate me. At noon, when the dead woman lost her shade, the neighbors began to disperse, astonished and full of sadness. I too made a point of moving away. My father prevented me, grabbing me by the arm.

"Stay here, my girl!"

Then, with unexpected agility, my father climbed the tree, armed with a big knife. With one stroke, he cut the rope. I thought the fallen body would produce an abrupt thud, as felled trees do. But no. There wasn't a sound. What fell was a severed cloud, soundless and insubstantial.

My crazy brother, Mwanatu, still tried to catch the corpse. He almost succumbed to the weight that fell on top of him, and for a moment, with both him and Mother spread-eagled, we feared we might be dealing with a double fatality.

◆

From the start, Mwanatu helped with our mother's obsequies and behaved as if he were at ease with both the village rituals and the Christian ceremonies. He seemed different, more lucid, when he offered to help Father, who was carrying the body as if his back were the earth where he was going to bury her. He bore her for longer than necessary, for he was determined, without anyone having spoken to him about the matter, that she would be laid to rest under the tree where she had hanged herself.

Father walked around the grave a few times and then dropped, helpless, to his knees. We all rushed forward to help the dead woman to settle in the hole dug for her. Then we closed her grave just as we had closed her eyes. I asked myself why we close the eyes of the dead. We fear they may contemplate us. Why do we hide their cold bodies in the depths of the earth? Because we fear we may recognize how dead we already are.

When the soil had been flattened, the sergeant stuck a metal cross over the grave, and, with his eyes closed, he invited us to pray. Only Mwanatu answered his call. Uncle Musisi pushed past those present and tore the cross out of the ground. Then, speaking in Txitxope, he started to invoke our ancestors in a loud voice. The sergeant looked at us as if asking for help, but Musisi ignored his silent plea and, making use of me to act as an interpreter, asked the soldier: "Let me ask you, Sergeant, since this God of yours is the Father of us all and Creator of all the languages, can it be that he only understands Portuguese? And you, niece, don't limit yourself to translating. Tell him what we blacks do. Or have you forgotten your race, Imani Nsambe?"

My race? I asked myself silently. At that moment, I understood how great my sadness was, but also that I had already been orphaned before. This vulnerability was not mine alone, but belonged to all my black brothers.

Orphanhood doesn't require death. It begins before we are even born.

I bent over the patch of sand where the cross had fallen and once again placed it over our mother's grave. And I recalled the words she spoke in that gentle way she had: "It's not the dead that weigh so heavily. It's those who never stop dying."

24

The Sergeant's Twelfth Letter

Nkokolani, July 29, 1895

Your Excellency Counselor José d'Almeida

Not knowing how to console her, I told Imani that her mother would return one day. "She doesn't have to return," the girl answered promptly. "She never left here." And she led me to an anthill behind the house, pointed at the mound, and said: "This is where we spend our life burying stars. This is my consolation."

Then she told me things that, though they might be considered blasphemous, are the most beautiful heresies I have ever heard. She told me that the dead don't walk the earth; it's they who make the earth walk. With a rope fashioned from sand and wind, the deceased fasten the sun so that it won't get lost in the heavens. And she also said that the dead open up the way for the birds and the rains. And they fall to the ground in every drop of dew, to fertilize the soil and give the bugs water to drink.

The girl said all this without pausing for breath.

"Where did you learn all this?" I asked apprehensively.

"I didn't have to learn," she answered. "I'm made of all this. What I had to be taught were the white man's stories."

"But aren't you a Catholic?"

"Yes. But I have many other gods as well."

I wasn't shocked by such a revelation. Perhaps because, like any good Republican, I am manifestly anticlerical. My anger against the priests was the only good thing I inherited from my father. My mother, for her part, left me a very different legacy. She lived for the mass, the only occasion when she was allowed to leave the house. I almost failed to recognize her in the way she would walk to church: modest steps, her face veiled, her hair covered by a black shawl. At home, she was forbidden to be a mother; in the street, forbidden to be a woman.

I came back from Chikazi's funeral rites with an unanswerable question: does one convey one's condolences to someone who doesn't believe in death? For that grieving African family, there was a dead person but no death. So what did they grieve for? These doubts, far from filling me with anguish, gave me, as I returned to the barracks, a sense of well-being that I had not felt for a long time.

It wasn't without surprise that I saw Mariano Fragata waiting for me in the living room, waving an envelope, which he promptly handed me.

"I've just arrived, and brought this for you," he said with an enigmatic smile.

He didn't go so far as to get up from the mildewed sofa before warning me: "Prepare yourself, my dear Germano. You're not going to like what's in there."

"What's this packet?"

"It's your letters, the ones you've been sending these last few months. They're all there."

I shook my head. My letters? Was it José d'Almeida who was returning them? And why was he sending them back to me now?

What Fragata then revealed to me was the final stab to be thrust into my already wounded breast: None of my letters had ever reached the counselor José d'Almeida. The person who had read them and then replied was invariably Lieutenant Ayres de Ornelas.

"I don't understand anything at all, my dear Fragata. All that I wrote ..."

Perplexity gave way to suspicion. What had caused the lieutenant to divert my letters and, more serious still, to pose as someone else? What secrets had Ornelas appropriated? And what use had he made of confidences expressed to someone I took for my own father? Not one of these questions could provide an adequate answer. All I could do was comment with a sigh: "I'm done for! This is going to be the end of me ..."

"It may not be as bad as you think," Fragata declared, pouring oil on my troubled waters.

"What do you mean, not as bad as I think? Don't forget, Fragata, that I'm in Africa on a suspended sentence. Now that my confidences have been revealed, they'll end up shooting me. I'll have the same fate as Sardinha ..."

And I reminded the counselor's adjunct how much I had exposed myself in that long exchange of letters. How many times had I cursed the monarchy and its government, how many times had I poured scorn on my superiors in rank? Why on earth had I not limited myself to the routine reports expected of an unknown sergeant?

"Don't dramatize things, Germano. There's no need."

"Unfortunately, I can only expect the worst. Look at this ..."

I showed Fragata an unusual document that had come into my hands by mistake. It was a communiqué about the diversion of telegrams that the royal commissioner had directed to the military commanders at Inhambane. Ayres de Ornelas himself had admitted responsibility for this. And I read out loud the letter in which he confessed his guilt, handwritten by Ornelas:

> I ask God to forgive me if I have become the involuntary cause of some problem for the implementation of the projects of Your Excellency, the royal commissioner. And I beg Your Excellency to forgive my error ...

Fragata interrupted me in order to allay my fears. Ornelas might be arrogant and ambitious, he might suffer from a persecution complex, but he wasn't a malicious person, capable of damaging me. And there was something else I didn't know. Ornelas was the person who received and replied to all correspondence addressed to the counselor José d'Almeida. Moreover, he proceeded like this with the assent of José d'Almeida himself, for whom he prepared a résumé of the news communicated in the various telegrams and letters.

I accepted his words of comfort without conviction. I opened the envelope and reread the letters that I had scribbled over the previous months. While I was doing this, Fragata fell asleep, exhausted. I gave him my own bed, because I knew that I wouldn't get any sleep that night. In fact, I don't think I'll ever sleep again.

25

Lands, Wars, Burials, and Banishments

The soldier gains his uniform; the man loses his soul.

After our mother's death, Mwanatu came back to live at home. Father received him as if he had never left—without a word or any attention. The person who returned was a stranger, a mere visitor, to whom one lends a sleeping mat. Mwanatu gave the impression of being less of a dimwit while still being at odds with himself. Sitting in the shade in the backyard, he was regaining his roots. We watched him with apprehension: his arm had gained the shape of the rifle he had held day and night.

That morning, however, Mwanatu Nsambe made a decision. Equipped with a shovel, he set off for the village cemetery. Someone coming from afar wouldn't call that patch of scrub by the river, just north of the village, a cemetery. But it was there, in a sacred copse, that the dead of the oldest family in Nkokolani—the so-called lords of the land—were laid to rest. The whites use the term "bury." We talk of "sowing the dead." Forever sons and daughters of the soil, we give the dead what the earth gives the seeds: sleep leading to rebirth.

Apart from the shovel that he carried over his shoulder, Mwanatu also bore his rifle, a Martini-Henry, over his left arm, with all the pomp of a parading soldier. In this particular case, my brother would not have been able to use the word "sow," for he was in fact going to bury the weapon that had accompanied him during imaginary battles against the Nguni invaders. He was thus entombing a part of himself. The other part had already been interred in the furthest reaches of his reason.

In his excursion to the cemetery, Mwanatu was fulfilling a command. Ever since his return home, he had been beset by the same dream. In this dream, the following happened: From the top of the tree where she had hanged herself, our mother ordered him to get rid of his rifle. And he should never again play the role of a Portuguese sepoy.

"Get rid of that weapon, my son! Take that musket and bury it near the river."

"Musket? Have some respect, Mother; this is a Martini-Henry"—pronouncing the name slowly, as if he were painstakingly drawing each syllable.

Pronounced like that, the name took on the sheen of a medal. Our mother was unaware of the care he took with this other creature: the special cloth used for its external hygiene, the oil to grease its most intimate parts, the felt cover to wrap around its barrel. All these acts of respect showed that this was much more than a simple weapon.

"I'm not asking you," Mother warned. "Nor am I alone in speaking to you. There are many voices here, and they are all saying the same thing: Get rid of that rifle."

The order was unequivocal, and was not the result of some personal whim. By burying the gun, Mwanatu would be laying the war itself to rest.

◆

On the way to the cemetery, my brother realized how heavy the rifle was, after all. In his forays as an imaginary soldier, he had never got as far as feeling its weight.

On the contrary, the weapon had always seemed to be part of him, an extension of his own body.

"It's a congenital arm," he argued when facing his mother.

She must understand. He had many people struggling against one another inside him: a corporal and a kabweni, a black man and a white, a Christian and a pagan. How could he possibly become one single creature? How could he return to being just her son?

As he descended into the valley of the Inharrime, my brother's step became vague and hesitant, revealing all these anxieties. Then, all of a sudden, he changed direction and made for the garrison. He was going to talk to Sergeant Germano before carrying out his promise. Although he had abandoned his duty as a sentry, he hadn't lost his soldierly discipline. And he needed his superior's blessing for such blatant disobedience.

◆

At first the Portuguese feigned a lack of interest, but after a moment he raised his voice as if baffled:

"You're going to do what? Bury your weapon?"

"That's what I intend to do, Sergeant, sir."

"And what do you want me to do? Go with you and bless the burial?"

Mwanatu was not so audacious. All he was asking was for the sergeant to approve his act of madness. He, the valiant soldier Mwanatu, a duly baptized Christian, was as defenseless as he was confused. He had always been puzzled, for instance, that a rifle should have a person's name. *Martini-Henry?* With all due respect, and not wishing to offend God, a black man would never give a weapon a person's name.

"I'm sorry, Sergeant, sir. I just came to ask your advice."

"You want some advice? Well, then, tell me something: It wasn't you who bought that gun, was it? Do you remember who gave it to you?"

"It was you, sir. The gun and the uniform."

"Have you forgotten that gun was given you to kill the enemies of God and of Portugal?"

"I don't think so."

"You don't think so? Well, if I were you, I would return that rifle. In fact, you should have done that the moment you stopped being a sentry. So you're going to give back the weapon and the uniform, the uniform you're still wearing. The weapons, ammunition, and you yourself belong to the Portuguese Crown."

"If I don't bury the weapon, what shall I tell my mother when she visits me in my dreams?"

"Tell her whatever you like. Lie, tell her you buried the goddamned gun. She'll never check your story."

"Don't speak of my mother in such a way! Don't ..."

Mwanatu withdrew, wringing his hands as if they were pieces of cloth. And for the first time, the Portuguese was scared of the dimwit sentry. It struck him that Mwanatu had undergone a catastrophic regression: he had gone back to being a mere black. And as such, he no longer merited trust. The sergeant's suspicions deepened still more. What if the boy were capable of killing someone with that weapon? It would surely be better if he got rid of it. And, feigning remorse, he authorized the Martini-Henry's burial. But before Mwanatu disappeared, he shouted after him: "What about your sister? She's never come back here ..."

"Imani's sad. That's all ..."

"Tell her I've unpacked some new cloth. If she wants, she can drop by. And you too, Mwanatu, drop by, because I miss having you around."

The young man waved a vague goodbye. And he even smiled sadly. How could the Portuguese miss him if he had never spoken to him all those months he had been there? Every time a white visitor greeted him, asking after his health, the sergeant would cut in: "Never ask a kaffir how he is, because, the next minute, he'll ask you for something."

When he remembered these incidents, the sepoy had an urge to kick the sergeant's pet hen. He didn't attack the creature, just spat at it. The spittle hung from its crest, but the chicken's expression remained indifferent and vacant. That's how Mwanatu wanted to be: with neither an inner nor an outer self, without remorse or fatigue.

What haunted him most were his memories of the advice given him by the Portuguese. To lie to his late mother? The sergeant must be a powerful man, yet he wasn't aware that other gods ruled there, as ancient as the land itself. And Mwanatu set off for the cemetery once more.

◆

It was noon, the hour when nothing moves, when shadows are devoured by the ground. In the sacred copse, my brother trod on the patches of shade with a leopard's caution until he chose a great tree, supported by roots that emerged from the soil and resembled dark elbows. It was here that he decided to dig the grave. He dropped to his knees and mumbled some monotonous gibberish. Was he praying? No. He was naming all those who had fallen in war.

His voice was unleashed in a continuous murmur, but each name was pronounced with the same care with which we help the elderly and children dress themselves. In the end, he fell into a heavy, embarrassed silence, after which he lamented: "I can't remember anyone else. Damned war ..."

Such is the cruelty of those who die in combat: they never cease to fall, their claws clinging to time like dead bats. Even so, Mwanatu took a breath and brought his ritual to a close. "I am here and call upon you, warriors of the Chopi nation!"

He caressed his gun before starting to dig. "The Chopi nation?" he asked out loud. And he was mystified by his own words.

◆

Mwanatu plunged the shovel forcefully into the hot sand. It was then that he heard a metallic sound, of iron striking iron. Once more he sank the shovel in, with the anger of someone killing a snake. And, yet again, sparks flew, as if lightning flashes were issuing from the ground. A somber presentiment caused the sepoy to look skyward in search of help. The sun in its entirety invaded his pupils, and this flood of light blinded him. That was his intention: Let the dead absent themselves for a moment. And let the gods, both dead and alive, forget him.

When he opened his eyes again, Mwanatu saw a javelin. This was the reason for the noises and the sparks. He loosened the sand around his discovery and saw, at the bottom of the grave, spears, bows, and arrows. The amount of weaponry was far too great to count. The relics from all wars were right there under his feet.

The sepoy did not fulfill his mission. Hurriedly, and with a frantic gait, he returned home. He dragged his rifle along the ground as if it were a useless hoe. He found the uncanny coincidence baffling: while seeking to bury his weapon, he had unearthed an old arsenal.

◆

After leaving his boots at the front door, Mwanatu hastened to hide the Martini-Henry behind a cupboard. Then he went looking for our father, to tell him what had happened. Or, rather, what hadn't happened.

He found his progenitor busy sweeping the backyard. Sweeping, his father argued, was like fishing: an activity that didn't require any effort. After our mother's death, Father gave up living for himself. "The less alive I am, the less they'll want to kill me." Those were his words. If it weren't for me, his only daughter, he would have got rid of his possessions, his house, his very existence. In truth, it would take him longer than that to get rid of his liquor still and his marimbas.

Sweeping was now his only occupation. And he didn't even put his broom down while Mwanatu was telling him what had happened in the bush—he couldn't be seen to look upset in front of the neighbors. After a while, he leaned on his broom, pulled his hat down over his forehead, and muttered: "There are matters we don't talk about out in the open. Let's go indoors."

In a corner of the room, Katini sank into a chair, overcome by apprehension. He took off his hat and placed it on his knees, and then, after a long pause, opened his heart:

"What you found out there in the copse is something we cannot explain or understand ..."

"Don't frighten me, Father. What happened?"

"What happened is what is going to happen."

He slowly rolled a cigarette, as if he were seeking strength. "No one likes tobacco leaf or smoke," he always told us. The pleasure the smoker gets is to be smoked by time. He coughed for a while and then, still breathless, he sputtered: "I want to tell you something: I'm the father of that hole."

"I beg your pardon, Father?"

"You dug where I had already dug before. That place was where I hid my javelin."

"Did you bury your weapon as well, Father?"

"You don't bury a weapon. You hide it while waiting for the next war. Now, let's go there, let's have a look at this grave."

Leaning on his broom as if it were a walking stick, he slammed the gate shut and set off along the road. They followed the path, Mwanatu in solemn silence, Father dragging his boots along. It was an indulgence to use the term "boots" to describe the two soles lashed to his feet.

Then they paused next to the tree where Mwanatu had busied himself digging before. The roots now seemed even more exposed, hugging the ground as if claiming it as their exclusive property.

Leaning into the grave, our father picked up the javelin and expressed his concern with a click of the tongue: "It's the same hole. And this is my javelin—see the mark here."

"So how did the other weapons end up here?"

"They didn't end up here."

"What do you mean?"

"They were born here. They're alive."

He asked his son to help him collect all this material and place it in different categories. They piled up the javelins on one side, the spears on the other, and the shields in a third heap. Old Katini then slowly surveyed these piles as if he were a general inspecting his arsenal. Finally, he said: "Let's leave it like this, the weapons well away from the grave. And let's get out of here as quickly as possible. And don't look back while we walk away."

◆

When Mwanatu joined me in the yard, where I was lighting the fire, he wore the burdened look of a condemned man. He told me what had happened during his frustrated attempt to bury the gun.

"Did the sergeant ask after me?"

"He says he misses you. I'll have to tell him something when I return the uniform to him. The weapon I'll keep, but this uniform I'll give back. If Ngungunyane's people come, I don't want them to get the wrong idea about me."

He insisted I should tell him the message I wished to convey to the Portuguese. I remained silent for a while, but then jumped up so quickly that I alarmed poor Mwanatu. "Take your clothes off, little brother. I'm telling you, I'm older. Take that loathsome uniform off."

"Now?"

"Yes, right now."

Trousers, shirt, tunic all fell to the floor like a sigh. I picked up the different bits of the uniform and hurled them into the fire. In a matter of seconds, the clothes were consumed by the flames, as Mwanatu looked on, dazed. And before he could say anything out of regret, I declared furiously: "It was men in uniform who raped the women in this village."

This is what men did, in obedience to the orders of war. They created a world without mothers, sisters, daughters. War required such a world, deprived of women, in order to thrive.

My brother withdrew, ashamed, when he sensed that our father was entering the house. Busy untying his boot soles, Katini mumbled as if he were addressing the ground, "I presume you've already cooked the food."

I suddenly had a thought about a lifelong burden of responsibility. Rather than ask for love, the men of Nkokolani ask their women to be punctual in serving them their meals. In this, my father was the same as all the other men in Nkokolani. He existed in order to be served. He was passing along this time-honored woman's duty to me.

Father and son sat down at the table in our backyard, under the old mango tree. I did what I had always done when my mother was alive: I brought the pitcher of water and a towel, and the men washed their hands. I served them their dinner in silence, as if I were paying heed to our mother's absence. Katini was perturbed, and served himself generously with nsope. His voice was thick when he declared: "Did you tell your brother to take off his clothes a little while ago? Well, I'm the one giving the orders now. Get up, daughter. Get up and unfasten your capulana."

Mwanatu went as far as making an indignant gesture, but Father repeated his command. I didn't obey him immediately. Father was drunk, incapable of linking words and ideas.

"You, my daughter, think you're very clever, dreaming of faraway places. Tell me something, Imani: Does that white man look at you? Has he ever touched you?"

"Father, please ..."

"Shut your mouth. Didn't I tell you to take your clothes off?" he suddenly remembered.

I undid the cloth tied around my waist and, stripped naked, stood there without moving, my arms straight down, like a soldier standing at attention. My hair was tangled; my legs were skinny and apart; my body was more fragile than the light of the fire that crackled next to me.

"You're thin—you look like a bullet," my father commented.

Katini Nsambe seemed surprised to see me like this, so womanly, so full of that sad silence worn by wives who, when they stop talking, cause the world around them to become speechless. He looked at the shadows that danced on the ground and told me to get dressed again. Then he affirmed: "Bullets are living things. That's why they kill—it's because they're alive. And you, dear daughter, seem like a dead thing."

To which he concluded: "No white man is going to want you like that, so lacking in pulp, so lacking in body."

Now that Mother was no longer with us, I couldn't revert to the excuse that I had been scrawny from birth.

"If you're thin, you're going to stop being so. Especially since you've got clearly marked tattoos on your waist, on your thighs. Did you see them, Mwanatu?"

"I'm not supposed to look, Father."

"But you've already had a look at your own body," Katini Nsambe cut in. "And you know that no man can resist those tattoos. That Portuguese knows very well that you won't prove slippery when he ..."

"The Portuguese have other customs ..."

"That's enough, Imani. Now come here and drink, so you can forget who you are: a poor black woman smelling of the soil ... Tomorrow go back to the Portuguese man's house and make that foreigner's head go giddy like the flames in that fire."

While he filled my glass, I set about thinking: Yes, I'm

a tattooed bullet. I'm going to fire off at that man's heart. And I'm going to get away from this godforsaken village once and for all.

◆

The day had broken overcast, and Aunt Rosi—who, following our mother's death, lent us a helping hand at home—wrapped herself up well before going out to tend the crops. In Nkokolani, when we wake up to a gray sky, it is time to prepare ourselves for the rigors of winter. It can be very hot, but on a cloudy day we all make use of warm clothing. Among the inhabitants of Nkokolani, the sky has greater authority than the temperature. And the colors have such authority that we don't even have names for them.

So it was with warm clothing on that gray morning that Aunt Rosi headed for the field. She carried with her all the sadness in the world. When she got to the plantation, she spread her legs and bent over slowly, like a dying star. The hoe rose and fell in her hands as if its blade were thumping the neck of a condemned prisoner. And this prisoner was her, unable to change her fate.

Little by little, the woman was assailed by an irrepressible urge to weep, but she didn't stop digging while her body performed an earthly dance. It wasn't long before she heard a metallic sound, as if her hoe had scraped against stone or bone. She scratched away the sand with her fingers and saw that there was a pistol buried there. She ran to call her neighbors. The women thought that it would be better not to touch the weapon, and that the only thing to do was to fill the hole and smooth the disturbed soil. They pretended that they hadn't seen anything, that nothing had happened. However, when they scratched away at the sand to cover up what had been found, they uncovered hundreds of bullets, all identical, like tadpoles recently born in a puddle of rain. They hurriedly gathered up their hoes and got out of there.

As soon as she got home, our aunt told us about the episode. The two men remained silent. It was a foreboding silence. Until Uncle Musisi spoke:

"Tomorrow, go and dig farther away. But don't go alone. Take the other women with you."

◆

In our house, Mwanatu awoke with a start in the middle of the night. Once again, his mother had visited him. She had reminded him that he was delaying in carrying out her order. But it wasn't his gun alone he should bury.

"All the guns?" her son asked.

"All of them. Those of the Portuguese as well."

"We can't bury the Portuguese ones, Mother."

"There's something you don't understand, my dear son. It's not that war asks for arms. It's the opposite—the arms give birth to war."

◆

Early the following day, Auntie burst into the house in a state of panic and shook her husband, who was still lying in bed.

"The war, husband ..."

"What's happened? Are we being attacked?"

She nodded by way of confirmation. Uncle Musisi jumped up and, still naked, crossed the room to take an old musket out of a leather bag. He shouted for Mwanatu. His nephew appeared in a flash, his eyes gleaming, clutching his rifle.

"What's happening?" he asked. "Is Ngungunyane attacking us?"

"I don't know. I haven't heard any shots," his uncle declared. "What direction are they coming from?"

Standing stock-still, Aunt Rosi contained herself, as if sensing an invisible presence inside the house, but then she pointed discreetly at the ground.

"I don't understand," Uncle said. "Is there someone underneath the house?"

She nodded. "They're everywhere," she added. With a subtle wave of her hand, she once again blamed the floor.

"But who?"

"Them."

Something seemed to groan in the skeleton of the house. So I tried to allay the existing tension and suggested, in a confident tone: "It's Tsangatelo. Grandfather has come to fetch us."

"Be quiet, Imani. Let me ask you again, wife: is there someone under the floor?"

"It's them, it's the weapons."

In a whisper, Rosi related what had just befallen her. Once again, she had set off to open up a new plantation, this time farther away, down by the riverbank. But it wasn't long before the previous macabre discovery was repeated: In this new terrain, among the smooth, round pebbles, she glimpsed the carcass of a horse. And a little farther on, a saddle and a pair of stirrups. Lying at her feet was one of those steeds that had galloped through her dreams. Who knows whether it wasn't the mount of Mouzinho de Albuquerque himself?

Around the carcass, countless cartridge cases were scattered, and Aunt Rosi swore that these capsules moved around like greedy insects now shorn of their feet, devouring everything they came across. This subterranean army was digging tunnels that extended beneath the entire world, and even at a distance, as she fled, she could hear their talons scratching away at the earth. The women in flight were yelling that they needed to get away from that place as quickly as possible.

"We are finished," she concluded, all the while preserving her contained, dignified pose. "We're going to die of hunger; we have nowhere else to plant crops."

This is what had happened in Nkokolani: War had turned our land into a cemetery. A cemetery that could accommodate no more dead.

26

The Sergeant's Thirteenth Letter

Nkokolani, August 11, 1895

Your Excellency Counselor José d'Almeida

I never imagined how much I would miss someone whose presence I never felt. A young idiot, silent and remote, has opened an abyss in my soul with his departure. Ever since Mwanatu returned to his parents' home, my loneliness and despair—which were already immense— have become unbearable. I always assumed that God would be the eternal companion of any Christian, wherever he might find himself. It's either one thing or the other: either I am not a good believer, or Nkokolani lies beyond the sphere of divine attention.

I don't know whether I miss Mwanatu more as a person or as a messenger boy. In truth, it is the absence of mail that causes me the greatest privation. These days, I am bedeviled by mad visions of my floor covered in papers. When I open my window, the breeze causes pages to flutter through the air and fly off into the distance. I look out at the surrounding countryside, which is entirely carpeted with sheets of paper. There are thousands of letters in one continuous sheet, letters as far as the eye can see. And in the middle of it all lies a dead youth with a tattoo on his arm, which reads: "A Mother's

Love." On closer inspection, one can see that his whole body is covered in tattoos. His body contains a whole book in minute script. The dead man comes back to life and sits up, fully awake. What he does is transcribe his writing from his skin onto paper. But then he soon realizes that a whole life is not enough to transfer all the letters, for there are more of them than there are pores in his skin.

Have I gone mad? That must surely be your judgment. And it must be mine as well. It was because of my insanity that I rejoiced, some days ago, when I received a visit from my erstwhile sentry. Had he returned to his post? My mistake. The lad hadn't come to stay. He was merely seeking my advice over some nonsensical mission. He wanted to bury the gun he had been given. I took advantage of the situation to ask after his sister, the beautiful Imani. He replied that he knew nothing. He was lying. It is obvious that the girl does not want to see me. And I respect her wish. Just as I respected the crazy intentions of her brother Mwanatu, feigning that I was listening to him and pretending to give him advice.

It happened, however, that I ran into Imani in the village this week, when she was buying fish. She didn't look at me. Her attitude was no different from what it had always been. That's how women talk to me, with their eyes looking firmly at the ground. She didn't look at me, but she spoke. And her question could not have been stranger:

"Do you think I'm a bullet?"

In the face of my incomprehension, she repeated the question. I invited her to come with me to visit her mother's grave. She agreed without a word. At the back of her house, we both sat down in silence.

"Elephants used to pass by here," she said, pointing to

the clump of trees. "Now there are none left. You've killed them all."

"We have killed them?"

"Isn't the one who kills the one who fires the gun, or who gives the order to kill? So, let me ask you, has all that ivory made you richer?"

"Not me, Imani. Not me."

And the girl pressed on: "That's how it will be when you've eviscerated the earth to steal all its minerals. You'll order the blacks to pile themselves up, one on top of another, until they reach the moon. And then Chopi miners will begin to dig for lunar silver."

In the girl's words, there was unconcealed rancor. I had lied, that was true. But there were other, more timeless reasons.

"Is it because I'm white? Is that why you're keeping your distance from me?"

"Life is like a tide."

I must confess, I have no preparation for understanding the metaphors that litter the speech of these Negroes. Imani has a soul that's all but white, yet she still surprises me with her use of language.

"Now I understand better," I said, to make peace, "this bitter feeling that blacks have against whites."

And I shared with her a recollection I had from my time in Lisbon. It happened the only time I watched a bullfight, having been taken to see it by my father. At one point, when the bull had tired and lost his aggression, half a dozen blacks were introduced into the ring, decked out with feathers and mounted on ridiculous cardboard horses. These ornamentations robbed them of their mobility but reinforced the burlesque tone that thrilled the crowd. The bull hurled himself against these poor devils, and they were all badly injured, to the delight of the spectators, who until then had been complaining about the paucity of the spectacle.

I looked up at Imani to assess the effect of what I had told her. Her face remained impassive.

"It wasn't racism. Or maybe it was. The truth is that they also threw Galicians into the arena."

"Are Galicians black?"

"No, they're like us."

"Us, who, Sergeant?"

I don't know whether I smiled, or if indeed I meant to. What I remember is that the girl got up and invited me to stand beside her, in silence, next to her mother's grave.

"Is your mother alive, Sergeant?"

I told her I didn't know. Imani stared at me aghast, and then shook her head. She told me that was the saddest reply she had ever heard.

Now, I have kept what made me rejoice most these last few days for the final part of this letter. For an unknown postman arrived at my house, a slim mulatto with slanting blue eyes like those of a fish. He had come from Inhambane, and, besides the routine items of correspondence, he was carrying—just imagine—a letter from my mother. When he held out the envelope to me, I stood there without moving, thunderstruck.

"A letter from my mother?"

And the lad almost had to prize open my fingers in order to give me the letter. Moreover, he apologized: the papers had been splashed with water as he crossed the river. I ran to the privacy of my bedroom in order to read the letter and enjoy it at my leisure. The moisture had caused the ink to run. But my eyes, watery from the emotion of it all, got the better of its apparent illegibility. The lines were few and the message vague: they expressed a mother's gratitude for her son's continuous messages of love and longing. I stopped reading, convinced of one thing: that letter was not addressed to me. And so I went and looked for the messenger. I had offered this new courier Mwanatu's quarters so he could rest. I interrupted his repose and returned the misdirected letter to him.

"This letter isn't for me!"

The lad half opened his eyes and once again curled up on his sleeping mat. It was only then that I realized I had never visited that minute cubicle before. And I felt a kind of remorse. I made the excuse of never having done it out of a sense of restraint at invading someone else's privacy. But deep down, I knew there was another reason.

I hurried back to my room in order to write to you. I sat down and began, as I always do, by filling the top of the page with the name of the recipient. Your name, my dear José d'Almeida. But at this point I stopped. And I pondered on the endless deceptions of this correspondence of ours.

I didn't understand, for example, the reason why you addressed to me copies of letters that Lieutenant Ayres de Ornelas had sent to his beloved mother. I must confess that I even thought Your Excellency had surpassed the limits of decency and consideration owed to another person's intimate feelings. But I now appreciate and thank you for your refined sensibility. Your Excellency guessed the most fundamental of my anxieties, the most hidden of my privations. And now that I have paused, my pen hesitating over your name at the top of the page, I reach the following conclusion: I cannot continue with this pretense. For I now know that it is not Your Excellency, the Counselor Almeida, who reads and replies to my letters. I should cross out the name of the recipient of this letter, and in its place insert the name of Ayres de Ornelas. For it is with you, dear Lieutenant Ornelas, that I speak, and indeed have always spoken.

I feel no offense at this deception. Quite the opposite. I ask you, dear lieutenant, to transmit my sincerest thanks to the counselor José d'Almeida. Tell him how happy I am with the trick played on me, just as I am grateful that he has been Ayres de Ornelas all along. And to you, my dear lieutenant, I say: Thank you for having pretended to be someone else. More than anything, I thank you for your kindness in having sent me letters destined for your beloved mother. You cannot imagine how much good these letters have done me, here in the depths of the interior. Imani was right when she drew my attention to there being no greater sadness than someone's not knowing whether his mother still belongs to this world. Your letters gave me the illusion of speaking to my mother as if she were providing solace for the pains of this infernal exile of mine.

I now know for certain that I have managed to survive in these backlands of Africa only thanks to the saintly woman who gave birth to me. And everything I have done that I may take pride in was due to the inspiration she provided. It was because of her that I joined the Republican revolt of January 31. As if, by wanting to kill the king, I were taking revenge on my stern, cold father.

In Batalha Square, it was to my mother that my thoughts returned when the bullets began to fly like sudden, tiny, ferrous birds. By a strange, sad irony, the shots fired at us came from the steps of a church dedicated to Saint Ildefonso, where the Municipal Guard were positioned. Although it was very different, this church seemed to me identical to the one my mother used to disappear into, and later reemerge from, with the lightness of an angel.

Next to me on the flight of steps, a companion from the same dormitory as me was shot dead. Along with him fell the red-and-green flag he was carrying in his arms. I leaned over the unfortunate man to try to help him. There wasn't a drop of blood, either on his uniform or on his exposed body. He seemed to have merely stumbled, and muttered something imperceptible without ever closing his mouth, until his gaze froze, fastened by some dark ribbon. It wasn't just a companion from my lodgings who was dying. My own life was seeping away too. At that moment, the tears I shed were only useful because they brought me back to my childhood bedroom.

And all this long journey that drew me away from my home was, after all, a slow, imperceptible return. The day I was left at the gate of the Military Academy, I took my time before entering the building. I knew that once I had done so a part of me would die forever. I lingered by the door, peering at the street to see whether my mother might yet come back, moved by a sense of remorse. But she didn't.

Years later, when I was leaving the trial of the mutineers in chains, I still believed my mother might be there to embrace me, on the quay where the families of the accused were waiting. But my mother was not among those present.

I do not know, from this distance, whether she is still by any chance alive. Deep within me, I can still hear the sweet, hoarse lullaby with which she sang me to sleep. And I hear her in the harmony of the marimbas, and in the prolonged silence of the savanna. Maybe that's all my mother ever was: a gentle voice, a tenuous silken thread from which the whole weight of the universe was suspended. This is what I should have given Imani by way of an answer when she asked me whether I had received news from my home in Portugal.

It was necessary for me to live among black folk and strangers to reach an understanding of myself. It was necessary for me to rot away in a dark, distant place to understand how much I still belong to the tiny village where I was born.

Maybe Imani is right that spiders and their webs can heal the world and repair the gashes in our souls. Maybe, during this time of exile, I have acquired a strange taste for inventing illnesses. But what I suffer from has nothing to do with medicine. In truth, Excellency, I haven't succumbed to sickness in Africa, like all the others. I fell ill in Portugal. My sickness is none other than my country's decline and putrefaction. Eça de Queiroz wrote, "Portugal is finished." When he wrote these words, he says, tears came to his eyes. That is his and my sickness: our fatherland without a future, drained by the greed of a handful of people, bent double under the whims and willfulness of England.

This decrepit garrison isn't fortuitous. Nor is my confinement within it fortuitous. As my grandfather aptly recalled, when we don our uniforms, we unclothe our souls. If I die now, Your Excellency will not suffer the inconvenience of having to return me to the fatherland. A naked soul bears no weight. I shall require no journey. For I shall leave no memory of me behind.

My mother said there were angels. And I, who was a child and had all the innocence of the world, didn't believe in such celestial creatures. There was something so sad about them that stopped me from believing. It has taken me all this time to understand that sadness. It is not a question of whether angels exist or not, but of the possibility that the sky might not be big enough to accommodate even one single angel.

27

Hands in Flight

What pains in death is falsity. Death exists only during a brief exchange of absences. In some other being, death will be reborn. Our pain is not knowing how to be immortal.

"Maybe," Germano said, "I lost my mother more than you lost yours."

The sergeant hugged me graciously. He had just arrived at our house. He wanted to repeat his condolences on the day when we were remembering our mother. I was alone in the backyard when, mournful, he presented himself.

"I don't know whether I want to see you."

It was as if he weren't listening to me, his hands resting on my shoulders. For a second, I had my doubts: were those hands so weightless, or were they the wings of an angel? What happened next left no room for doubt. The Portuguese gave me a lingering hug. Never before had I been held with such conviction. I allowed myself to remain in his embrace, more still than a stone. In a mere instant, every one of my fifteen years nestled in that man's arms. I was puzzled by the sergeant's stillness, as if he had suddenly ceased to exist. However, his hands gradually loosened, and they began to descend, mapping my back and navigating my thighs. I was so far away that I didn't react. When I tried to protest, I couldn't find my voice. With a vigorous push, I removed the foreigner from me. At that instant, I was a bullet, a bullet capable of piercing the wings of that angel. His eyes fixed on the ground, he withdrew, so fragile that I almost called him back.

That night, I went to bed early, hoping sleep would visit me as gently as a caress. But such a visit was not to be. Instead, I dreamed there was a huge fire that set the night ablaze. Mother danced barefoot over the flames while Father played a marimba. Every time he touched a key, a bat flew up from the marimba and fluttered above our heads. At one point, mother took a burning coal in her hands, raised it to her mouth, and swallowed it whole. And, with her tongue reddened and her lips burning, she shouted to her husband: "Fire doesn't hurt me. My body knows no pain. And know this: I never felt anything when you beat me."

Katini continued playing, as if he hadn't heard her. And she wheeled around the fire and the marimba. Her face raised high, her voice brimming with pride, she proclaimed: "Now I'm really dancing, husband. Now I can dance, and not just when you tell me to."

Later, she got tired, and, sweating and shaking, she snuggled up to me. I wiped off her perspiration and gave her some water to drink. Then I told her that every morning Father would leave a little tobacco and flour next to the tree where she had hanged herself. And he would stay there for hours, his eyes unfocused on anything.

"I know, daughter. Your father has never kept me company so much."

Then I confessed my inner misgivings. I told her about the Portuguese sergeant who caused me simultaneously such disgust and such fascination. How could I love a man who had so betrayed us?

"Do you want a man who doesn't lie to you or betray you? You'll die single, my dear daughter."

Early next morning, I threw the clothes I was wearing on the floor, and tied a simple capulana around my perspiring body. I set off for the garrison, fleet of foot. I found the Portuguese, stripped to the waist, cuddling his old pet hen. Surprised and embarrassed, Germano rushed into the house to make himself respectable. I blocked his path, and the soldier collided with me. Then I whispered voluptuously: "Hold me, Sergeant. Hold me tight."

The man was struck dumb and petrified. After a moment, he looked around in a panic to see whether anyone was looking. "Please, girl ..."

In silence, I took his hand and led him inside. His steps were those of a blind man, and, maybe because of that, he hadn't noticed that I had let my capulana slip to the floor. When he saw I was naked, he quivered uncontrollably.

"Sergeant, I want to be a woman," I said, my lips next to his sweating face.

I expected him to fondle me. But the soldier was paralyzed, looking left and right in despair.

"I'm a marimba," I murmured in his ear. "Men who play me will hear music they've never listened to before."

"I can't, Imani. I'm not alone."

A shadow glided across the floor. At first, there was nothing more than the swish of a skirt. Then, out of the half-light, a white woman appeared, her fair hair hanging loosely over her shoulders. The vision made me feel dizzy, as if I had been given a hefty push. Then I realized: never before had I seen a woman of another race. The whites I had known had all been men. In shame, I wrapped my capulana around myself again. But as I walked toward the door, I was stopped by the visitor. She was tall and pale, like the plaster figure of the Virgin Mary that adorned the ancient church by the seashore. Her dress brushing the floor made her seem taller still.

"Who's this?" she asked, addressing the Portuguese.

"This? Oh, this is a … a girl who runs errands for me."

"I can see what sort of errands …"

"Don't make me laugh, Bianca …"

The intruder circled me, examining my body as only a man might do.

"Don't think you're getting out of here just like that," she told me severely. "Sit down; I'll be back in a minute!"

She disappeared down the hall, leaving behind her a trace of a sweet fragrance. His shoulders hunched, the Portuguese whispered to me that she was an Italian friend who had arrived from Lourenço Marques. Her name was Bianca Vanzini Marini. Everyone called her the "white woman with the hands of gold."

"Call her Dona Bianca," he advised me.

The visitor returned, bringing a dagger partially wrapped in a cloth. I shuddered, terrified. I was about to end my days there because of jealousy.

"Don't hurt me," I implored in a voice that was almost inaudible.

The Italian woman pulled up a stool and sat down behind my chair. She began to unwrap the dagger and told me to sit up straight while her fingers felt my neck. I began to weep, my soul emptied. Those minutes seemed endless. Then, slowly, the visitor began to smooth my hair. Suddenly, a metal comb emerged from the cloth. I smiled, relieved: what I had imagined to be a deadly knife was, after all, a harmless object.

The white woman murmured in a strange accent, "Let's fix this beautiful hair."

No one had ever praised my hair before. On the contrary, my father thought I should wear a headscarf to hide the sin of my curly hair.

While she was combing me, the foreigner said: "Your mother hanged herself from a tree. I came to Africa to die."

She got to her feet so she could work better. Her fingers were busy plaiting the mass of my frizzy hair. But as I was still in doubt, my neck remained tense while she went on talking.

"I'm going to tell you my story. That's why I'm combing your hair. I learned from black women that there's no better way to make conversation."

The Italian woman certainly had a point. Men observe women making braids and think they are just taking care of their beauty. But they are sweetening the passage of time.

◆

The first time Dona Bianca came to Mozambique, she got pregnant, and her husband fled in the direction of South Africa, or so people said. She returned to Italy to have the child, but her son died right after he was born. There was only one way to face up to her loss, and that was by committing suicide.

"I wasn't brave enough to put an end to it all. I didn't have your mother's nobility of spirit."

Then she remembered there was one place in the world where one dies easily and quickly: Lourenço Marques. That would be a good place to die. The end would come without any drama, without her having to make a decision: the heat, the pestilence, the fevers, the dirty, muddy streets, all would conspire to bring about her demise without any one of them being the sole cause.

And so she returned to Africa in order to die. In the house where she found lodgings, she discovered an album containing photographs of well-known Portuguese military figures. One of these was of an attractive man whose uniform endowed him with manly elegance, but whose face betrayed a strangely melancholic air. It was Mouzinho de Albuquerque. In no more than a fleeting moment, the Italian woman detected death in the captain's gaze. In his eyes, she saw the same tragic destiny that she was seeking so hard for herself. She was told the handsome captain would be sailing for Mozambique. I shall await that day, she said to herself with a sigh. Surprisingly, this man—whom she had only known through a faded photograph—gave her back her will to live.

"I have set my hopes on meeting him during the course of his journey— so as to restore to him the life that he gave me."

In Lourenço Marques, Bianca did a bit of everything. She worked as a milliner, a seamstress, a trader in liquor. And when she had nothing left to sell, she sold herself. But it was in gambling that she gained her fortune. She accumulated enough money to stop working, and she set off on that journey to Inhambane, where she was going to visit the Fornasini, who were Italians like herself.

When Bianca finished her story, a long sigh of relief ran through my body. The Italian woman was not Germano's spouse; she was there quite simply as a traveler. And I sank into the torpor that her pale hands had induced.

◆

Away from the barracks, disorder had become general chaos. The unearthed arms created a sense that Nkokolani was being besieged from the bowels of the earth. And there was talk of curses, vengeance, and wizardry. Fear is the most powerful of generals. From the belly of its autocratic leader, there now appeared soldiers, eagerly awaiting the voice of command.

That afternoon, while Dona Bianca was combing my hair, the village's inhabitants assembled in the main square. There were requests for a *chidilo*, a great blood sacrifice, a celebration directed at all ancestral entities. They chose the men who would visit the highest terrain, the top of the dunes overlooking the ocean. These lands lay beyond the first line of fortifications designed to protect the village. Next to these khokholos, they would slaughter a goat and speak to the spirits of the "lords of the land."

"Over there, there will be no hiding place for arms," Aunt Rosi assured them. "There no one can dig a hole, for that is where the founding fathers of our land are buried."

Musisi walked by his wife's side at the head of a huge, panicking crowd. Armed with the old Martini-Henry, which had escaped burial, the sepoy Mwanatu marched on one of the flanks. And he saw that everyone, without exception, was carrying a weapon: cutlasses, knives, javelins, bows and arrows, pistols, muskets. Alarmed, Mwanatu asked, "Why are all of us armed? It looks as if we're going to war ..."

No one answered. And the sepoy began to hang back, as if doubting the wisdom of such a demonstration. That was when he noticed our father at the rear of the procession. Mwanatu had never imagined that Katini Nsambe would join such a noisy horde of people. He greeted his progenitor with a timid gesture.

As he began to walk more quickly, so as to get away from the arresting sight of his father, he saw Uncle Musisi approaching and, out of breath, asking him anxiously, "Were you ordered to bury all the weapons?"

Without pausing in his march, Mwanatu nodded. "It was my dead mother who told me to," he said.

"In that case, we'll have to eliminate the weapons belonging to the Portuguese as well," his uncle commented.

◆

In military formation, the villagers' caravan crossed the river and entered the bush on the other bank. The clouds on that day were so low that the warriors had to stoop to preserve their frame.

Farther ahead, the men paused at the entrance to a copse. Before digging a hole, they tied a piece of white cloth to the trunk of a mafura tree and spilled a few drops of liquor on the white sand. In this way, the dead knew they were being remembered.

Then they rose as one and, to the rhythm of a virile chant, began to scratch away at the ground. From the entrails of the earth they gradually uncovered a ghastly sight: a vast arms dump gleamed in the sunlight and caused the terrified men to throw their picks and shovels aside and step back. Holding her arms wide, Aunt Rosi hurriedly invoked the ancestors and begged them for protection against vengeance and witchcraft.

After their initial shock, the men peered into the hole. They saw an accumulation and variety of weapons of war never seen before: cannons, machine guns, all manner of rifles and munition, most of them still in rotting wooden crates.

Uncle Musisi climbed up onto a termite mound and surveyed the crowd haughtily. His hoarse voice hovered over the silence:

"It is sad what is happening to us, my brothers. Are we scared of the strangers who have come to dominate us from afar? Well, let us fear ourselves more, for we are losing our very souls."

This was when my father stepped out from the throng and faced Musisi.

"Brother-in-law, the people want peace."

"They want peace? Then leave these hiding places in peace. If the earth is brimming with arms, so much the better. Rifles give greater sustenance than hoes ..."

"Let us return to Nkokolani, my brothers ..."

"Nkokolani doesn't belong to us anymore."

"My brother ..."

"Never call me brother again, for you are the white men's brother ..."

My father bowed his head but didn't withdraw—he had something else to say. And he declared in a loud voice:

"I have an explanation for all that is happening."

His explanation was simple: The earth is a womb. That which nestles within it must be born and multiply. And when weapons were deposited in the ground, the earth thought they were seeds and caused these materials to germinate and proliferate as if they were plants. That is what Katini Nsambe said, perched precariously on the trunk of a fallen tree.

"The earth is in a state of confusion, my brothers," he added. "I have journeyed through its interior, and I know what I'm talking about. Did the dead woman say we should bury all the arms? Well, then, let's unbury them."

Without waiting for the reaction of those listening to

him, Father got down from his improvised platform and vanished into the crowd. Uncle savored his adversary's retreat and waited for silence to spread. Only then did he speak once more, to demonstrate that the last word belonged to him.

"Listen to my orders: No one is to open another hole. And no one is to take any weapon out of the pits that you opened up willy-nilly around here."

He, Musisi, was the only one in whom the ancestors had any faith. The dead had complained to him how forgotten and defenseless they felt. And they begged him not to leave them unarmed.

"We must leave them with the weapons," Musisi continued. "That is what they ask: these pits must be filled in with everything in them, do you hear?"

Those present looked down at the ground with modesty and respect. Without anyone's noticing him, my brother Mwanatu walked past the crowd to stand next to the termite mound. That was when everyone realized that Musisi's nephew was now his bodyguard.

"When the next war comes, the dead will be my only army. Do you people want this?"

And, as of one voice, everyone answered *no*. Standing upright, Uncle raised his arm as if it were a flag and declared: "Then, my brothers, let us go to the Portuguese garrison and take all the weapons stored there. We should take control of those weapons. If they won't defend us, we shall have to do it ourselves."

◆

When they got back to the village, the men were held back by the womenfolk who had packed into the square. A babble of protesting voices pervaded this other throng.

A fat woman was the first to complain:

"There's no land left for us to sow. We're going to leave; if not we'll die."

"The arms that have been planted are so many that the rain and the river are full of rust," another woman added.

"And what's worse," a third woman yelled, "we can't even die anymore. Where would they bury us?"

So the divine message, according to them, was very clear: There was nothing left but to emigrate. There are places where people have had to abandon their homeland. In Nkokolani, it was the land that had abandoned its people.

Uncle Musisi, who had listened to all this in silence, started pushing away the women in front of him while shouting encouragement to the men marching with him: "Are we women? Are we going to allow ourselves to be held up by all this weeping, all these words that seek to bend our will? Forward, my brothers, let us march on the barracks and let us redeem the arms that are ours by right."

◆

Sergeant Germano de Melo looked in the direction of the square to confirm the greatest terror any European could feel: the sight of thousands of armed blacks emerging from the ground like dark ants, and advancing with the fury of a sudden storm. This was what was erupting in front of his blue eyes, suddenly turned green with fear. The hordes were still far away, but he hurried to erect his defenses. He ran to the obsolete armory to fetch the only weapon that was still working: a machine gun, with a couple of cartridge belts. He barricaded the doors with heavy crates of bullets and did the same to the windows.

Then he ran back to the house. He was puzzled to see the door open and got a fright when he saw me, Imani, and the Italian woman in the living room, looking outside through the wooden shutters.

"Have you seen what's coming? I'm done for."

"I came to warn you," I explained.

"Well, you came too late. Now God alone can defend me. Wait here for me—don't move. I'm going in there to get the Bible ..."

He dashed into his bedroom, almost treading on the chicken, and I even heard the thud of his body hitting the ground. I went to help. The sergeant had stumbled over a goat that was wandering around the house. On all fours, the Portuguese came face-to-face with the animal's snout. It was then that he noticed a white paste seeping from the goat's mouth. Germano forced open the creature's jaws to reveal the crushed remains of the book in his cupped hands.

"It's the Bible," he lamented. "The goddamned goat ate the Bible."

It had been chewed up. More than just chewed, it had been pulped. The divine word, that word he had been looking for so urgently, had been chomped by a goat. I looked on the floor for anything that might remain of the Sacred Scripture, while Germano hurried to look out of the window. I managed to salvage a few pages and presented them to him, before his feverish gaze.

"This was left," I announced apprehensively.

Soaked sheets of paper fell to the floor. The soldier got as far as touching them with his fingertips, but then he jumped up and kicked the goat outside. Right there, by the door to the house, he fired a shot at the animal that blew its head away. A horn was hurled violently into the room and rolled across the floor as if it were alive.

The sergeant then busied himself setting up by the window the machine gun that he had taken from the armory. "Keep away from here, both of you; go into the bedroom," he ordered, with a voice that was unrecognizable. I ignored the order. I noticed how the Portuguese was aiming at the raucous, approaching throng with his weapon, already loaded and ready. And I saw that my brother Mwanatu was at the head of the crowd. I screamed: "Sergeant! Don't do it!"

He didn't answer, but turned the barrel toward me, and his look betrayed his intention. He would fire at me if I distracted him from his fanatical objectives. From the wall, I took down the Martini-Henry, which had been hanging there the whole time. When I called his name again, the sergeant had already taken the first shot. He glanced at me out of the corner of his eye. Then his look turned to one of disbelief. He barely had time to shield his face with his hands, and when the gun went off, my body was thrown back and I was deafened by the explosion.

28

The Sergeant's Last Letter

Inharrime, August 26, 1895

Most Esteemed Lieutenant Ayres de Ornelas

You will be unfamiliar with this handwriting, Excellency. But it is your humble servant, Sergeant Germano de Melo, who is writing to you, or, rather, who has ordered this letter to be written. It is Imani's writing, and if there are to be more letters, she will write what I dictate. The reason for this is straightforward: The horror that so often assailed me has now become a reality. I have no hands; they flew away like an angel's wings, ripped apart by a bullet fired from close range. The person who shot me was the woman who occupied my heart, the one who, time after time, gave me back the hands that, in my delirium, I was convinced I had lost. If I recover from this frightful injury, then I shall be able to compete with One-Arm Silva, the deserter who ended up a hero. Maybe I shall be granted a reprieve in my sentence, and be able to ride proudly down the streets of Lourenço Marques. Perhaps they will erect a statue of me in the Terreiro do Paço, in Lisbon. But this one would be different from all the others, which display an entire body without any sign of an amputation.

When the fateful shot was fired, I lost consciousness.

And when I came to, I was being carried to a large dugout. Katini, Imani's father, and Mwanatu, her faithful brother, were rowing the craft away from Nkokolani. They rowed against time, they rowed against the current. Seated in the stern, Bianca and Imani were occupied with their tasks as nurses.

We were heading for the house of the only doctor in the region, a Swiss man by the name of Liengme. The doctor maintained a field hospital at the source of the Inharrime, and although he was an adversary of Portugal, he was my last hope of being saved. As I lay on the bottom of the boat, figures hovered above me, silhouetted against the intense moonlight. I could hear voices, at first faint, but then clearer. From time to time, a figure would lean over me: it was Bianca, changing the improvised bandages and cleaning my wounds, which I dared not look at. The river was like a silver mirror, and at that hour, the hippopotamuses had already left the water to graze along the riverbank.

Suddenly, there was a red flash on the horizon: a huge fire had been lit somewhere in the belly of night.

"They've seen us," Katini affirmed.

The fire must be a signal transmitted from one village to the others, telling them of the arrival of white men.

"And are we those whites?" I asked.

"Yes. They think that this is a military craft and we're transporting arms ..."

Later, it became clear that this wasn't a beacon for sending a warning. For the next thing that happened was a huge explosion from within the fire's reddened heart. The flames rose so high that they illuminated the whole of the surrounding grassland. The dugout pulled into the riverbank, hidden by a thick mass of trees. This was when Bianca unexpectedly jumped ashore and started rushing across that glimmering piece of open ground, attracted like a moth to those whimsical flashes of light. I sat up in the boat so as to get a better glimpse of the frightful sight, and to witness the Italian woman's madness as she surrendered to the horrific conflagration. We shouted at her not to get too far away; we begged her to come back. But she persisted insanely in her demented rush. Katini yelled at his daughter to go get her.

After hesitating at first, Imani eventually ran after the frenetic Italian woman. All of a sudden, there was a thunderous roar, and a whirlwind of dust and smoke enveloped us. That was when, like some apparition originating in the depths of the night, the horses emerged. They were advancing in a frenzied, hectic gallop, their manes lit up by the flames, their eyes glinting in the firelight. They passed by us like winged creatures of the apocalypse. Then they disappeared. We could still hear the sound of their hooves plunging through the darkness for some time afterward.

Later, we began to hear human voices. Someone was shouting in Portuguese. From the darkness emerged a military figure who, unaware of our presence, was busy peering through the gloom that had swallowed up the frightened steeds. Her face radiant, Dona Bianca stared fixedly at the stranger, and then abruptly threw herself on her knees, her hands clasped together, as if she were before some divine being.

"Captain Mouzinho! I can't believe it!"

"And who are you, madame?"

"I am Bianca. I am the woman who was born to meet you."

"This is no place for a woman. How did you end up here, my lady?"

We listened from a distance to their astonishing dialogue, and even today, I find it hard to believe. The truth is that Mouzinho, or whatever other compatriot of mine it was, looked for a moment at Imani, seeking, who knows, an explanation for that white woman's presence there. The captain's face was a mask: not a muscle in his face moved because of his apprehension. He seemed to be serene, but, according to what Imani told me, his eyes were those of an animal faced with flames. Then he stopped paying attention to the two women so he could issue orders to his soldiers, who by now were gathering around him: "Take care, because there may be enemies hidden here. The fire may be a trick, an ambush laid by those damned Vátuas."

The intense redness of the light threw into relief the pallor of the white soldiers while they sought some confirmation of their deepest fears in the surrounding darkness. Then they hurried away. Along with their commanding officer, they plunged into the pitch black of the night.

Bianca, led by Imani, returned to the boat as if she were in some sort of a trance. The black girl had heard one of the soldiers explain what had happened: a fire had destroyed the Portuguese encampment, causing the munitions to explode and the horses to gallop off in a frenzy. This disastrous fire, Imani said, was nothing compared with the fear that blazed in those soldiers' eyes. That was a timeless terror. In each face, the most ancient monsters could be seen. The fire began to abate, but these monsters still devoured the souls of those young soldiers.

Bianca was speechless, as if turned to stone. She obeyed the order to hide, along with the rest of us, in the bottom of the boat. And on we went, rowing silently, so as not to become a target for the terrorstricken soldiers. In their fearful state, they would have riddled our poor boat with bullets.

I lay down in the bottom of the boat once more, shaking with pain amid all the commotion. I had seen myself in the dismayed look of the horses. A river galloped inside me, and I slowly sank into its murky depth, where the only ground is water.

29

A Road Made of Water

I've known rivers:
I've known rivers ancient as the world and older than
the flow of human blood in human veins.

My soul has grown deep like the rivers
...
I've known rivers:
Ancient, dusky rivers.

My soul has grown deep like the rivers

—FROM "THE NEGRO SPEAKS OF RIVERS" BY LANGSTON HUGHES

In the dugout's prow, my father and my brother rowed vigorously, taking turns with the oars so as to overcome the current. In the belly of the little boat traveled the sergeant, lying stretched out. What remained of his arms was wrapped in blood-soaked cloths. The disappearance of his hands—which before seemed only a hallucination—had now become a reality. Never again would the sergeant turn his gaze to his own fingers.

The blood accumulated in a pool, and each drop dripped onto my sense of guilt. Upon me, who had returned his whole body to him so many times, fell the sin of having caused his hands to fly away.

With us traveled the Italian woman, Bianca. From time to time, the woman would untie the unhappy sergeant's cloths and dip them in the waters of the river.

The Inharrime was stained red.

"Do you know the story of this river?" the European woman asked me.

And, without waiting for a reply, she began telling me that Vasco da Gama had once given it a name, the River of Copper. And they had once confided in her that, on the south bank of the river, the king of Gaza had buried a fortune in gold sovereigns. "Well, there's neither copper nor gold: the only things around here are grasses and stones." That's what Bianca said, only to muse, immediately afterward: "Why do we persist in giving names to things that belong to no one? And tell me, my dear: why in heaven's name did they decide to call me the 'woman with the hands of gold'?"

I ceased listening to her. And I found myself swaying this way and that over the feeling that had rendered me breathless ever since I had shot the sergeant, some hours before. I know I did it to save my brother. But this reason wasn't sufficient for me to face the suffering I could see stamped on his face. Ever since I embarked in this boat, I had been unable to stop looking at him, as if my gaze might relieve him, and his pain and suffering might be shared between two souls.

The sergeant's arms became gradually redder and redder. It was a strange coloring, peppered with the gunpowder that burned him. And his face had now gained a bluish hue. There seemed to be no border between the blue of his eyes, the blue of his skin, and the blue of the river. The man was groaning, his mouth open. The Italian woman told me he was calling my name. I tried to ignore him. I was scared he might be asking me to confirm the existence of his hands, now that he had lost them for good. At a certain point, however, I had to lean over his tortured face. It seemed that he wanted to dictate a letter, an urgent letter to the "Most Esteemed Sir."

Our journey was interrupted by the strangest of episodes. On the left bank of the river, a huge fire spread light and flames that were so bright, they were enough to turn night into day. The Italian woman got out of the boat and dashed off in a frenzied rush. When I went to retrieve her, we ran into some Portuguese soldiers who were chasing horses that had fled the chaos.

When we got back to the dugout, the Italian woman was very disturbed and kept repeating: "I saw him, I saw him!" My father told her to keep quiet, because he feared that the soldiers, in their state of alarm, might take us for an enemy target.

And we rowed on in silence until day broke. Those strange events had distracted me. The moment the sun came up, I began to be tormented by guilt once more; without my being aware of it, tears rolled down my cheeks, thick and fast.

"Don't cry, Imani," Bianca begged me.

"Let her cry, lady," my father interceded. "Those tears aren't hers."

And Bianca smiled tolerantly. She had returned to her senses, as if she had no memory of what had happened the previous night. She was, on the other hand, more forlorn, and her gestures more abrupt and restrained. Ever since she had come back to the dugout and recovered from her frenzy, the Italian woman had done justice to the nickname that had gilded her hands: she fulfilled her role as nurse with rigor. And she assumed a certain cold distance as she told him, by way of consolation, "There are two or three fingers we might yet save."

"To hell with my fingers," Germano mumbled. "I've died, my dear friend. I'm already dead."

"Now, now, Germano, you'll bury me yet."

"I like your accent, Bianca. Go on talking; don't stop talking to me."

The Italian woman's faulty pronunciation made the Portuguese language seem sweeter. She opened up its vowels and ignored the silences after its consonants. For sure, she would fail the exams set by Father Rudolfo. But this double standard was clear to see in the sergeant's words. Whites can speak in various ways: people say they have an accent. Only we blacks are not allowed to have another accent. It's not enough for us to speak another people's language. In that language, we must stop being ourselves.

◆

There are many things Bianca doesn't know about. She doesn't understand my father when he says my tears are not mine. These tears belong to a river inside of us that overflows through our eyes. In Nkokolani, we know that which cannot be explained in another language. We know, for example, how my little sisters were taken away by the flood. Mother wept; she wept every night. Not a single tear brought them back. Tired of crying, our mother traveled to the source of all the rivers. That source isn't a place we give a name to. It's the original belly, where those who arrive and those who depart lie nestled. The Italian woman doesn't know any of this.

When Dona Bianca travels on a river, she sees time. In the swirl of the current, she contemplates that which never returns. But for us, time is a drop of water: it is born in the clouds, enters the rivers and the oceans, and falls again the next time it rains. A river's estuary is the sea's source.

The Italian woman spoke of the names the river had.

When she announced them, I felt uncomfortable. For she spoke as if the waters of the Inharrime belonged to her. The truth is, Bianca is far from knowing how these rivers are born. Busy endowing them with names, she had neglected their history. The Italian woman doesn't know that in the very beginning, when the earth as yet had no owners, the rivers and clouds flowed under the ground. Then the demon arrived and stuck his finger in the sand. His long nail scratched around in the depths. He was looking for stones that shimmered in the sunlight. Our mothers begged the gods to protect the stars they had hidden under the sand. They begged the devil to cease tearing out the gleaming minerals and delivering them up to the covetousness of those seeking to enrich themselves. But the devil didn't stop. For there were those among the power-hungry who worshipped him. And his nails broke, and his long, thin fingers bled. For the very first time, the demon's contaminated blood coagulated in the earth's belly. The riches that lay below the ground were cursed. The clouds and rivers abandoned the planet's belly in order to escape this curse. And they became the earth's veins and hair.

This is the story of the rivers. The greedy may steal their water until they run dry. But they won't steal their history. Now I understand: I learned to write in order to relate better what I had lived. And in this narration, I tell the stories of those who have no form of writing. I do what my father does: In the dust and ashes, I write the names of the dead. So that they may be born again from the footprints we leave.

It is strange how our farewells shrink the size of time. My fifteen years pass by me in a flash. My mother's body is now that of a child. And it grows smaller and smaller, until it is no bigger than a fruit. And she tells me: "Before you were even born, before you first saw the light of day, you had known rivers and oceans." And something within me is torn apart, as if I know that I shall never go back to Nkokolani.

On the Design

As book design is an integral part of the reading experience, we would like to acknowledge the work of those who shaped the form in which the story is housed.

Tessa van der Waals (Netherlands) is responsible for the cover design, cover typography and art direction of all World Editions books. She works in the internationally renowned tradition of Dutch Design. Her bright and powerful visual aesthetic maintains a harmony between image and typography and captures the unique atmosphere of each book. She works closely with internationally celebrated photographers, artists, and letter designers. Her work has frequently been awarded prizes for Best Dutch Book Design.

The image on the cover is detail from a fabric created by Vlisco, a Dutch company who design distinctive fabrics inspired by African motifs. Many of their designs have become cultural treasures bestowed with special names and meanings by the merchants of Central and West Africa. This particular fabric has been given the name 'The Eye of My Rival' and is claimed to symbolize family tensions, particularly between wives and husbands, and the resolution of conflict through dialogue.

The cover has been edited by lithographer Bert van der Horst of BFC Graphics (Netherlands).

Suzan Beijer (Netherlands) is responsible for the typography and careful interior book design of all World Editions titles.

The text on the inside covers and the press quotes are set in Circular, designed by Laurenz Brunner (Switzerland) and published by Swiss type foundry Lineto.

All World Editions books are set in the typeface Dolly, specifically designed for book typography. Dolly creates a warm page image perfect for an enjoyable reading experience. This typeface is designed by Underware, a European collective formed by Bas Jacobs (Netherlands), Akiem Helmling (Germany), and Sami Kortemäki (Finland). Underware are also the creators of the World Editions logo, which meets the design requirement that 'a strong shape can always be drawn with a toe in the sand.'